GW00778028

LOOK, STRANGER

When Matthew Vereker arrives from the American Mid-West on a year's exchange as vicar of All Hallows on Helmsley Island, he finds that 'England' is more complicated than he had supposed. The Island is cluttered with smart bungalows, decaying cottages, day trippers, squatters, agitators, followers of the Ancient People, and the ghosts of nuns. Vereker's problems are many and diverse, but one at least he can hope to solve : his own. When the time comes for him to return to America he knows that things will never be the same for him again.

Look, Stranger

By

MARY HOCKING

1979

CHATTO & WINDUS

LONDON

Published by
Chatto & Windus Ltd.
40/42 William IV Street
London WC2N 4DF

*

Clarke, Irwin & Co. Ltd.
Toronto

British Library Cataloguing in Publication Data

Hocking, Mary
  Look, stranger
  I. Title
  823'.9'1F   PR6058.026L/
  ISBN 0-7011-2368-0

© Mary Hocking 1979
Printed in Great Britain by
The Bowering Press Ltd.
Plymouth and London

To my godchildren

Allison, David and Marian

Acknowledgements

The lines from the song, 'When I needed a neighbour', from Sydney Carter's *Green Print for Song*, are reproduced by kind permission of the publisher, Stainer & Bell Ltd.

The verses from Roy Campbell's translation of a poem from St. John of the Cross are reprinted by kind permission of the Harvill Press and Hughes Massie Ltd., on behalf of the executors of the Roy Campbell Estate.

Look, Stranger, on this island now

A U D E N

1

Time was when the island was known as Smugglers' Island. That was over a hundred years ago; but as late as the nineteen-thirties children played out epic chases between smugglers and customs officials along the lonely sand dunes. There were two villages, one to the east and one to the west of the island; in the centre there was farmland and woods where the children could play when they got tired of being smugglers. Only a few families came to the island for summer holidays because there was nothing for the adults to do except walk and swim. After the war, some of the summer visitors, nostalgically recalling those tranquil holidays, bought plots of land and built bungalows or renovated old cottages. It was then that the estate agents realized that there was money to be made out of Helmsley Island, 'where everyone can have a cottage by the sea'. Bungalow estates sprouted all along the coast, and when the coast was built up, the estate agents began to extol the unspoilt beauty of the interior. The County Council, anxious to save the green acres on the mainland, many of which were owned by members of the Council, saw the island as part-answer to its housing problem and filled in some of the gaps left by the private house developers.

There was no planning, it was a happening. By the nineteen-sixties the island looked as though a gigantic aircraft had flown overhead and jettisoned a load of matchboxes which had fallen higgledy-piggledy all over the land. By the nineteen-seventies, the gap-fillers were having to use all their ingenuity to squeeze in yet more matchboxes, but they weren't doing anything as restrictive as planning. Planning was for the mainland. 'The island,' said the mayor, who was an estate agent, 'is one of the places which always says "yes" and as long as I have any say in its future it always will say "yes".'

The island said 'yes' to day trippers who came in their hoards because parking was free on the beaches; and with the day trippers came the fruit machines, the bingo halls, and the fairground. A narrow causeway which took single line traffic connected the island to the mainland. There was no other way off the island. At week-ends there were traffic jams morning and evening and during high summer the traffic was packed solid all the way to the big roundabout where the London road crossed the main road from Folkestone to Portsmouth. While this bottleneck was very annoying for motorists, it had the advantage that the gangs on motor bikes avoided Helmsley : if they caused havoc on the island all the police had to do was wait to pick them up as they came off the causeway. In Helmsley, crime, at least, was home produced.

There was one small stretch along the lee shore which remained much as it had always been. There were marshes here and fields which were known as the Priory Grounds, although the priory had been crumbling away since the time of Henry VIII and only low walls and disconnected arches remained to make mute protest. This area was too remote to tempt children brought up to be dependent on Dad's car for their outings. Also, after the noise and bustle of the rest of the island, the priory grounds were 'different' and regarded with suspicion. The few cottages, built from stones taken from the ruined priory, were not picturesque, they had small windows and looked like prisons; it was sometimes difficult to tell whether anyone lived in them or not. The dogs weren't friendly.

All Hallows at West Helmsley was on the edge of the populated area and beyond it lay the alien priory fields stretching away with nothing to break the green monotony but a line of poplars here and there. It was a bad position, parishioners had to come from the centre of the town to reach the church and this was asking a lot of people who seldom ventured further than the nearest parade of shops.

The vicarage was alongside the churchyard. It had been built in the days when the vicars of Helmsley had large families and could afford to keep servants. Now it was a severe drain on the physical and financial resources of the incumbent and it looked rather shabby; but it was a well-proportioned, sensible house and contrived to keep a pleasant aspect in spite of the poor state in which it found itself. The big garden was given over to grass and clover; there were daffodils in the spring and dandelions in the summer.

10

This was daffodil time. The front door of the vicarage was open and morning sunlight shafted into the hall. A woman was scrubbing the flagged floor while another woman stabbed flowers into a huge earthenware jug on a chest against the staircase wall. The chest was very strong and ancient and looked as though the house had been built around it. The woman in charge of the flowers used its surface as a base on which to hammer the stems of tulips: she was a more efficient smith than flower arranger.

'... lived like pigs,' the scrubbing woman was saying. 'What will the new man think of us when he sees this?'

'He won't know, you've got it so clean.'

'I couldn't do anything about the marks on the dining-room wall, could I? Or the enamel in the bath.' She sat back on ample haunches and wiped a forearm across her sweating, purple face; she was elderly for so much effort and self-pityingly aware of it. 'I wonder what sort of house our lot is going to in Iowa or Minnesota or wherever it is....'

'Clinically clean, I expect. Americans are so up-tight about cleanliness, aren't they?'

A shadow fell across the doorway and the cleaner turned to see who was standing in her light. 'He's not here yet,' she rebuked the newcomer. 'Aaah! Don't tread on that floor! Stand over there by the little window, *not* the big one, 'til I've put the polisher over it.'

The newcomer did as he was bidden. He was a tall man wearing a navy anorak; he had untidy hair of a dusty hue and a crumpled face with the pliable features which can register at one moment a range of emotion through sorrow and pain to gaiety and joy; in another age he might have been a strolling player.

'Who is he?' the flower arranger lowered her voice minimally as she propped up the tulips with strategically placed twigs of laurel.

'From the *Herald*. They rang up to say they wanted someone to interview the new vicar.'

'Bit hard on the poor man to jump on him immediately he crosses the threshold.'

'That was the idea – "a spontaneous impression of England," they said.'

'Does the editor think Helmsley is England?'

'I expect the new vicar will, won't he?'

'Poor sod! But perhaps it won't seem too bad to him. After all, he's from the Mid-West, isn't he? One of those awful little towns that looks as though it's been jacked up temporarily for an exhibition and then forgotten about.' She jammed the head of a tulip between two laurel leaves, 'The sort where the inhabitants think Canada is still a colony.'

'Do you think he'll have us square dancing on the lawn?'

'I could put up with the square dancing if it wasn't for the folksy sermons we shall have to sit through.' She stood back to regard her work. She was a lean, swarthy woman, carelessly dressed; one could imagine her selling flowers at a wayside stall – she had sharp brown eyes and would strike a hard bargain.

'Miss Draisey says a lot of advanced thought has come from the American church.'

'But not from the Reverend Matthew Vereker. They wouldn't let him within a hundred miles of this place if he had an advanced thought in his head.'

'Helmsley's not as bad as all that.' The cleaner wrung out the cloth over a bucket.

'But it's hardly worth crossing the Atlantic to spend a year in it. He must be desperate for a change.' She cuffed the clippings into a heap, caught the expression on the cleaner's face as she was about to sweep them onto the floor, and screwed up her skirt to receive them instead. 'I'll put these in the bin.' She disappeared into the darkness beyond the stairs.

'You're certainly doing a wonderful job on that floor.'

The cleaner looked around her, startled by the deep voice with its unmistakably American intonation. There was only the "reporter" still standing by the small window. He smiled a wry apology.

'Oh, my goodness!' Her hands flew to her face. 'What can you think of us?' Steam came from her puffy red fingers.

'It's my fault,' he said hastily. 'I thought before we settled in, I'd like to look around, informally. But I guess I ought to have warned you.' He paused, rubbing his nose with his knuckles, afraid that if he said any more he might become folksy.

'Gwynneth!' The cleaner got to her feet, painfully, with a

look of reproach on her heavy face; then she backed down the hall, keeping her eye on the new vicar as though he might attack if she turned her back on him. 'Gwynneth, come here!' She vanished into the dark region beyond the stairs and after a whispered exchange Gwynneth emerged.

Gwynneth was not abashed. 'Well, now you know what happens to those who arrive early for a party!' She spoke as though she had known him for years – probably in another life, he thought, looking at those piercing brown eyes in the swarthy face. She walked firmly across the still-wet floor to where he was marooned beneath the window. 'I'm Gwynneth Jarman.' She extended a strong, brown hand stained by wounded flowers. 'My husband is your churchwarden.'

They shook hands.

'And what do you think of Helmsley now that you've looked around it informally?'

'It's like a building set someone has tilted so all the pieces have got jumbled on top of one another.' He looked out through the open door. 'I guess there's more to it than that.' He sounded unhopeful.

'I'd love to say that it's the warmth of the people that counts,' Gwynneth Jarman said, not noticeably regretful. 'But it wouldn't be true because I've lived here most of my life and I don't know half of them. It's that kind of a place now.'

'Ugh-hugh.' He nodded his head gloomily. Then, making an effort, he excused himself, 'I've been travelling the best part of a week.' But his eyes had been tired longer than that.

The cleaner appeared at this moment to say she had the kettle on. 'Is it tea, or coffee, vicar?'

Over tea the cleaner was introduced as Mrs. Maud Hooper. Her husband, now deceased, had been the verger at All Hallows for thirty years and she served the church as part-time cleaner. Matthew Vereker, feeling something was required of him, opined, 'Thirty years is a long time.'

A contemptuous smile dragged at Mrs. Hooper's weary mouth. 'Alf wasn't ambitious.'

Vereker selected what looked to be the least rock-like of Mrs. Hooper's scones and glanced round the sitting-room. The Reverend Hilary Roberts might well by now be drinking coffee in the sitting-room at Coopers Town: Vereker won-

13

dered whether Roberts was finding his surroundings equally depressing. Roberts had four children, and no doubt they had brought so much life to the vicarage that it was neither necessary, nor desirable, to take much thought for the furnishings. Over the years all the tapestried upholstery had faded to the same greyish-beige as the carpet, while the worn leather armchair appeared, from its sagging cushion, to have broken springs. The velvet curtains were bleached a dusty caramel but showed a richer brown in the folds. There was a large picture on the wall of shaggy cattle paddling in misty fields with fuzzed mountains in the background.

'I guess this place is pretty old?' he hazarded.

'About seventeen-sixty,' Gwynneth Jarman shrugged.

'Indeed?' Vereker was impressed. His ancestors would still have been in England in seventeen-sixty.

'Carrick Farm is much older. Early Tudor.'

For no good reason that Vereker could see there was some kind of silent communication between the two women at this point. Mrs. Jarman raised her eyebrows and Mrs. Hooper pursed her lips; then Mrs. Hooper, who appeared to be the loser in this exchange, bent her attention to a small piece of scone, pressing it against her plate with one thumbnail until it crumbled. Gwynneth Jarman went on, 'You can just see the chimneys of the farm between those trees.'

Vereker looked out of the window and saw, at the far end of a distant field, a row of trees; he thought he could just make out a chimney.

'Is it still a farm?'

'No.'

Mrs. Hooper smiled unpleasantly at her crumbled scone.

'Zoe and Tudor Lindsay live there,' Gwynneth Jarman said. 'Zoe'll be keeping house for you here. Hilary Roberts said you would need someone to help your daughter. That is right, I hope?'

'I guess we'll need a bit of help with a place this size.' Vereker was cautious; he didn't want to make excuses for Nan, yet he felt a need to ease the way for her. 'She hasn't got a lot of experience. We haven't lived a very normal life, my wife being ill for such a long time. . . .' He was so concerned for Nan; if he said too much he would show his distress. He broke off and muttered, 'It's very kind of Mrs. Lindsay.'

'The kindness will be as much on your side as hers,' Mrs. Jarman said crisply. 'She needs something to occupy her.'

Vereker gazed out of the window, giving himself time to think about the occupying of Mrs. Lindsay. 'Would that be part of the farm?' he asked idly, pointing at a jagged wall some distance to the right of the row of trees.

'No. That's the priory ruins; the nuns owned all the land around here, but that was a long time ago.' Mrs. Jarman regarded Mrs. Hooper menacingly while she dismissed the priory from the conversation. Mrs. Hooper looked rather furtive.

'Roberts didn't say anything about a priory. Nan will be interested. She likes old things, furniture, buildings . . . we don't have much in that line where we come from.'

'Where is your daughter now?' Gwynneth Jarman nailed the conversation to Nan.

'We stayed the night in town. She's coming later today with the luggage.'

He didn't want to talk about Nan. He must leave her to make her own impression on these people, anything he said would be wrong – parents are always wrong. He got up. 'I think perhaps that now I'm here I ought to stroll across and meet Mrs. Lindsay.'

Mrs. Hooper seemed to gather herself to speak, her shoulders braced, her bosom swelled, but all this took time and the redoubtable Mrs. Jarman had ushered Vereker out of the room before Mrs. Hooper's lips so much as parted.

'There are two rights of way; one from the church graveyard and one at the end of Virginia Close. Both will lead you across the fields to the farm.' She saw him out of the house and pointed him in the direction of Virginia Close. As they parted, she said, 'And it's *Miss* Lindsay : Zoe and Tudor are cousins.' She remained at the front door, watching him as he walked down the drive to make sure he didn't play truant. On an impulse he turned at the gate.

'Mrs. Jarman,' he called out to her. 'Are you a school ma'am?'

'Yes.'

'I thought you might be.'

She closed the door.

To his right was the church, a little grey stone building

with a cone-shaped tower. He could see a group of people in the porch reading the notices on the board. Tourists : parishioners don't congregate in the church porch to read the notices on a mid-week morning, not in this or any other country. He would go into the church on his return.

He headed obediently towards Virginia Close which was a turning to the left just beyond the vicarage. It was a short road with a T junction at the far end. Vereker walked slowly studying the solid, well-built bungalows on either side. He was drawn to other people's homes; gazing in at lighted rooms to see a family gathered together gave him a feeling of warmth which he recognized as a sad reflection on his own lack of such joy. The bungalows were brick, but some had been painted white and there were at least two pinks and one blue among them. They all had glass porches full of healthy pot plants and the front windows were big, but, alas, most of them had blinds or net curtains to protect the inmates from ill-mannered people like Matthew Vereker. There were cars on the concrete outside several of the garages, and one or two boats. The gardens were neat in a rather fussy way and there was a profusion of hydrangeas. The other main feature was the dogs. The dogs had had a dull morning; he was the first happening of their day and they all came down to their gates to greet him, snuffling, yapping, baying according to the custom of their breed. The human inhabitants were more reserved, although a man in a thick ribbed sweater clipping an already immaculate hedge observed that it was another fine day, wasn't it? The man was watched by a neatly dressed woman with blue hair who obviously didn't want a stranger to intrude at this moment – perhaps at any moment?

The people and their properties seemed reasonably prosperous and Vereker was puzzled as to why, this being the case, they chose to live with so little space around them. There was just about room for two good-sized dustbins to stand side by side between the bungalow walls. Where Vereker came from space was one thing they had plenty of and until now he had always taken it for granted, as essential as air to breathe.

He came to the T junction and paused. To the right, on his side of the road, were more bungalows which he judged to be older than those in Virginia Close. At one time these bungalows had faced fields, but now the ground on the opposite side of the road was being torn up to make way for buildings that resembled the lakeside shacks of his childhood holidays. Vereker stared in dismay at a large notice which informed him that sixteen "luxury town houses" were being erected on this site. If he hadn't seen it with his own eyes, he would not have credited that, even if a prize of a million dollars had been offered, it would have been possible for any architect, however greedy and ingenious, to have got sixteen houses on this pocket-handkerchief of a site. In comparison, the bungalow dwellers were living in spacious luxury. He looked at the notice again. "Sixteen luxury town houses each with two garages." Thirty-two cars, on a site that size, would mean that all the outside area would have to be tarmac to provide driveways. The people in the bungalows, who had looked out on green fields, would now be living in the shadow of a car park, and a shanty town car park, at that.

Further down the road, beyond the bungalows and the new development, big-bosomed houses bedecked with gables and wooden balustrades billowed onto the street, each hoisting private hotel notices. These buildings belonged to a more expansive age and at one time had probably stood in their own grounds. No doubt the coming of the bungalow estates had seemed as odious to their owners as the town houses must seem to the bungalow dwellers. Perhaps the town-house buyers would come out of it best. At least they wouldn't have anything to lose; everything that could happen to this area would have happened with their advent.

To his left, the road curved out of sight so that the promised right of way was hidden from view. He followed the curve of the road and stopped, surprised by what he saw. The road had became a narrow lane meandering between tall hedges, and opposite to where he was standing there was a white five-barred gate with a stile beside it. The gate was padlocked and there was enough barbed wire festooned about it to make it seem as though some kind of trench warfare was going on in Helmsley. On the other side of the gate he could see a track running down the side of a barley field; beyond was pastureland with cows, and then marshland running out to the sea. It was a different world, existing simultaneously, but separately from the world of the new Helmsley. The people lived in their respective camps and it didn't look as though any fraternizing was encouraged. This is bad, he thought as he climbed the stile.

He got down from the stile without impaling himself on the barbed wire and set off across the field towards the trees he had seen from the vicarage window. The chimneys of Carrick Farm were clearly visibly now and he forgot about the two Helmsleys in the more immediate problem of Miss Lindsay. He must see Miss Lindsay and find out what it was that ailed her; those two women had made it quite clear between them that *something* ailed her. He didn't mean to have Nan saddled with another invalid, however pitiable. 'Miss Lindsay, now that I've seen the house I think maybe we'll manage without troubling you too much,' he rehearsed as he walked.

In the event, the rehearsal was unnecessary because there was no answer when he knocked on the door of Carrick Farm. It was a long, low house and it was only too easy to look in at the windows. At first, Vereker looked through the small window to the side of the door. He saw a square, dark hall with wooden beams sagging beneath the weight of the ceiling; to the left several doors led off the hall and on the far side was a staircase with predictably worn treads; immediately opposite the front door was a brick fireplace, the grate stuffed with what looked like paper wrappings left over from last Christmas. Guiltily, he picked his way along the front of the house, treading carefully on the springy turf. The garden was his idea of an English garden, with its deep green lawn and haphazard flower beds, and he didn't want to disturb any precious part of it. He stood on tiptoe and looked through a narrow window into a small room with a table just below the window sill stacked with files, typewriter, copy paper and two unwashed cups. Vereker moved on to a more generous latticed window which revealed a sitting-room. Vereker loved sitting-rooms and this was the sitting-room of his dreams. In spite of his intellectual pretensions, his was a simple soul which cried out for just the rumpled comfort this room offered. It had at least one deep winged armchair where a man could rest both limbs and head while he contemplated next Sunday's sermons, it also had a sofa long enough to stretch out on if a man fancied an afternoon nap after he had written those sermons. He hadn't much experience of the kind of chairs a woman preferred, Alma having spent so many years on her back; but he could imagine her as a young woman curled up in the capacious velvet tub affair, or sitting on one of the big cushions that were scattered around the floor, firelight playing on her face. As he gazed at the fire in the big hearth, the flames sputtering from the pyramid of logs, he felt suddenly desolate. He turned away from the house and made his way across the lawn in the direction of a small orchard.

He fought the desolation as he walked through the orchard and was saved from defeat by his first glimpse of the priory ruins. The right of way from the church would have led him to Carrick Farm via the priory, but Mrs. Jarman had turned him in the direction of Virginia Close. No doubt she had her reasons. Someone had certainly made a good job of ruining the priory; it was possible to make out a doorway here, the base of a chimney there, an archway or two which might or might not have been a part of the cloisters, but to his un-tutored eye this was all that was identifiable. He sat on the chimney base and wondered idly what the island had been like when the nuns lived there.

Beyond this field the marshes ran out to the sea; he could see water glinting in the sun and a few sailing boats bobbing about. It would be nice if Nan could get in with some young-sters who would take her sailing. Friends had told him that Nan ought to have a change, that she was becoming with-drawn and needed to get right away from Coopers Town. The opportunity to do this exchange with Roberts had seemed God-sent; but more recently he had had doubts. Perhaps he should have sent her to his cousin in California, encouraged her to start a life of her own instead of shackling her to him? The trouble was that neither of them had felt they could bear to lose the other so soon after Alma's death. They weren't companionable, just unable to get along without each other.

The sun was pleasantly warm but not uncomfortable. He listened to the scuttering of rabbits in the long grass, the chirp of birds, the rustle of the wind in the trees. It should have been peaceful but, perhaps because of the nearness of the marshes, there was a rather unpleasant smell which he soon found oppressing his spirits.

He got up and retraced his steps. As he went past the front of Carrick Farm he saw a woman watching him from a first floor window. He only had time to see the oval of her face before she withdrew into the shadows; there seemed little doubt that she had been in the house all the time. He was too ashamed at the thought that she had probably witnessed his behaviour to question hers. He retreated hastily towards "new" Helmsley.

2

It was nine-thirty, so she had missed breakfast. There was a notice stuck to the back of the door which gave the times of meals : breakfast was between eight and nine. This business of serving meals at set times and firmly closing the pantry door in between was one of those quaint English customs no one had told her about. Another custom was that beds were made up – or stripped down, as the case might be – while guests were having breakfast. At eight-fifteen a woman had come to do the bed, only to find it occupied by Nancy Vereker. Nancy's offer to make the bed herself hadn't been well-received. The woman had said she would come back later and she had given Nancy a look which made it clear she had fouled up her entire morning.

Nancy put one arm over the side of the bed and hauled up the eiderdown. There was no central heating and the morning air was cold as if it had come straight out of the ice-box. She would lie here for another ten minutes while she got warmed through again; then she would go into town and see if there was some place that served coffee after nine in the morning. She didn't think she could organize herself for the journey to Helmsley without the stimulus of coffee. She propped herself up against the pillows and set to work filing her nails.

Now that she was sitting up she could look out at the sea if she chose. 'I hate the sea,' she said aloud, as though someone had contradicted her. But in spite of this protestation she very soon put the nail file down on the bedside table and stared out of the window at the blue-green mass. She had seen it heaving about just like that through the porthole while the Irish steward relieved her of her virginity. She closed her eyes and waited for her body to give some sign that it, too, remembered his exploits. Nothing happened.

It seemed that every generation had its myths : hers was sex, and she had just exploded it. Friends had assured her that she couldn't savour anything in life without sex : music, art, literature, dancing, even eating and drinking, couldn't be

21

experienced fully by a virgin. But breakfast had tasted much the same après sex, and she had still been afraid of diving into the pool. Far worse, her confidence was as impaired as ever : she hadn't found it any easier to mix on equal terms with the other youngsters on the boat, she still felt a resentful muddle when she was with her father, and she was going to be quite unable to cope with getting herself and their luggage to Helmsley Island. She had lost her innocence but she didn't seem to have acquired anything to replace it.

It wasn't even as if she had enjoyed the experience. Worst of all, she didn't think the steward had, either, because he hadn't bothered her after that one occasion. She swung her legs over the side of the bed and felt for her slippers. The bathroom wasn't as bad as she had anticipated and the water was hot; she felt better when she returned to her room. Even if the experience hadn't been all she had expected, at least she had got it done; she wouldn't ever be sorry about that. She was in line with all the others now.

But the others got more fun out of things than she did. They really enjoyed sex, just as, when they were younger, they had really enjoyed their love affairs with other girls. She had had Angela Parrish. Her parents had not approved of Angela; but the attitudes of her companions were more important than her parents' views and she had persisted with Angela although their loving had never got beyond putting their arms round each other's waists in the playground and pinching each other in the wash-room. She wished she could get the knack of *enjoying* experience.

She sat on the stool in front of the mirror and had a good look at herself. Her face, like the rest of her, was small. People had always commented on how small she was; she had small bones and a small frame, she was small in every way it was possible to be small. 'A bright little bird,' her mother had called her. 'My Nancy bird.' Nancy brushed her cropped chestnut hair, trying to make it lie down like a sleek cap round her head, but it bounced up wirily. She spent hours trying to create a different personality for herself by changing the way she dressed and doing something about her eyebrows; but in the end her hair always defeated her efforts. She wondered if a person could ever become mature with hair like hers.

So many of her friends had become mature. She had watched it happening to them, seen them settling into their skins, each day they added a line to the portrait until it became formidably clear and bold. Whereas she was one person one day and another the next. Although she was nineteen she looked fifteen and sometimes acted fifteen. Her mother's illness had retarded her emotional development; yet she sometimes had insights beyond her years. One way and another she was as mixed up as it was possible to be.

There was the sound of voices in the corridor. It was ten past ten and other guests were departing. The woman would come back to do the bed any minute now; if it had not been for her Nancy would probably have remained staring in the mirror most of the morning, wondering what she was to do about getting herself and the luggage to Helsmley Island. The night before she had told her father, 'Leave it to me. I'm not a child.' When he had tried to give her advice, she had interrupted, 'You want to do all my thinking for me.' So he had gone early this morning, leaving her to do her thinking for herself. Or had he? Perhaps he had left a message for her downstairs telling her the times of trains and explaining that he had ordered a cab to take her to the station. Fortified by this thought, she dressed quickly, finished packing, and was ready to leave the room when the bed-making woman returned. She carried her cases down to the hall and saw that her father's cases were already stacked beside the front door. The proprietress was welcoming new arrivals and a cab driver was waiting to be paid.

'You'll need a taxi, won't you, Miss Vereker?' the proprietress said and signalled to the driver.

'Did my father leave a message for me?' Nancy asked anxiously. But the proprietress was too busy with the new arrivals to pay attention to her. The cab driver said, 'Central Station?' and picked up her cases without waiting for a reply. When they arrived at the station, she overtipped him to such an extent that he summoned a porter for her.

The porter, a depressed man with a running nose, asked Nancy where she was going.

'Helmsley Island.'

'Helmsley Island! You won't get a train direct to Helmsley Island.'

'How *will* I get there?'

He told her that she could take a train to some place the name of which she did not catch and from there she could hire another cab; or she could go by coach, but that would mean three changes and the coach drivers might not be too pleased about all that luggage.

Nancy, who was ready to abandon the whole project if he would go away and leave her alone, said, 'Well, I'll think about it, thank you very much.'

A train came in on platform three and the porter went in search of better-motivated travellers. Nancy sat on the largest of the cases. Nearby a man and a boy were talking in front of the entrance to platform three; it was hard to guess the boy's age because he had one of those pinched faces that change little from youth to old age.

The man said, 'There'll be someone to meet you at the other end.'

The boy said, 'I'll have jumped out by then.'

As Nancy looked at the thin, bespectacled boy she was aware of an almost total deprivation which turned her heart. The boy's companion, apparently unimpressed by the suicide threat, said :

'Try to write a few lines to your mother.'

'Much she cares!'

The arriving passengers had alighted now and the first few carriages were empty. The man put a hand on the boy's shoulder and propelled him gently towards the ticket barrier. Nancy, moved by a wretchedness greater than her own, walked to the barrier and stared across it at the man and the boy. The boy had a mulish expression clamped on his face but it was plain that he was unable to offer effective resistance; when the whistle blew and the train moved off, he would be on it and would remain on it until he reached the station where someone was to meet him. How awful life was! She stood at the barrier repeating under her breath all the four-letter words she could call to mind. The boy was too preoccupied with his misery to notice anything extraneous but after a time the man glanced across at her. So far she hadn't paid much attention to him, but she took stock of him now. His tall, thin figure gave the impression of being cast in something more unyielding than flesh; he reminded her of

24

one of those emaciated Giacometti figures. He had wiry brown hair, just short of shoulder length, and was dressed in an old blue sweater and brown corduroys; but in spite of his casual appearance there was a professional aloofness in his attitude to the boy which suggested he was performing a task for which he was paid.

The whistle shrilled. The man gave last-minute instructions to the boy, a porter walked along the train slamming doors and Nancy turned away unable to watch as the train moved out. She sat on one of the cases and shed a few tears for the wickedness of the uncaring world.

'And what were you muttering about?' a voice asked. 'And why the tears?'

'I was damning you to hell for being so cruel to that poor boy.'

She realised with a start that she was talking to another person and looked up. His narrow face was deeply tanned and his blue eyes were so pale that they looked as though the sun had bleached them. It was the pale eyes that held her attention, so cool and appraising in that thin, brown face. 'I wouldn't trust him,' she thought. In that fleeting moment when she judged him unreliable, she also sensed that he was not a happy person, that there was something unresolved about him which might be his undoing. She saw all this quite clearly, and then the impression splintered and she was never subsequently sure what she thought about him.

'*Life* has been cruel to that boy.' He looked down at her in amusement. 'Life *is* cruel, don't you know that?' His eyes focussed on the cases and he bent forward to read a label.

'You're going to Helmsley Island.'

'There isn't any way of getting there,' she answered dejectedly.

'Six days out of seven you'd be right. But today I had to see that poor little beast off on his way to school.' He stopped, tantalisingly, so that she was forced to ask :

'Are you going near there?'

'I live there.'

'You live there !'

He laughed. 'It's not as rapturous as all that.' He made her feel self-conscious; she could not bring herself to ask if he would take her to the island. Perhaps he realised something of

25

this because he became more business-like. 'Let's see if we can find a porter.'

In the car he introduced himself as Tudor Lindsay and she told him that she was Nancy Vereker.

'I guessed that. Only a preacher's daughter would damn anyone to hell these days.'

'Do you go to the church?'

'No, I do not!' He sounded quietly savage and this greatly impressed her.

'If you don't go to the church, how did you know about me?' she asked timidly. 'I mean, that my father was a preacher. . . .'

'Because Helmsley is one of those old-world islands on which no stranger can set foot without all the locals knowing about it; as you walk along its quaint cobbled streets everyone will give you the time of day; and Mrs. Gubbins in the post office will tell you all the village scandal because she opens all the mail.' He gave her a sideways glance. 'Wasn't that what you were expecting?'

'I don't know.' His manner made her uneasy; she wondered how she was going to keep up her end of the conversation all the way to the island.

'I'm sorry.' He sounded genuinely contrite. 'I've had a bloody awful morning. Do you think coffee would do us both good?'

They stopped some distance out of town at a hotel called *The Barley Mow* and had coffee in the bar; the only other person in the room was the woman who served them and she paid little attention to them as she washed down the bar counter. A radio in a room at the back of the bar blared folk music. Tudor Lindsay asked Nancy about her life in America. She told him about Coopers Town, about her mother's illness with sclerosis which seemed to have gone on as long as she could remember, about how much she wanted to get away from it all and really start living. Then he told her that she wasn't ready for much living yet because she hadn't had a chance to get her growing up done properly; her emotional life had been submerged and she hadn't learnt how to form relationships with other people. She said wasn't it bad to be like this at nineteen and he said, yes, it was bad, but she would come out of it, given time.

'Time is what I don't have,' she said, feeling very old.

'You're going to have trouble, let's face it; but there's a lot that can happen between nineteen and old age.'

Then he asked her if she had grieved for her mother, and she wasn't sure because it had seemed to happen too gradually for grief; but he insisted it was important to get her grieving done and she promised to try. She felt she was reading a book someone had written about her. She asked if he wrote books and he said he didn't have time even to read them, he was a social worker.

'That must be wonderful! To do so much good for other people.' Why, in just under half an hour he had told her more about herself than anyone ever had in all her nineteen years!

He said bitterly that you couldn't do anything worthwhile until the system had been changed. As they continued their journey, he told her how the system should be changed. She was so absorbed she didn't even notice that they had left the mainland until, just as the car turned into a country lane, she had a fleeting glimpse of sea behind her and the tall masts of sailing boats.

'I can't tell you how grateful I am!' she said when he stopped the car outside the vicarage.

'Try.' He looked at her, smiling in a way that made her feel foolish. She wished she hadn't sounded so enthusiastic; he would think she was just a silly kid. Then he bent forward and kissed her on the mouth. It was such a shock she didn't respond, but sat there meekly while his mouth pressed harder and harder against hers until she could feel his teeth cutting her gums. When he was finished, she said breathlessly, 'Thank you,' which was a silly thing to say. He remained bending over her, leisurely examining her face; she felt her cheeks burning and she wanted to get out of the car and run away somewhere to hide her shame. Then he took her hand and pressed it. 'Never mind.'

He got out of the car and began to put the cases down in the road. 'Do you mind if I just stack them here? I've got to see a family in East Helmsley and I'm late.'

She realized after he had gone that he hadn't told her how he came to have heard of her father; but her father himself explained that later as they had supper together.

They had unpacked and tried to establish a presence by

scattering a few of their possessions about, but the house hung around them ill-fitting as borrowed clothes. People had called bringing flowers, jam, home-made cakes, notices to read in church on Sunday, invitations to lunch, tea, supper, summonses to attend a vigil, choir concert and a meeting of the Bible Society; the rural dean had telephoned to say he would refrain from pressing invitations until they had settled down.

It was nine o'clock, dark and cold by the time they sat down to a supper of ham and eggs, provided by Mrs. Jarman. They ate in the kitchen which was at the back of the house; they had drawn the curtains in the front rooms, switched off all the lights which could be seen from the road, and taken the telephone receiver off the rest. It was not a cheerful meal. Nancy was overwhelmed by the effort of being sociable to so many people whom she had never met before and Vereker was depressed by the threat of imminent social engagements with the rural dean.

Nancy was about to collect their plates when she was conscious that her father had mentioned the Lindsays in connection with help in the house.

'Is that his wife?' she asked sharply.

'No, they are cousins.'

'I think we ought to accept,' she said, brightening a little. 'We can't start by refusing help.'

'We should start as we mean to go on.'

He spoke quite mildly, but she snapped back at him. 'But I don't know how I mean to go on until I've started.'

'There's some sense in that,' he said pacifically.

This annoyed her, too. When he disagreed with her she felt obscurely threatened, when he agreed with her she felt he was undermining her in a more subtle way. Everything he said and did annoyed her, from his slow manner of speech to the way he held his knife. Yet the more he annoyed her, the more she loved him; love and annoyance seemed inextricably tangled in her. She took his plate from him as soon as he had finished torturing the last piece of ham. 'Now just leave the dishes to me for once, will you? Why don't you put the kettle on for coffee?'

He fumbled in the cupboards and by the time she had dried the dishes, he had located the coffee.

28

'When I've drunk this I'm for bed,' she said. 'I'm so tired I could drop.'

He looked unhappily at her cup but did not say that she wouldn't sleep if she drank strong coffee.

'Do the Lindsays live near here?' she asked.

'They live in a farmhouse way across the fields. You'd like it, Nan. Oh, and there's a ruin of some kind, too: a priory that is much older than the farmhouse. Mrs. Jarman and Mrs. Hooper made quite a mystery of it. Do you suppose it could be haunted?'

'More like those are two silly women!' She was aware that he was trying to cheer her up and miserably unable to respond.

They sat in silence for a few minutes, then he said, 'Do you think you'll like it here, Nan?'

'I can't tell until I've seen the place properly, can I?' She scraped back her chair and carried her cup to the sink where she poured away what was left of the coffee. 'Too strong,' she said, wanting to make amends. Then, looking at him hunched wearily over the table, she thought what an ungenerous little beast she was and how dearly she loved him. She went across and hugged him.

'Goodnight, Our Dad.' This was a family joke; a Yorkshire couple had stayed with them in Coopers Town when she was a toddler, in the days when her mother was well and laughed a lot.

'You remember the Dempseys, do you?' He was immensely cheered, bless him! 'Perhaps I could get in touch with them. Yorkshire's not all that far, I expect they come south sometimes.'

She took a glass of water and turned resolutely to the door, determined not to show how little she relished her first night in this big, echoing house. 'Don't stay up late, you've had a long day.' She didn't like to think of him down here alone in this enormous old kitchen. Since her mother's death she had been afraid that he might do something dreadful. She wanted to get away from him, but the thought that he might get away from her was beyond bearing.

When she got into bed she could not sleep; but it was not the coffee, or the strangeness of the house, or her fears for her father, which kept her awake; it was the memory of Tudor

Lindsay's kiss. The kiss pervaded her whole body with warmth and set up a throbbing agitation in that area which had so recently been the steward's province. All sorts of conflicting feelings came flooding in now, complicating what had been effected with so little fuss and bother. She wished she had not let the steward touch her when he came into the cabin as she stepped out of the shower; he hadn't been very forceful, she would not have had a lot of difficulty getting rid of him if she had tried. But as though in a trance she had allowed him to carry her to the bed and while he was arranging her to suit his inelegant purpose she had thought that it was a good thing it was happening at last; she had fixed her eyes on the porthole and when he lunged on top of her she had not cried out even if she had not enjoyed it. Why hadn't she enjoyed it, when now she wanted him, or if not him, she wanted someone rather badly? She drew her knees up tight and folded her arms about them, pressing them to her small breasts; and she cried because her father would be sad if he knew what she had so casually permitted.

While Nancy was suffering pangs of guilt and desire, her father had stepped out into the garden, tempted by a white cat. The cat had appeared at the kitchen window, its pink nose pressed against the pane, its wide green eyes pitiful as a soul locked out of paradise. But as soon as Vereker went out with a saucer of milk, the cat became disdainful and strolled off into the shrubbery. Vereker remained in the garden. There was no moon, but it was a cloudless night and the stars were bright. It was quiet; not the quiet of the vast American open spaces, but a small, individual quietness, as though somewhere a current had been switched off. He was a stranger here; if he went out of the front gate he wouldn't know which way to turn to look for the first lighted window. The fear that from now on he was always going to be on the outside of the lighted window had been terrifying him ever since Alma's death. But in Coopers Town he had been able to keep the fear at bay because he had a role to play; he had carried on with his pastoral work and it had carried him through. Now, in a strange place which had no need of him, he felt in full the loneliness of life without Alma. Nan would go, and the sooner the better for her sake. When she had gone there would be no one for him to love. People would be kind, of course; they would throw him crumbs of comfort, make sure he didn't eat alone too often, but really he would be an awful nuisance to them. His faith told him otherwise; it told him that God always has use for His creatures. But panic clamped his tongue and he could not pray. It was only when he was in his bedroom that the habit of many prayerful years reasserted itself and he repeated over and over again, although he felt no response and there was darkness without and within, 'Lord, save me from too much concern with myself. Teach me to love you in all your creatures.'

3

The next day the squatters moved in. There were two women, three men and five children accompanied by their guardian angel, a stocky, trousered woman with cropped hair slicked across her forehead to conceal a disfiguring scar. She had a cigarette stuck to her lower lip and regarded Vereker through a blue haze while she talked to him in a harsh, gasping voice as though she was functioning on only half a lung. It seemed that she had had much experience of commandeering property. Vereker decided that this was the time to play the waiting game; he was good at the waiting game, patience was his long suit. While the trousered woman talked, he studied the human casualties that she had deposited at his feet.

The squatters looked at him as though he was a potential enemy : he was, after all, in possession of a house. This much they had in common, otherwise their attitudes differed sharply. The men, rank and dishevelled, with long dark hair parted neatly in the centre (the only neat thing about them), sat cross-legged with heads bowed like beggars in an eastern bazaar – or Lazarus at the rich man's gate. The women stood aloof from the men. The older of the two was in tears. She was a big, soft brown creature with the bewildered air of a pet rabbit who has been abandoned to fend for itself in the wild. Her tears came easily as though crying was her first, and perhaps only, response to difficulty. Her companion, on the other hand, had been bred over many generations for the situation in which she now found herself. From her narrow, sharp-featured face looked out the hungry extras who had crowded the sets of the London of Gay, Hogarth, Dickens, cunning, vicious, resourceful, derisive and tenacious. She looked at Vereker with the indifferent assurance of one who is well-aware of the problem she poses. When society came up with a solution, she would present it with another problem : this was a game in which she held all the good cards. Vereker decided that he was not taking her on if he could help it.

Only last night, he had prayed that he might see God in all His creatures : one puts oneself in grave peril when one talks to God. Vereker played for time with God and the squatters' guardian angel. 'I only arrived here yesterday. I don't know what accommodation there is in the house.'

'*I* know.' She threw the damp cigarette butt on the floor and ground her heel on it.

Vereker was unimpressed by this display. If she knew the house so well, it was a mistake not to have taken possession while it was empty. It was just possible that this lady was not so formidable as she appeared. He said, 'I haven't had a chance to meet my churchwardens yet. I don't even know who owns the property.'

'The Church *own* the property.' She said "own" as though the Church was engaged in an obscene practice.

'So I can hardly talk terms with you,' Vereker went on determinedly. 'But if you and our friends here like to go into the garden, I daresay we can rustle up some breakfast while I make a few enquiries.'

At the mention of breakfast the squatters betrayed signs of willingness to agree a truce. Vereker led them down the corridor to the back door. It was a pleasant morning and the garden looked inviting; two of the younger children immediately began to chase each other, jumping over the daffodils and burrowing into the shrubbery, while the older children made for the nearest climbable tree. The men sat on the grass and contemplated their navels while the women sat one each end of a garden seat with broken slats. Vereker returned to the house. The guardian angel was waiting in the hall; she seemed unsurprised by the defection of her charges.

'What organisation are you working with?' Vereker asked her.

'My own. I used to be with Shelter, but not any more. Shelter's not effective out of London and the big cities.'

'Shelter is shit.'

Vereker looked round, surprised, and discovered that not all the squatters had defected. The oldest of the children, a youth with long, curly red hair, was sitting on the stairs whence he regarded Vereker. Although he was small and slight, he was older than Vereker had at first imagined. Sixteen, possibly seventeen, Vereker thought, looking at the pale freckled face.

'I don't want breakfast so you'll have to think of another way of getting rid of me.' He managed to convey quite clearly that he thought the offer of breakfast about as well-intentioned as the kiss of Judas.

'This is Milo Anguilo,' Meg Jacobs said to Vereker.

The red-head bowed in mocking acknowledgement of the introduction. Then the boy looked up and smiled into Vereker's face and Vereker was aware that he was confronted by no ordinary personality. The smile sweetened the face and bestowed on it a kind of elfin grace, a strange blend of shyness, warmth and malice. There was no suggestion of contrivance, the smile was a gift with no conditions attached to it; yet Vereker was conscious of a number of usually disparate, even explosive, qualities contained in what appeared to be a fragile vessel : a highly strung, and possibly unstable creature, this.

Vereker said, 'I sent the others into the garden because I wanted to talk to Miss Jacobs alone.'

'About how to get rid of us?' The question was not entirely cynical; although the mouth was wry, the violet eyes manifested a naive belief that the truth might still be told. Vereker said, 'I can't possibly take all of you.'

'That's fair enough,' Meg Jacobs intervened. 'I think Sir here may be prepared to help us. Leave this to your Auntie Meg and get some breakfast, old son.' She placed nicotine-stained fingers on the boy's shoulder. The boy laughed uneasily, not liking the gesture; nevertheless, he did not allow himself to shrink from her touch. Vereker wondered whether, at Milo's age, he would have been capable of such forbearance.

'All right, Meg; I'll leave it to you.' Milo disengaged himself gently and got to his feet. He looked at Vereker. 'You've got to take my mother.' He made the statement simply, without any suggestion of appeal or threat. 'She can't cope like Mrs. Peters can.'

Vereker watched as the boy moved away, walking with the dancer's light step which, for all its ease, conceals a formidable flow of energy from the top of the head to the tips of fingers and toes.

Meg Jacobs said, 'You can't take on the Peters family, I

34

know that. And the odds are they wouldn't stay anyway. But you must take the Anguilos, for Milo's sake, not his sodding mother's.' She lit another cigarette and placed the spent match carefully in the matchbox; she had become quite friendly. 'Father is an Argentinian diplomat, or so Mother says.' For all her concern, Vereker noticed she had the regrettable habit of depriving people of their identity. 'He went back to the Argentine years ago and they haven't heard from him since. So, Milo is the man of the family; that means keeping Mother and his two sisters, and that will soon mean stealing and anything else that comes his way, including drug peddling. He's very worried about Mother. For years she has "shared" all her problems with him because "it will help him to grow up". Without him, she'd fold up altogether and he knows it.'

Vereker could hear distant screams. He said, 'That's bad.'

'It's worse than bad. He's sensitive and she'll get every ounce of emotion out of him until she's sucked him dry.'

Vereker, from his brief glimpse of the boy, suspected that his survival chances might be higher than Meg Jacobs rated them. Nevertheless, he could well imagine that Milo's present problems might lead him into crime. He said, 'I'll do what I can.'

'You will?' For a moment Vereker was afraid she would embrace him; she looked as though she might be given to bear hugs. He muttered something about telephoning Donald Jarman and she said, 'He'll be at his office now – six-nine-o-four, Jarman and Laker, chartered accountants. Don't let his secretary put you off, tell her we've set light to the place.' There were more screams from the garden. 'I'd better go and see what they are doing, otherwise you may have a fire for real.'

Vereker went into the kitchen. Nan, who had been having a late breakfast, was standing by the window. 'Who is that lovely red-head?'

'They are all squatters.'

'We have squatters? That's great! Are they going to stay?'

'Some of them might. I'm going to telephone Mr. Jarman. Would you be able to make coffee and toast for them?'

She looked doubtfully out of the window, counting. 'Do you think the kids want coffee?'

'Make it for the others and then ask what the kids would like.'

'Suppose we don't have it?' She was losing ground already. 'There's only one bottle of milk and . . .'

Vereker left her to sort this out and went to telephone Donald Jarman who had little practical advice to offer, but promised to come round.

By the time Vereker returned to the kitchen, Nan was out in the garden with the squatters. The kitchen smelt of burnt toast; coffee had boiled over on the stove and the sink was coated with charred toast scrapings. In spite of this, Nan appeared to have satisfied the squatters and she looked as though she was enjoying talking to Milo. Meg Jacobs was playing with the younger children who were holding hands and dancing round her.

Donald Jarman arrived in a quarter of an hour. He was a tallish man, with a heavy body sprucely controlled by a dark grey suit; he carried a rolled umbrella. He had dark hair, short, but with a crinkle here and there not entirely ironed out by careful grooming. His face had humour and a certain urbanity, the eyes smiled and the brows lofted in rueful resignation, but the jowls were those of a heavyweight. It was a face which had contradictory elements held together by some ruling principle which might be the public school ethos, or, just conceivably, the belief that most things are permissible provided one is not found out. For some reason, he reminded Vereker of a latter-day Stanley Baldwin; a man with a comfortable, bluff exterior cloaking a more subtle, even devious, personality. Vereker was an avid reader of biographies and had recently read one on Baldwin.

'I've been in touch with the rural dean,' Jarman told Vereker.

'What did he say?'

' "Get them out". Which is fine for him, away on the mainland.'

'It's a very big house just for Nan and me,' Vereker said.

'We may have to take the Anguilos, but don't promise anything. I'll give the rector of Doddlecombe a call and find out how he managed; I know he had a bit of trouble with squatters at one time.'

'What kind of a person is Meg Jacobs?'

'Meg Jacobs?' Jarman smiled. He had oddly-shaped triangular eyes with a sense of mischief in them kept under superficial control. 'She's well meaning enough, but not very effective – frightens herself as much as anyone else. We ought to come to terms with her before someone really nasty takes over.'

The morning passed. The squatters were taken away in relays to a home for unmarried mothers where lunch had been laid on for them.

Jarman had spent the morning on the telephone with little to show for it. The rector of Doddlecombe had gone on a sponsored walk and Tudor Lindsay was in court. 'I suggest you go over to Carrick Farm this evening and get Lindsay on the job. He probably knows more about sorting out this kind of mess than anyone else.'

'Is he helpful?'

'He'll have to be over this. It's his job.'

Jarman departed for a late lunch and Vereker and Nan sat down to the remains of the cold ham and salad. She seemed in better spirits than the night before. 'I've made a list of things we need.' Her tone challenged her father to question her list, but when he failed to do so she hung around for a few minutes to give him another chance; eventually, however, she set out for the shops looking resolute, if not exactly confident.

The squatters returned and seemed content to amuse themselves in the garden. The reporter from the *Herald* arrived, delighted about the squatters, and asked Vereker for his views on squatting. Vereker said that he had not been here long enough to have any views.

'But doesn't Christianity involve loving our neighbours?' the reporter asked predictably.

Vereker said that indeed this was so.

'Then aren't these your neighbours?' the reporter persisted.

'Well, in a way they are, and in a way they aren't, because this isn't my house.'

At this point they were interrupted by the arrival of the other churchwarden, Colonel Maitland, an old man in tweeds and a hat which Vereker associated with Sherlock Holmes. The old man had watery blue eyes and was a little hard of hearing; he was, however, in full possession of his wits and proceeded to interview Vereker on his life in America on behalf of the reporter. He spoke in a series of short barks, turning every now and again to the reporter to snap, 'Got that?' 'That what you want to know, eh?' When the reporter had the temerity to mention the squatters, he was put down with a growling, 'Can't talk about that now. Later, later. Always in a hurry, you fellahs.' When, like a sheepdog protecting a particularly foolish sheep, he had nosed the reporter away from Vereker and out of the front door, the old man said severely, 'Should have waited for me before seeing that fellah.'

'I didn't know you were coming,' Vereker pointed out.

The old man stared at him in angry reproach; obviously he considered that he had reached an age when occasional unreason is allowable and should not be questioned.

'But I was very glad to see you,' Vereker assured him.

'Humph.' The old man walked to the window and looked at the squatters, screwing up his eyes in the bright light. 'Bad business. Just when you've arrived. Drifters and spongers most of them. Still, there are reasons why we ought to take the Anguilos.' He did not say what those reasons were.

Vereker said he would like to take the Anguilos. He also said that it had been suggested he should see Tudor Lindsay in the evening. He did not want to get involved with the Lindsays and hoped that this wily old man would take the task from him, but Colonel Maitland merely nodded and asked, 'D'ye have this sort of caper in America?' Then, before Vereker could answer, he went on, 'When I was a child I knew an old man who saw Abraham Lincoln. How old d'ye think that makes me?'

'Eighty?' Vereker hazarded.

'Eighty-three. That was a bad business, y'know. A country can't afford to squander its great men like that.' He looked at Vereker shrewdly. 'What happened to Kennedy, eh? Was it that fellah, forget his name. . . .'

The telephone rang before Vereker could confess his ignorance. It was a Miss Draisey who was a member of the parochial church council; she had telephoned to welcome Vereker and to give him a list of people who were sick on whom he should call preferably today but certainly before Sunday. When Vereker had taken down the list of names,

38

Colonel Maitland went through it, crossed off three names and added two others. Then he told Vereker about an old man he had known who had seen Disraeli drive up to Gunnersbury Park to greet Baron Rothschild. After two more telephone calls, a discussion of church business and the casualties at Passchendaele, the old man departed.

It was half-past four and Vereker was eager for tea; this was one English habit he seemed to have acquired instantaneously. The hall was dark now, but the kitchen door was open and sunlight slanted in at the window and cast a cone of light on the floor. As Vereker walked towards the kitchen, a shadow blocked part of the light. Nan must be back. But instead of going forward to greet her, he stopped. It was quiet. Nan was a hurrying person; she would be at the table by now, banging down her purchases and calling out to him that she was back. Whoever was in the kitchen was having second thoughts about being there. One of the squatters, another parishioner with pickles, fruit-cake? He had so wanted a few moments alone. Whoever it was, wasn't welcome.

He went into the kitchen and found a strange woman standing by the back door; a tall woman, in a dark-green, belted coat, wearing a dark-green felt hat which dipped on one side so that only the plane of one cheek and a shadowed eye were visible. She remained quite still, her back against the door, perhaps startled by his sudden arrival; she reminded him of a figure in a 'thirties movie, one of the 'heavier' actresses, Garbo or Dietrich, who were always standing around looking fraught with their backs to doors.

'Mr. Vereker?' She took off her hat and looked for somewhere to lay it down. 'I'm Zoe Lindsay.' He did not respond, but she seemed unaware of any lack of courtesy on his part. 'I said I'd help with the house.' She glanced around the kitchen; Nan had left it in a mess, but this did not seem to concern her. She still had not found anywhere to put her hat and had not moved away from the door.

'We've got squatters,' Vereker said. His mind was not on the squatters.

She ran her fingers through her hair which had been flattened by the hat; she did this in an abstracted way, as a man might have done. The problem of making the best of herself was not one with which she would ever have to contend : beauty was hers whether she wanted it or not. Your less fortunate human being, such as Matthew Vereker, must try to make the best of a face for which mouth, eyes, nose have been chosen at random, rejects from other models. Her face and features were all of a piece; the cavities between the finely arched brows and the high cheekbones had been hollowed for just those almond eyes, while the elegant ripple of the nostrils and the swell of the long upper lip belonged ineluctably to the oval frame in which they were contained. Unnecessary generosity would cloy such sculptured beauty : her eyelashes were not long, the light brown hair was not exceptional in colour or texture, the skin was dry and too pale.

For how long Vereker gazed at her he could not have said. No doubt he behaved rudely, but then she had not been very polite yesterday when she observed him from an upstairs window of her house. She took his scrutiny calmly. She had found out about her beauty a long time ago and the knowledge had left her free to concentrate on other worries. Certainly, she had worries. Her face had the gentle, dazed expression of the person who has gone into retreat from life. Looking at her, Vereker heard a voice inside him crying out angrily, 'I have had enough of ill women !'

'Have you had tea yet?' She came forward at last and laid her hat on one of the kitchen chairs. Her voice was low and subdued.

'I was just coming to make it.'

'You really want tea? I can make coffee if you prefer it.'

'I have become addicted to tea.' He was brusque.

She went to the sink to fill the kettle. 'Are those the squatters?' she asked, looking out of the window neither surprised nor interested.

'Yes. Do you know any of them?'

'We all know the Anguilos, of course.' She did not explain why this should be so. 'Tudor will know the others, I expect.'

She poured tea for herself and Vereker and they sat at the kitchen table. 'I feel I ought to take in one or two of them,' Vereker said. 'This house is so large.'

This surprised her. 'But our house is large, too. I suppose we ought to take someone in. I hadn't thought of that.'

'Have you lived there long?'

'All my life.'

She sipped her tea slowly, lacing her fingers round the cup to warm them although it was not cold in the kitchen. Outside the light was beginning to fade. Vereker wished that Nan would return.

'I'll come in the morning tomorrow,' she said. 'I meant to come this morning, only. . . .' She lost the thread of her thought.

'We don't want to put you out in any way.'

'Why should you put me out?' She looked at him with hostility as though he had said something presumptuous.

'You've got your own house to look after.'

'That doesn't take me all day. I shall be pleased to come here. It's a nice old house.'

Vereker, feeling uncomfortable, said, 'I'll leave you, then. I don't suppose you want me under your feet.'

He went to the study and looked through the notes which Roberts had left for him. Then he made a few notes of things he might say at the social evening on Friday at which he was to meet his parishioners. At six o'clock he went into the church to say the evening office. Zoe Lindsay was about to leave when he returned.

'Your daughter is in the bath,' she told him. 'And I've let the squatters into the cellar. I didn't think they should have the run of the house until you've sorted things out.'

'The cellar!'

'It's more of a basement,' she assured him. 'The Roberts children used it as a play area and there's a lavatory and wash-basin down there.'

He opened the door for her. The air was sharp and smelt of frost.

'It's dark now,' he said, not sure what was expected of him. 'Should I walk you home?'

She smiled and for a moment all the cobwebs were blown away and her face was clear as crystal. 'There's no need, I'm used to the dark. I'd be a prisoner all winter if I never went out at night unaccompanied.'

'You're not afraid of ghosts down at the priory?' he asked, a little sorry that his offer had been refused.

'There's no need to be frightened of them; they're quite harmless.'

He leaned against the lintel of the door, prepared to chat.

41

'Now I've heard that said often, but it doesn't convince me. If I went down to that priory ruin and saw a lot of nuns there in the moonlight, I'd be plain terrified.'

'It's not just in the moonlight,' she said. 'They're there in the day, too.'

There was a pause. The evening air blew in between them and it seemed to Vereker to be degrees colder. He said, keeping his voice carefully unemphatic, 'You see them?'

'Yes.'

'And do they talk to you?'

'No.' She put on her hat; it shielded her face, but her voice sounded sad. 'At first I tried to talk to them; then I realized that although I see them, they don't see me.'

They bade each other good night and Vereker shut the door sooner than was strictly polite. He did a rapid tour of the house. She had left it in good order. That was fine : he and Nan could carry on from here. Later, he would tackle Tudor Lindsay about the squatters and he would make it plain, even at the risk of giving offence, that he and Nan did not need any more help from his cousin.

Jarman called on his way home from the office and Meg Jacobs returned from some unspecified errand. Vereker had little chance to talk to Nan alone, but when he went into the kitchen where she was preparing sandwiches, she said, 'I *like* Zoe Lindsay. She's got a very special aura. Didn't you feel it?'

'She's unusual,' Vereker conceded.

'Yes.' Nan sighed, as though to be unusual was the ultimate in personal achievement.

'I thought she looked rather strained,' Vereker felt his way carefully. 'Maybe it's asking too much of her to look after this house as well as her own.'

'She likes the house. She told me so.'

'I'll have a word with her cousin,' Vereker muttered. 'I'm going over there now.'

'You could ask them to have dinner with us sometime. Don't you think you should?' Nan looked doubtfully at the hunks of bread, thick at the top and tapering to mere crumble at the other end, and quailed at the thought of producing dinner for four. 'Or drinks, maybe; or coffee.'

'Maybe.' Vereker had no intention of offering hospitality

42

to the Lindsays; Zoe Lindsay was another of God's creatures whom he was rejecting. He told himself he was doing it for Nan's sake; but Nan hadn't been in his mind when that inner voice had formed those shocking words, 'I have had enough of ill women!'

Nan started to say something about Tudor Lindsay, but as she was speaking Meg Jacobs came in and offered to help with the sandwiches. Vereker, glad of the interruption, said, 'I'll be on my way now.'

As he shut the door behind him, Vereker blew out his cheeks in a gusty sigh. If he walked slowly it could take him all of half an hour to get to Carrick Farm. He walked down the drive, opened the front gate, and turned in the direction of Virginia Close, moving with the taut restraint of an escaped prisoner who may at any moment break into an ill-considered run. His heart was pounding and he steadied his pace. Friends at home had warned him that life in England was very different to life in America; it would take him a little while, they had said, to acclimatize himself to the slower pace. His heart was still pounding as he walked down Virginia Close; the difference in pace would be the death of him if he wasn't careful.

The bungalows all had their porch lights on, it was like walking through a glow-worm camp. It was quiet; no one clipping a hedge, no dogs barking. The inhabitants, human and canine, were presumably holed up in their sitting-rooms. "Camp" was the wrong word, "camp" suggested a community of people living together and that was too primitive for what was happening here; these people had refined themselves out of tribal existence, they might be housed together but they did their living very privately.

At the T junction the moon shone on the concrete mixer and the crane and the derelict buildings, roofless with empty windowless eyes. An illuminated tag at the top of scaffolding hoisted the builders name among the stars. Far in the distance, towards the town centre, a traffic light blinked. There was no traffic in sight but now all around him he could hear the banshee wail of police sirens; he stood listening for a moment, puzzled, until a rapid burst of machine-gun fire brought the realization that the noise was coming from dozens of television sets.

43

He turned gratefully towards the darkness of the country lane, found the stile and climbed it. The right of way was by no means easy to follow in the dark so now he had to walk slowly. It was good to have more space around him, but he still didn't feel right. He saw a line of trees strung out stark against the sky, he heard the wind in the long grass, he smelt the salt tang of marshes, but he had no feeling of liberation, and the dim light from a solitary cottage brought no sense of warmth and comfort. There was an older way of life trodden under foot here. There was an older way of life in America, too; but Indian territory wasn't peaceful, not for the white man, anyway. It was absurd to make comparisons. Yet the feeling remained strongly with him of a life to which violence has been done. There was no peace here.

There was no peace for Tudor Lindsay, either. At first, Vereker thought that this was his fault. Lindsay was eating his supper in the sitting-room when Vereker arrived. Vereker said, 'I am sorry about this,' but Lindsay accepted the interruption with thin-lipped satisfaction as though he had been waiting for something to spoil his evening.

Zoe said to Vereker, 'I'll get you coffee,' and Vereker accepted because he thought this might make Lindsay more relaxed so that he wouldn't hurry over his meal. In fact, it made little difference as Lindsay was a compulsively quick eater.

'Squatters,' Lindsay said when Zoe had gone out to the kitchen. 'How does the Christian Church solve that one?' He hitched himself back more comfortably in his chair and re-settled the tray on his knees.

Vereker said, 'Yes, it's an awkward one.'

'What did the Christian Church do before the social services department was set up, I wonder?' Lindsay addressed his plate.

'Are you going to rehouse the squatters?' Vereker asked.

'How neat and tidy that would be, wouldn't it? A wave of the fairy godmother's wand, and hey presto, a neat little house appears in a clearing in the wood. I'm afraid I don't deal in magic.'

'Then I suppose the Christian Church will have to carry on much as it did before the social services department was set up.'

Lindsay looked angry. He might make mock of others, but he expected to be treated with respect himself. He attacked his food in silence. The waves of unrest were very strong.

After a few minutes, Vereker got up and went over to a bookcase on the far side of the room. No doubt it wasn't polite for a stranger to make himself at home in this fashion but he felt an imperative need to remove himself from Tudor Lindsay's magnetic field. The books were old and had leather bindings with gilt lettering : *Lorna Doone, Sir Nigel, Masterman Ready, The Lamplighter, From Log Cabin to White House*; he took down the latter. Dust tickled his nose but he managed to stifle the sneeze. On the yellow, pock-marked fly leaf were inscribed with decorative flourishes the words "Silas Duverell on his ninth birthday from Father". A photograph slipped from between the leaves of the book, a studio portrait of a woman with her hair knotted up beneath a lace cap. This must surely be a relative of Zoe, the bone structure was unmistakable. He closed the book and replaced it on the shelf. He looked about the room for something else to occupy his mind. Lindsay was eating cheese and biscuits; he seemed to have forgotten about Vereker. The door of the room was open and Vereker could see part of the hall with the fireplace stuffed with Christmas wrapping paper and an oil lamp on a chest near the stairs. He wished that the fire and the lamp were alight, they would give such a welcoming glow to the hall. This house should be welcoming, there was nothing sinister about it; it had been built at a time when people first sought a degree of comfort in their homes, but before there was any thought of luxury. It was sound, secure, comfortable, unpretentious. So why did he have this feeling of something in the house that was trying to get out? Did every English country house have a prisoner in the East Wing?

Zoe came with coffee. 'What a pity you've had all this trouble so soon after you arrived,' she said.

'The dispossessed *are* incredibly inconsiderate,' Lindsay said.

Zoe said to Vereker, 'Milk? Sugar?' Apart from a slight drawing together of her features as though she had a headache, nothing in her manner suggested that she was aware of her cousin or had heard him speak. When Vereker had accepted milk and sugar she seated herself on a cushion on the hearth and gazed at the log fire.

There was an awkward silence which Vereker broke by asking Lindsay, 'Have you lived here all your life?'

'God forbid! Don't be misled by my ridiculous name. My mother saw a film called *Tudor Rose*; that was how my mother reached the important decisions of her life, such as giving a name to her first born. In fact, I come from a working class background.' Lindsay looked at Vereker as though he was hoisting a banner.

'Go back one or two generations and most of us are sons of the soil,' Vereker said easily.

'Not in England. In fact, you are speaking in the presence of a sprig of the oldest family on the island. The Duverells came over with William the Conqueror, they belong to the real aristocracy, undiluted by the vulgar Tudors.' He made a gesture towards Zoe.

Zoe held a poker against the largest of the logs, turning the tip slowly, boring into the log so that eventually it fell apart and a shower of glowing ash fell into the grate. 'Edward the Fourth did his share of the diluting,' she said.

'And what is that supposed to mean?' For the first time since Vereker had arrived, Tudor Lindsay looked directly at his cousin.

'Edward the Fourth came before the Tudors, that's all.'

'Thank you for the history lesson.' His anger was intense.

She took no notice of him and went on poking the log.

'It was a scandal in our family when Zoe's mother married Jonas Lindsay.' At first, Tudor Lindsay spoke quietly, with an electric amusement which struck sparks from the atmosphere; but as he failed to gain her attention his voice grew louder. 'My mother was terribly shocked about it. Whenever Jonas' name was introduced into the conversation, she would explain to any stranger who happened to be present, "Jonas married above himself"; it wasn't "fit". To do something that wasn't "fit" was a crime to her.'

'Have you ever thought of leaving England?' Vereker asked in the hope of deflecting some of this bitterness.

'For America, the Land of Liberty?'

'You think that even worse?'

'Let's say I'd sooner stay in England.'

'Russia, then?'

'As bureaucratic as America!'

'China?'

Lindsay picked up the tray and hurled china in the hearth. 'Can't you ever attend to anything that's said?' he shouted at Zoe. 'Can't you ever be part of anything that's going on, here, now, in the twentieth century?'

Zoe gave a start and the poker dropped from her hand; this apart, she remained absolutely still until Lindsay had gone out of the room saying that he would go across to the vicarage in a few minutes. When his footsteps sounded on the stairs, she said, 'I'll get the dustpan.'

Vereker was left alone feeling like a bit player deserted on-stage by the two principal characters. The fire was almost out and the room was distinctly chilly. He locked his fingers together and blew on them. Zoe came back with a dustpan and brush and began to sweep up the broken crockery. Vereker did not know what to do. He felt that his presence had barely registered with these two and that it might be tactless to intrude at this particular point. While he was still undecided, Tudor Lindsay came back, struggling into a raincoat.

'I think I should make it quite clear,' he said, 'that my sympathy is with the squatters.'

'I have sympathy for them, too,' Vereker answered.

'Moreover, I don't believe in God.'

'No?'

'Don't you mind?' Lindsay had himself well in control now and seemed genuinely amused.

'It's an occupational hazard,' Vereker answered. 'I've noticed people seem to have a compulsion when introduced to a writer to confess that they don't read his books. With a clergyman, they don't feel comfortable until they've told him they don't believe in his God.'

'Let's go, shall we?' Lindsay was rather deflated.

Vereker said goodbye to Zoe. She answered, 'Goodbye' and then, as the two men went into the hall, she called out, 'I'll be over in the morning, Mr. Vereker.' Lindsay had the front door open and Vereker followed him without replying.

A mist had come up from the sea, trailing a grey shroud over the fields, and without Lindsay beside him Vereker would not have known which way to turn. Sound was muffled. Vereker rubbed a finger in his ear but it made no difference.

He felt chilled to the marrow. Lindsay, however, seemed in better spirits now that he had got his adrenalin going and said cheerfully, 'You really dislike me, don't you?'

'Why is it so important to you to be disliked?'

'Because you know where you are with people who dislike you.'

Lindsay opened a gate. 'This way,' he said to Vereker who was trying to go through the hedge.

Vereker said, 'But you must have some friends, surely?'

'I prefer women.'

'And that excludes friendship?'

'With a woman, for God's sake!'

'I've often thought women have a greater gift for friendship than men,' Vereker said.

'Can you imagine being friendly with a woman like Zoe?'

Vereker did not answer. He was beginning to understand Zoe's attitude, silence was probably the best defence against Lindsay.

'She retreats from all confrontations, takes herself off into a world of her own and puts up the shutters. People with that gentle, impervious manner always *are* utterly selfish, but they never get found out.'

'*You've* found out.'

'But at a price; oh, believe me, at a price. Do you think I enjoy scenes like that one this evening?'

'I had an idea you might.'

'You don't know anything about psychology. Hasn't it reached the Far-West yet?'

'Middle-West.'

'You shouldn't stifle things inside you; it rots your guts. You've got to be prepared not to give a damn what other people think and just holler.'

Vereker stumbled over a clump of grass and remained crouched forward.

'Hurt yourself?' Lindsay put a hand on his shoulder; he sounded concerned.

'No, just getting my breath back.' Vereker's heart was thumping again. 'I hope you know where we're going.'

'To hell. All of us.'

'For an agnostic, you have an odd turn of phrase.'

'Atheist.'

48

They stood silently with the mist swirling round them thicker than ever.

'Hell,' Lindsay said, 'is oneself.'

'*That* thought has been around a long time, even in the Middle-West.'

They walked on. The mist played games with them; sometimes it was dense, sometimes it parted so that they could see quite clearly. In one clear spell, Vereker saw a wall jutting up like a fang.

'We're in the priory grounds,' he said.

'The grounds were extensive. We are actually inside the building.' Tudor Lindsay slowed his pace. 'Go carefully, there are heaps of stone and rubble everywhere. If I had my way the whole site would be levelled.' As they threaded their way in and out of the low walls, he said, 'Can't you do something about this nonsense?'

'Exorcism? I'm surprised you ask.'

'I've tried psychiatry; she wouldn't go.'

'So the alternative is to make the nuns go?'

'Something has to be done. Other people are beginning to get in on the act. Did you know that?'

'Mrs. Hooper?'

'Not only Mrs. Hooper. She's harmless. Something has to be done. I'm serious about this. Think about it. You came to me quick enough when you were in trouble with the squatters.'

The mist cleared abruptly as they reached the church. By the time they arrived at the vicarage, Tudor Lindsay had assumed his professional role. He played it well and Nancy was very impressed.

'Isn't he terrific!' she said, as Lindsay talked to Meg Jacobs and the squatters.

Undoubtedly, here was a man who was prepared to be endlessly patient with those less fortunate in their circumstances than himself and less well-endowed intellectually; a man who was also a capable negotiator, and had the judgement to know when to stand firm and when it is safe to give way.

'He managed that well, give the devil his due,' Donald Jarman said when eventually it was agreed that Milo, his mother and his sisters should remain in the basement rooms.

Vereker made no comment on Lindsay's performance. There was a sterile violence about the man which roused a response in Vereker which, if not actually violent, was far from peaceable.

Later, the mist cleared from the priory ruins and Zoe saw Dame Alice making her nightly round. She christened her Dame Alice because it was convenient to name those of the nuns whom she saw most often.

Zoe was sitting on a low wall in the middle of a field where cattle pastured during the day. Diseased elm trees had been cut down only that afternoon and now lay twisted on the ground like prehistoric monsters. Although the mist had cleared damp air still rose from the grass and Zoe in duffel coat and Dame Alice in hood and habit were sensibly dressed each in her own fashion. Dame Alice walked purposefully across the field towards Zoe, then for no apparent reason did a sharp right turn, walked a few paces, did a left turn and proceeded calmly and without deviating through two felled elms, bowed her head and crossed herself as she walked through a thorn bush, and entered the complex of low walls where Zoe was sitting. Now, Zoe knew that Dame Alice had reached the corridor leading from the great hall to the dorter. Zoe herself was seated in that corridor.

Dame Alice paused just outside the great hall, standing with her head to one side in a listening attitude. Hopefully, Zoe sang "We'll all go to sea in a yellow submarine" which was the only song that came into her head at that moment. Dame Alice lifted up her voluminous skirts and after some fumbling produced something which she crammed greedily into her mouth. Scarcely a response to a song sung some seven hundred years hence, Zoe thought resignedly. As Dame Alice moved forward again, Zoe kicked a stone into her path, but Dame Alice did not respond to that, either. Now she was within a foot of Zoe. Her face looked as it always had looked since Zoe first saw her, like a russet apple which has been stored too long and is not quite wholesome. There was a sour smell as she passed by.

Zoe did not wonder where Dame Alice was going, or how she would spend the hours until the morning. She simply accepted what Dame Alice communicated to the night air as she did her lonely round. Zoe prayed, 'Good Lord, be merciful to your servant Alice who didn't choose to serve you in this way and doesn't understand what it is all about.' Then she got to her feet, holding the hood of her duffel coat around her face, and turned towards Carrick Farm.

Poor Dame Alice, an obdurately cheerful middle-aged woman whose good-nature had been eroded by the wear and tear of the uneventful years: yet, in some ways, lucky Dame Alice, not so aware as some of the others that she was caught in a trap. Zoe could see Carrick Farm now, solid against the sky. As she looked, a light snapped on in Tudor's room. Now that he was awake he might read or he might turn out the light and go to the window. If he went to the window he would see her coming back. She began to hurry. What fools women are! she thought angrily as she stumbled over the twisted branches of an elm. Life can't be as difficult as we make out; there must be a knack about springing the trap, something quite simple, all the great discoveries are simple. The light went out in Tudor's room. He was waiting at the top of the stairs when she came in from the kitchen entrance.

'How many nuns did you see tonight?' he asked, brittle as a character out of Coward.

'One.' It would have been easier to lie to him, but she wasn't prepared to do that.

He switched on the light and came half-way down the stairs, blocking her way; he had a nice sense of the dramatic had Tudor. His face was expressing strong emotion, but whether rage or desperation, she could not tell since she never looked at him for long nowadays. Each glance was like exploring an exposed nerve.

'That priory was in use for two hundred years at least,' he said in a low, tight voice.

'Yes, I know.' She folded her hands and looked down at them, wondering whether she could make the thumb and middle finger of the one hand meet across the knuckles of the other.

'And how many women have passed within its walls in that time? Four or five hundred, would you think that a reasonable estimate? And you see – how many? Six or seven? Scarcely a representative sample, is it?'

'No,' she agreed, smiling as though she had made some silly mistake in ordering the groceries; the knuckle bones were too big, the fingers failed to meet.

'Does the action all take place over one decade or does it span several generations?'

She shrugged her shoulders and tried the experiment with her hands reversed. The knuckle bones didn't seem so big; she wondered if she had arthritis in the other hand.

'Don't you ever subject these apparitions to rational scrutiny? Do you really think it is likely that out of all the women who have lived in that priory you should be visited by only six or seven?'

She shook her head. She did not think it likely, it just happened.

'They are creatures of your mind.'

He meant this to frighten her, but it would have been kinder were it true that they were a product of her sick mind. These women had minds of their own which meant that their pain was their own, too. She felt their pain.

'I'm tired, Tudor,' she said. 'I'll go to bed now.'

'We've got to talk about this.'

'Not now. It must be three o'clock.' Almost imperceptibly the balance of advantage was shifting.

'It doesn't matter if we talk all night, we have got to talk!'

'I'll go to bed now.'

'THIS IS MAKING ME ILL!' He shouted as he had shouted as a child, so loud that his parents gave in to him for fear that otherwise he would harm himself. 'DON'T YOU CARE THAT YOU ARE MAKING ME ILL?'

He was barring her passage up the stairs and had manoeuvred her against the wall; yet in spite of this, she seemed to elude him.

'You wouldn't mind if I died.' It had been his ultimate threat to his parents and he had never found a way of going beyond it.

She said, 'Don't be silly.'

He put his hands to his face and began to cry.

She said, 'No, Tudor, no,' in a quiet, cold voice. She could pass him now, and did.

Tudor remained on the stairs crying as though his body would break apart. She was not afraid that he would do anything desperate, he was too afraid of death for that. He was trapped, too, poor Tudor! But she would not weaken. He had invaded every corner of her life save this one. When he

52

became her lover he had walked around her, slamming all the doors, closing all the windows, because he must have complete possession. But she had found a world into which he could not follow her and she was prepared to guard that territory.

She went to her room and walked across to the window without turning on the light. She had been born in this room and it was from this window that she had first glimpsed the nuns. She had been thirteen then and she had known instinctively that there was something wrong about seeing them, so she had not run to tell her mother. She had kept the nuns at the edge of vision and sometimes they had seemed to fade, merging to a grey blur which might have been indicative of a slight visual defect. But when she was nineteen her father had died and her mother had decided to die, too. Zoe had given up her art course to nurse her mother in her long dying, had had a love affair with a married man, and grown almost imperceptibly into her thirties. At some time during that unhappy period the nuns had advanced beyond the edge of vision. It was only when Tudor became her lover, however, that she had finally turned to them and allowed herself to know them.

'Scarcely a representative sample, is it?'

Tudor's voice came to her as she stood by the window. Tudor was good on samples; he used them as he used statistics, to disprove anything and everything. Disproof was important to Tudor. Fortunately, in this case it had been the numbers involved in the sample that concerned him. He was a long way from her problem. There *was* one odd thing about the nuns whom she saw. Some accommodated themselves well to their prison, others were unable to do so; but they were *all* imprisoned. Her "sample" did not include one who lived in the priory voluntarily because God had called her. And there must have been some in each generation. Yet she never saw them. She longed to see them, hoping that it might be catching, this glory that was theirs.

'Why?'

So many questions, questions, questions; questions without answer of everything and everyone, since Tudor came. Yet here, where she was safe from him, here in her private world, she was plagued by this question that was all her own.

4

The Jarmans lived in a mock Tudor house in Elm Lane. Elm Lane still had elms; it had an unmade road, too, which was full of pebbles and shells having at one time led straight off the beach from which it was now separated by the coast road. The unmade road was the devil on car tyres but most of the householders had lived there a long time and liked it that way. The Jarmans' house had been built in the early nineteen-thirties and stood in an acre of ground with an untidy lawn on three sides and a small orchard at the back. Some of the people in the lane had compromised with modernity to the extent of selling off part of their land so that here and there new properties had been eased in between the old. This infilling had been done discreetly; the buildings were of the log-cabin type and peeped shyly from between the branches of trees. Barbara Jarman, who felt embarrassed by their subservience, called their owners the Disney Folk. In spite of the Disney Folk, the lane still looked much as it had in pictures taken before the war when it had been the only residential area of the west village.

The elms, the unmade road, and the more generous gardens were all that remained of those rural days. Elm Lane now ran like a natural fault across a complex of well-surfaced roads where sensible people who wanted neat pavements and sodium lamps lived in bungalows and chalets in close proximity to amusement arcades, launderettes and supermarkets. The seascape, however, had not changed much, although old people said there had been more sand before the war. If one blinkered one's eyes one could still look down Elm Lane to an unspoilt vista of pebble beach and sea merging imperceptibly into sky. Unblinkered, one would be primarily aware of the fairground to the right. At night, the Jarmans could see the lights of the ferris wheel from their sitting-room window and they could hear the noise of the fairground all over the house.

The Jarmans were unlike any family Nancy had ever known. She had led rather a subdued life and her idea of a happy home was a place where peace, however fragile, is maintained intact. On the first occasion when she went to supper with the Jarmans, her arrival coincided with Mrs. Jarman's return from a school staff meeting. The moment she set foot in the house Mrs. Jarman shouted to her daughter, Barbara, 'Is the kettle on? I'm in shreds!'

Barbara Jarman, seventeen and remarkably self-possessed, said to Nancy, 'Mother believes it would be bad for her to stay at home, intellectually starved; it would make her neurotic and bad-tempered and we'd all suffer. So instead we have her like this. Aren't we lucky?'

'Tea first, darling,' Mrs. Jarman said. 'Analysis can wait.'

She and Barbara went into the kitchen whence their raised voices could be heard, Mrs. Jarman talking about the staff meeting and Barbara saying couldn't she ever talk about anything but school? Mr. Jarman regarded Nancy over the top of *The Financial Times* and said, 'Supper *will* come in time.'

Mrs. Jarman came immediately, a cup of tea in one hand. 'Where's Jeremy?'

Her husband lowered the paper and looked around the room as though he expected Jeremy to emerge from behind the furniture. Barbara called from the kitchen, 'He's gone to supper with Mike Hanley.'

'He wouldn't have thought to tell me?'

'Yes.' Barbara appeared in the doorway looking amused. 'He did think; he told me and I'm telling you.'

Mrs. Jarman sank into an armchair and sipped her tea. 'There's a parents' meeting at school next week,' Barbara called from the kitchen.

Mr. Jarman turned the pages of *The Financial Times*. Mrs. Jarman watched him for a moment or two and then said, 'How long is it since you've been to a parents' meeting? Not since the children were in junior school, I should think.'

Mr. Jarman put *The Financial Times* down on the floor and went out of the room. Mrs. Jarman followed him and could be heard calling up the stairs, 'That's right! Retire to your favourite place the moment something is said you don't want to answer.' She went up a few steps to ensure that her words carried. 'This is almost a one-parent family, the amount you participate in your children's activities.'

She came back to the sitting-room looking refreshed, drank

her tea and went into the kitchen where she began to bang pans about. 'Go and talk to Nancy, I can manage here,' she instructed Barbara.

Barbara came out of the kitchen and sat on the hearth stool. She was a compact-looking girl who was probably good at games and most others things as well; she had her mother's dark brown eyes, a clear English complexion and she spoke with immaculate precision.

'Are you shocked by us?' she asked. 'Didn't you have rows in your house? We have them all the time.'

'I couldn't ever have talked to my mother in that tone of voice,' Nancy said. 'She would have been hurt.'

'But you can't live with someone for years without hurting them.'

Nancy tried to win sympathy which was her inevitable response to situations where she felt herself out-classed. 'My mother,' she said quietly, 'was very ill.'

Barbara looked annoyed and said, 'I'm sorry about that,' as though she did not really mean it.

Mrs. Jarman came in with a laden tray and Barbara put out the cutlery. Mr. Jarman returned and talked to Nancy about America. He seemed to know more about it than she did. He also gave the impression that there were things he knew about her. It wasn't the same kind of knowing as that displayed by Tudor Lindsay. Tudor had told her about her psychological situation and had explained her hang-ups in language that was as impersonal as a case history; but Mr. Jarman looked at her as though he knew what she was like under her skin. He was an accountant, but sitting here in his own home he was Nancy's idea of an English country squire. There was a suggestion of the stables about him. She was glad when Mrs. Jarman summoned them to the table.

'How are your squatters?' Mrs. Jarman asked Nancy.

'Mrs. Anguilo has been in and out a bit. She couldn't get the stove in the basement to light. . . .'

'My dear, she'll never get anything to work if there's someone else around to do it, so be careful.'

Nancy said she would be careful, although she had enjoyed Mrs. Anguilo's helplessness which had made her feel efficient in comparison.

'Milo had a long talk with my father.'

Barbara said, 'Beware of Milo! Did you know that he belongs to the Ancient People?'

'And who are the Ancient People?' her father asked.

'They are the people who worship the old gods who were driven out by Christianity. But they've been waiting around and now that Christianity's on the way out, their time has come.'

'What do they do?' Mrs. Jarman said. 'The worshippers, I mean, not the gods.'

'Whatever turns them on.'

'I wouldn't have thought they needed to bring back the old gods to do that,' Mr. Jarman observed, helping himself to another slice of ham.

'That shows just how out of touch you are, Daddy. You don't begin to understand how serious things are getting. "Way out" means "everyone's been"; and soon there'll be more people "underground" than above. You've got to be pretty ingenious to find something to be "outside" of nowadays.'

'So, what's the answer?'

'You introduce another dimension, I suppose. Give the supernatural a whirl.'

'How do you know all this?' Mrs. Jarman asked.

'Cam told me. Ronnie Smart, their lodger, is a member of the Ancient People. He keeps the Smarts awake at night making strange noises. Apparently to be an Ancient Person you must empty yourself and see what takes possession, and he has difficulty emptying so he practises in bed at night. Cam's mother thinks he's making himself ill.'

'I wonder if anyone possesses Milo.'

'He has quite a success apparently. It's understandable, don't you think? If I was a spirit and I had to choose between inhabiting Milo or Ronnie Smart I'd go for Milo every time.'

'What is all this about Ronnie Smart? *I* don't know any Ronnie Smart.' Mrs. Jarman sounded as though his existence must be proved mathematically if she were to accept him.

'I *told* you, he's the lodger. He's a computer programmer at the university.'

'Why ever does he live on Helmsley, then?' Mrs. Jarman pushed the salad dish towards Nancy. 'It all sounds very

57

unlikely to me. I wouldn't have thought a computer programmer would be interested in the old gods, or whatever they
call themselves.'

'Wouldn't you?' her husband looked surprised. 'I would
have thought computer programmers would be rather a long
way out.'

'What do *you* know about being a long way out?' she
turned on him. 'You're the most conventional man I know.'

'It would be nice to have placid, dumpling sort of parents,
wouldn't it?' Barbara said to Nancy who didn't know how to
answer.

'Would you rather I was like Cam's mother?' Mrs. Jarman
asked. 'And took in lodgers like this unpossessed computer
programmer, instead of going to work?'

'Yes, I should love that. Cam says that her mother is
always there when she comes home in the afternoon. She
thinks it's important that a teenage daughter should have her
mother there so that she can off-load on her. Can you imagine
that?'

Mrs. Jarman pushed her chair back and began stacking
the dirty plates. 'I think you are very unkind. Perhaps I'd
better give up my job. Would you like that?'

'It's too late for me.' Barbara took a stick of celery before
it was whisked away. 'But Jeremy might benefit, I suppose.'

'Perhaps teenage boys need their fathers to be at home?'
Mr. Jarman said. 'We'll have to ask Jeremy about that.'

Mrs. Jarman went into the kitchen and Nancy followed
carrying the bread-board. Mrs. Jarman heaped the dishes in
the sink and turned the hot tap full on so that water squirted
off the crockery onto her jumper. She began to attack the
saucepans with vigour; her expression was as fierce as her
movements. After a minute or two Barbara came in carrying
the remainder of the dishes. She put them down on the draining board and picked up a tea-cloth; then she bent forward,
looking up into her mother's face, and said, 'Woof!'

'Woof, woof!' her mother replied.

Barbara wiped a plate and she and her mother talked com-
panionably. Nancy thought the Jarmans were an upside-down
sort of family. She was familiar with tension beneath a calm
surface, but here, although things seemed rather rough on the
surface, there was a strange absence of tension. She felt in-

explicably happy and hoped she would come here often and help with the dishes.

When they returned to the sitting-room Mr. Jarman was watching a film about a Special Branch officer who at that moment was in bed with a blonde. Mr. Jarman said, keeping his eyes on the screen, 'This is what we pay our taxes for.'

His wife said, 'I don't suppose Nancy wants to watch this.'

Before Nancy could answer there was a knock on the front door. The caller was Mrs. Hooper. She came into the sitting-room looking deeply offended. The sight of Nancy seemed to make matters worse.

'I hope I'm not intruding,' she said stiffly.

'That depends on why you've come, Maud,' Mr. Jarman said as his wife turned off the television. 'If it's church business, then you *are* intruding.'

'Oh, I don't know anything about church business!' Mrs. Hooper's face flushed and her lips trembled as though her dentures had slipped. '*I'm* too old to be of much use to the church.'

Mrs. Jarman, who was standing behind Mrs. Hooper, caught her husband's eye and a signal passed between them.

'These young people want to watch television, Maud,' Mr. Jarman said. 'Suppose we go to the breakfast-room?'

But Mrs. Hooper, having reluctantly consented to seat herself, was not to be easily dislodged. She said, as though continuing an interrupted conversation, 'And what's all this about "no man is an island", then?'

'It's a quotation from John Donne,' Barbara said uppishly.

'You don't have to tell me it's a quotation,' Mrs. Hooper snapped. 'But it's a funny thing to preach a sermon about when you've just come to an island, isn't it?'

Nancy looked at an old copy of the *Radio Times* which was used as a wedge under the castor of the television trolley; it had a picture on the front of a complacent ginger cat sitting in a winged armchair. Her mouth had gone dry. If this acid-faced woman was going to criticise her father she knew she wouldn't be able to take it calmly.

'I don't think I've got the connection between your being of no use to the church and the vicar preaching a sermon about islands.' Mr. Jarman fumbled for a pipe in his jacket pocket.

'He was standing up there, his first sermon in our church, and telling us he didn't like our way of doing things. That's what it boiled down to, John Donne or no John Donne.' Mrs. Hooper shot an aggrieved glance at Barbara.

'I thought it was our way of *not* doing things that bothered him.' Barbara took up the cudgels before Nancy could intervene. Her parents looked at her dubiously, but neither of them interrupted her. 'But I don't think he was getting at you particularly, Mrs. Hooper. I thought he was probably getting at me.'

'You!' Mrs. Hooper put a world of outrage and disdain into this one word.

'Older people like to be with people they have things in common with. And the things people at All Hallows have in common are that they've been brought up to support the church and listen to the Queen's speech on Christmas Day; they have standards and values and they sell flags for voluntary societies.'

'*I* see. And those things are wrong, are they?'

'They're not what the other half of the island is about. That's why I think the vicar was getting at young people like me; we're the ones who want to break down the barriers.'

'You'd like to see the church filled with people from the Manning estate, would you, like the Roman Catholic church is; the parents in dirty jeans and the children running up and down the aisle during communion and pop groups playing the hymns?'

'I don't know that I would like that myself,' Barbara said judicially. 'But then I think I shall probably end up agnostic, so I suppose my vote doesn't count. But Jeremy is very much for bringing in the Manning estate people, dirty jeans and all.'

'Jeremy!' Mr. Jarman exclaimed.

'He's gone to a meeting at Mike Hanley's. They're going to organize a door-to-door evangelical campaign. I'm not sure that's the way to set about it. For myself. . . .'

'I think that's enough,' Mrs. Jarman said. 'Why don't you take Nancy for a walk?'

Mrs. Hooper, however, was not willing to let Barbara get away so easily. She leant forward and pointed a finger at her.

'How long are the young young? Tell me that!' She sat back in her chair and folded her hands over her stomach. 'We have the church turned upside down for them, and then they aren't young any more and there's a new lot of young who want something different and everything has to be turned upside down again. And who keeps the church running while all this is going on? *Old* people! Old, out of date people who, even if they do listen to Her Majesty on Christmas Day, are prepared to go down on their knees and scrub floors, and clean brass, and make coffee, and put the chairs out in the church hall, and clear up afterwards. Are Jeremy's groups going to do all that?'

'It's not just groups of young people,' Barbara said. 'There are old people on the Manning estate, and middle-aged people.'

'Put your raincoat on,' Mrs. Jarman said to Barbara. 'It looks a bit misty outside.'

Once outside the house, Barbara said to Nancy, 'We'll go down to the beach, shall we?'

A mist was coming off the sea. The trees looked insubstantial and the houses of the Disney Folk had disappeared. When they had gone a hundred yards the Jarmans' house had disappeared, too. It was hard to believe that Mr. and Mrs. Jarman would still be talking to Mrs. Hooper in that comfortable room. The lights along the coast road were blurred and the great slab of the near by hotel had lost its concrete outline although lighted windows floated disconnectedly like hanging lamps. There was no sound from the fairground which didn't do much mid-week trade until the summer season began. A few people were walking their dogs and one or two cars were crawling with dipped headlights. Beyond the road the shingle beach shelved down to the sea. Barbara and Nancy passed a row of bathing huts and a rowing boat lying on its side. Then there was nothing but the mist although not far ahead they could hear the waves hissing on the pebbles.

Nancy said, 'Do you think my father's sermon has upset many people?'

'I hope so,' Barbara answered. 'There wouldn't have been any point in it otherwise, would there?'

Nancy felt desolate. She had the wrong shoes on for walking on a pebble beach, and she didn't like their being alone with the sea so near and unseen. After they had walked a little way the mist parted for a moment and she saw the sea, inky black, only three feet away. She said involuntarily, 'I hate dark water.'

Barbara said, 'You're very inhibited, aren't you?'

She said this quietly and without malice. It would have been easier to cope with aggression or bitchiness which could be answered in kind. Nancy bit back a reference to her unfortunate childhood; she had made a resolution only an hour ago not to rely on this to get her out of trouble and it was a bit soon to break it. Then Barbara said, 'I'm sorry if I seemed rude.'

Nancy stumbled against a breakwater and nearly fell over. Barbara helped her to her feet. 'You haven't got the right shoes on,' she said. 'Why ever didn't you say?'

They made their way back to the road and Barbara said, 'I'll walk home with you.' As they walked down the quiet, blank streets, she said, 'Is there more going on in American towns at night?'

'Not in Coopers Town,' Nancy answered. 'But it's always there; it doesn't just suddenly die on you.'

'This place is like a morgue at night. No wonder Milo and his friends have to go back to prehistoric times to get a bit of life out of it.'

'Do you think they really go back to prehistoric times?'

'Want to judge for yourself?'

They had come to a crossroads; to the left and to the right, behind and ahead, the neat little bungalows were bedded down for the night. It was like standing on the corner of a Hollywood film set when all the studio workers had gone home. Nancy felt an icy trickle of despair run down her spine. Life couldn't just peter out like this! 'How?' she asked Barbara.

'I know where they'll be tonight. Ronnie Smart told Cam because he wants her to join them. But she's afraid there may be a sacrificial element – a virgin to be offered up each new moon!'

Barbara turned to the right, walking briskly now, her fists bunched in her pockets. 'I've been dying to do this,' she said. 'But I didn't think it would be much fun on my own.' It was the first time she had come within hailing distance of an admission of weakness since Nancy had met her. A man passed them on a bicycle, riding slowly; for a time the tail-light wobbled in front of them, then it disappeared as he turned into a side road. 'They probably have a curfew,' Barbara said. 'If he's late home, he'll have to go before a tribunal of blue-rinsed matrons.' There were three street lamps still to go, then darkness. Something moved in the shrubbery of a garden just ahead, a pair of jewelled eyes turned momentarily in their direction, then a lean shadow darted across the road.

'The saucy thing!' Barbara exclaimed. 'That was a fox.'

'Doing a bit of garbage collecting,' Nancy said as a dustbin lid clattered on concrete.

Now the last street lamp was behind them and it was dark. A slight breeze was stirring, however, and there was a smell of damp earth. 'With any luck, this will blow the mist away,' Barbara said. They came to a stile. 'You know where you are now? There's All Hallows over there, behind those trees. And this footpath leads to the priory ruins.'

The mist cleared slowly, clinging to their eyebrows and forming in drops on their hair. Nancy shivered. 'Do they dress up for these rites?'

'The reverse, I gather.'

The mist parted suddenly as they came in sight of the priory ruins. The moon lit up the scene so clearly that they felt they had stepped onto a stage; automatically, they both crouched down in the grass. 'We'll have to creep along behind that hedge and get in the shadow of the trees,' Barbara said. Nancy's heart was thudding, but they reached the shelter of the hedge and made their way safely to the trees without disturbing so much as a rabbit. From beneath the trees they could look out over the priory ruins without any fear of being seen themselves. The walls were low, but here and there part of an arch reared up; it was easier, at night, for the eye to complete the broken curve, while imagination constructed a flying buttress from a strand of cloud, a roof of vaulted trees. The breeze was blowing more strongly now, but it failed to disperse a rank smell which seemed to rise from the ground.

Barbara said, 'Look!'

A troop of nude figures came trotting out from the Carrick Farm entrance to the site. 'Just like a circus! Where's the ring master?' Barbara spoke in a whisper although there was little danger of her voice carrying at this distance. The figures now broke from their close formation and pranced round rather aimlessly. 'Each doing his own thing.' Barbara seemed to find it

63

necessary to punctuate the proceedings with comments. Nancy felt depressed. The figures looked pathetic and vulnerable as children, and it was obvious from their awkward footwork that they were not used to dancing about in fields barefoot. Some sort of order was being established now, however; one of the men had scrambled onto a great stone slab and was standing with his head tilted upwards, making a noise as though he was gargling. A woman crouched beneath the stone slab; she arched her back, then eased down on her haunches, brought her body forward, low so that her breasts touched the ground, then arched her back again and repeated the catlike motion. 'That's our P.E. mistress!' Barbara exclaimed. 'That's her favourite exercise for relaxing the muscles around the pelvis. Do you relax the muscles round your pelvis? You've no idea what a difficult sex-life you're going to have if you don't.'

'I think that's Mrs. Anguilo.' Nancy was peering at a pear-shaped outline which looked as if it had been blown up by a pump, one could imagine the breasts, stomach and thighs gradually inflating. 'Poor Mrs. Anguilo!' Nancy said, as the body revolved unsteadily. 'I'm sure she isn't enjoying this.'

'Neither is Ronnie Smart. He's got his back to us and his buttocks are moving left, right, left, right, as though he was on a parade ground. Poor little Ronnie! No gift for improvisation.'

'It must be awfully cold out there.'

'Yes, not very conducive to ecstasy, or whatever. . . . Hullo, hullo! How's that for scene stealing?'

The broken arch must have worn away in a series of steps, but that was not apparent from this distance, and it seemed as if the light figure which ran nimbly up the arch had taken wing. Milo stood at the top, one leg thrust forward, the knee slightly bent, perfectly balanced; then he raised his hands slowly above his head in a gesture of supplication. Nancy said, 'I hope he isn't going to fall.' Now, it was Barbara who was silent, gazing at the slim body which topped the jagged column like a Greek statue, beautiful, noble, imbued with that pagan sadness for life that is sweet as honey and fleeting as a dream. Barbara's eyes glistened. Milo's companions had unravelled themselves from their antics and now trotted across to the base of the arch. The man on the stone slab hesitated a moment before he, too, joined the gazing circle. Milo shifted his weight; standing with legs a little apart, he slowly arched his body back, the shoulders braced as though a tremendous weight had been entrusted to his outstretched arms. His concentration was such that he might have been holding an unexploded bomb up there above his head. He began to rotate slowly on his precarious perch and this movement was accompanied by a noise that was like a long sustained howl, but strangely distant, as though it came from far away across the fields and the sea and further even than that. His hands began to move; slowly, slowly, he was bringing the thing down to earth, it was there, palpable, becoming flesh between his fingers.

Barbara said, 'I'm not having any more of this!' She put her fingers in her mouth and emitted a piercing whistle. Nancy clapped her hands to her eyes and waited for she knew not what, the end of the world, Barbara's instant demise, or, at the least, someone, probably Milo, to have a bad accident.

'It's all over,' Barbara said. 'You can look now.'

'What's happened?' Nancy still wasn't looking.

'They're going home in rather bad order. Milo jumped. His reactions are really extraordinarily quick.'

Some of the Ancient People were coming towards them. Milo and Mrs. Anguilo passed quite close. Nancy had a glimpse of her terrified face. After they had gone a small man limped past; his screwed up face looked like that of a little boy who has gone after stolen fruit and got a belly-ache from eating green apples.

'Why did you whistle?' Nancy asked Barbara.

'I had the feeling it wasn't good for Milo to be up on that pillar.'

'Why wasn't it good for him?'

Barbara said infuriatingly, 'Ah, there's a lot you don't know. We're very behind the times in Helmsley. We have witches and warlocks.'

'Now you're teasing me.'

They retraced their steps across the field.

'Was that really your P.E. mistress?' Nancy asked. 'Surely she wouldn't do that sort of thing with a pupil?'

'She's done most other things with him, so why not this?' Barbara kicked a stone out of her path. 'Silly bitch!'

'Do you . . .' Nancy fumbled awkwardly for words. 'I mean, have you . . . ?'

'Goodness, no. I've got a lot of studying to do before I get to medical school.'

Nancy walked on in silence. She felt that Barbara had the map of her life traced out, and at some stage in the future there was a notice which read "have intercourse", suitably placed so that it did not interfere with her studies and was not so late as irreparably to damage her development. Barbara, Nancy told herself, was cold and calculating. But Barbara, sparkling in moonlight, looked far from cold. The hard truth was that she was seventeen and virgo intacta, and it didn't seem to have done her the slightest harm.

They came to the stile and Nancy watched as Barbara, in a display of spritely exuberance, vaulted over it. When she has a man, she'll make a success of that, too, Nancy thought wretchedly. They walked towards the lighted streets and turned in the direction of All Hallows. As the bulk of the church loomed up, Nancy wondered what she was to do with the knowledge she had acquired.

'Ought I to tell my father?' she asked Barbara.

'I shouldn't if I were you. It would be difficult for him to ignore it, in his position. And you don't want to get the Anguilos into trouble, do you?'

'I suppose not.' Nancy was not accustomed to keeping problems to herself.

'Why not talk to Tudor Lindsay about it?' Barbara suggested. 'He might be able to put a stop to it. He knows the Anguilos quite well. If they dropped out of the magic circle, it wouldn't matter about the others, would it?'

Nancy hesitated, thinking about Tudor. 'Do you think he'd mind?'

'Why should he? It's his job.'

'You don't sound as if you think much of him.'

'Oh, he's great, for all I know. It's just that our family has been mixed up enough with the Lindsays.'

She gave no explanation of this remark, and Nancy, who was savouring the pleasures of a future meeting with Tudor, was not curious.

It was half-past ten when Nancy went into the house. She expected her father to be waiting for her, but instead there

66

was a note on the hall window ledge, which read, 'I have gone visiting. Back by ten.' Nancy wrote under it, 'In bed. Ten thirty!'

Her father had to go to a meeting of the parochial church council the next evening and soon after he left the house Nancy set off for Carrick Farm. By the time she reached the farm she had lost her nerve and had Zoe not caught sight of her as she hovered at the gate, she might well have returned to the vicarage and transacted her business over the telephone.

Tudor was in his study writing up his case notes. He was wearing spectacles which he took off as Zoe led Nancy into the room.

'Nancy wants to talk to you about the squatters,' Zoe said.

'Come in, Nancy.' There was something familiar in the absence of fuss as if she was keeping an engagement with him. 'I hope they haven't been bothering you?'

'Well, a little. . . .' She looked about uncertainly. There was barely room for two in the room, let alone three.

'Sit down and tell me about it.'

Zoe went out and shut the door. Tudor seated Nancy in his desk chair and drew up a stool for himself. She told him what had happened. He watched her face, quizzically, as if she was telling him about herself. When she had finished, he said, 'You shouldn't be upset by these poor people. They can't find any other way of acting out their fears and repressions, that's all.'

'It was . . . sort of blasphemous.'

'Blasphemy against what?'

'Well, God . . . and Jesus, I suppose.'

'Do you know what I think? Gods, ancient and modern, are a blasphemy against the human spirit. Mature people don't need gods, Nancy.'

She did not answer and he said, 'I've shocked you, haven't I?'

'No . . . I . . .' She turned her head away.

'Don't always back out of situations.' He put his hand beneath her chin and turned her face towards him. 'If you're shocked, say so.'

'I can't,' she mumbled.

'Because you don't like to bother other people with your feelings?'

'Something like that.'

'That's a lie. You know that's a lie, don't you? Self-exposure is a risk and you're not prepared to run risks, that's the truth, isn't it?'

She bit her lip. He ran his finger lightly down her throat. 'Isn't it?' She shivered and he said, 'Now don't be silly about this. You've got to grow up one day. Are you a virgin?'

'No.'

'Just once, because you were curious? Is that it?'

'Something like that.'

'Do you want to talk about it?'

'I . . . yes, I . . . that would be great, it would be a very real help to me, Tudor.' She gave an idiotic little laugh. 'But not right now, I mean, when you're busy and. . . .'

He let her flounder. Then there was silence. Nancy thought of Zoe, perhaps in the hall, listening to the silence.

Tudor said quietly, 'What are you frightened of, Nancy?'

Nancy wondered what he expected her to be frightened of, but the room was too small and he was too near for her to be able to think.

'I must go now.' She got up abruptly and upset some of his papers on the floor.

'Must you?' His eyes were slate grey.

'I hope you're not angry?'

'My dear girl, why should I be angry?' he asked coldly.

'Perhaps I could see you when I'm a bit more sort of settled?'

He gave the faintest shrug as though the conversation had become boring. For a moment as she looked at him it flickered across Nancy's mind that he was cruel. There has to be a way of escape, a rope up which one can climb; that brief intimation of his cruelty would one day be the hemp of her rope. But now as she went out of the room her only thought was that she might have lost the chance of getting to know him better.

Zoe, coming out of the kitchen, said, 'Aren't you stopping for coffee, Nancy?'

Nancy shook her head, fumbled at the door and let herself out.

'That's an odd little girl,' Tudor said, coming out of the study.

Zoe looked at him as if she had made a discovery, although it was difficult to imagine what else she could discover about Tudor.

5

All the trees were pricked with green and Mrs. Hooper told Vereker she could never remember the catkins being so enormous in other years. Vereker responded warmly to the catkins because he wanted to win favour with Mrs. Hooper. It was difficult having a member of the parochial church council who wasn't on speaking terms with the vicar. He thanked God for the miracle of the catkins.

Easter came. There were seventy-five people at the Good Friday service, which was a post-war record, and on Easter Sunday the church was packed for the eleven o'clock communion.

'The Kingdom of Heaven is spring,' Vereker said. 'The green after the winter. You and I made green, here and now. Now. Always now. Now for Zacchaeus, now for Mary Magdalene, now for us in the sacrament here in All Hallows.'

In the vestry afterwards, Miss Genevieve Draisey helped the churchwardens to count the collection.

'He's advertized the event well enough, I suppose he was bound to draw a crowd,' Miss Draisey said in her hoarse, theatrical voice. Miss Draisey was a very important person, but Donald Jarman was never able to take her seriously because she looked so unnervingly like a comedian in drag with her bracelets and bangles and bulging sausage curls. 'I wonder he didn't stand outside the church door shouting, "Roll up! Roll up! All the fun of the Easter Festival!".' She pushed a bundle of pound notes to one side with as much distaste as if they were thirty pieces of silver.

'He's done a lot of visiting. No harm in that,' Donald Jarman said. Vereker, in agreement with the Reverend Roberts, had donated his Easter offering to the church and neither of his churchwardens was disposed to quarrel with the means by which he had got people to the church.

'When I was head of Creighton Manor School, I always advised the Governors against any form of advertizing,' Miss Draisey said. 'I used to say, the *product* advertizes the school.'

'You mean your gels?' Colonel Maitland asked, putting a rubber band round a packet of five-pound notes.

'Indeed.' She bent towards him and Donald Jarman thought for a jubilant moment that she was going to dig the old man in the ribs. 'And we were never short of pupils. Never!'

'But we are short of church members,' Jarman said. 'That must mean there is something wrong with our product.'

'I don't feel there is anything wrong with you and me, do you, Colonel?'

'We're getting on a bit, my dear,' he said philosophically, writing figures on an envelope. 'We're getting on a bit. How much have you got there, Donald?'

The next Sunday was Low Sunday and Vereker, in common with most other clergymen, was well aware what that meant in terms of congregation. He went visiting again. This time he went to the area between the fairground and the new block of holiday flats where the poorer people in his parish lived. At one time this had been a pleasant neighbourhood consisting of well-built terraced houses each with gardens back and front. But some of the little terraces had been pulled down to make way for the new flats, and then the fairground had completed the breakdown. Now the houses stood in twos and threes and the place had the gap-toothed look of the bombed sites he had seen in pictures of war-time London. When Vereker first saw the area, he hoped, being something of an optimist, that here he might find that the people had been drawn together by the disaster that had befallen them, that they would have established a community life of a kind, coarse, rough, perhaps, but real. It wasn't like that. Some of the men were out of work, others were waiting for the blow to fall. There was resentment about the Common Market, capitalism, the unions, the Socialist right and the Socialist left, but no one had anything positive to say about the situation. After supper, the men went to the pub, or to the working men's club near the harbour, or they sat at home dully watching television. Here, as elsewhere on the island, people stagnated. When asked whether they would come to All Hallows most of them said 'no' and when asked why, they said that the church was not for them. The Anglican Church, he was told time and time again, was a middle-class institution.

70

Occasionally, however, he had a sensation that a signal was being sent out, very faint, overlaid with the meaningless noises he and others were making. 'Help me! Help me!' the signal said. The need could not be defined; it was simply there in a troubled eye, in the silence after the voice gave up its struggle with words. Vereker dared not say too much to these people because the signal was so weak and he was so unsure of himself. He could only say, 'Come to All Hallows. At least, give it a trial.'

In Virginia Close, the trial was over and the case had been lost. They were polite, they poured sherry and gave donations, one or two offered him a day's sailing; but as far as they were concerned, the Church had outlived its purpose. They were sophisticated people, moderate and sceptical, and they had outgrown religion. If there had ever been a voice inside them that cried out for help, they had rationalized it away. When he left, they would turn on the television and settle down to watch a play about the struggle of the working classes, written by a member of the middle-class. Class. Class. Always class. There weren't any people in England, only members of classes dying behind their stockades. England had no breadth; he felt it crowding in on him, over-peopled and cramped, bedevilled with intricate, baffling complexities which can only ravel up existence when people are closely confined. Yet there were depths. Suddenly, without warning, they were there at your feet, black, bottomless, terrifying; you skimmed along on the surface thinking you were managing pretty well, then suddenly the ground had shifted and you had stepped into a well.

He had this feeling particularly strongly when he visited the rural part of his parish. It was a grey day with a wrinkled sky and water lying in the furrows of the fields. There was a screen of poplars shielding a big, square old house which was in a shocking state of disrepair but still retained a weary air of breeding. A little further on there was an even larger house sprawling behind unkempt hedges. He had never met the people who lived in this little pocket which lay away to the east of Carrick Farm. As he walked along the road one or two cars went by, travelling fast, and a boy on a motor bike who rode as if he had far to go. They made a noise and churned up mud, but they did not impinge on whatever life went on in this place.

He called at both the big houses but got no answer. At the first, he was astonished to see a goat peering from one of the ground floor windows. At the other house, an upper window was occupied by a tattered red setter who watched him sympathetically but showed no sign of rousing such of the inhabitants who might be hidden in the more remote regions of the house. Further down the road, there was a row of farm cottages which, he had been told, were no longer attached to a farm; they had the look of places which have outlived their usefulness. He worked his way down the row.

The people who lived in this row were tenants, and the owner, knowing that the property was scheduled for demolition, had refused to carry out repairs; the sentence of death hung over Mutton Row. But in spite of cracked plaster and rotting window frames, life lingered obstinately, and dingy curtains, a pot of African violets, a packet of Daz on a window sill, gave evidence of human occupation in all save the last cottage. Here, Nature appeared to be doing the work of the demolition men unhampered by any effort on the part of the occupants. Not only was plaster cracked and woodwork rotten, but all the windows were broken and so many tiles were missing from the roof that one suspected a more profitable use had been found for them elsewhere. Only the sound of a child crying indicated that the place was inhabited. The front door swung open into the living-room when Vereker touched the knocker. Something not human scuttled across the uncarpeted floor. As far as he could see there was no furniture in the room except for a settee resting against the far wall; it had one leg missing and the stuffing was ripped out of its belly. There was a smell of bad drains and damp which would have been a good deal worse had the place not been so thoroughly ventilated.

The woman came down the stairs and Vereker announced himself while she was still in deep shadow. '*My* parish church?' There was triumphant malice in her voice; too late, he recognized his erstwhile squatter. 'You and God weren't bothered with me when you talked to me last time, were you? Couldn't get rid of me fast enough.'

'I'm afraid there wasn't room in the vicarage.' The words had a dismally familiar ring.

'There was room for the Anguilos, though. Didn't tell her to fuck off, did you?'

The curtains of the house next door parted and a white, ferret-face peeped out, topped by a wounded head bound in gauze and malformed by curlers.

'I can understand how you must feel,' Vereker mumbled.

A child had been wailing from somewhere above for several minutes and she went to the foot of the stairs and shouted, 'Are you going to shut up?' The wailing continued and she ascended three steps. 'You know what I promised you!' The child hiccupped a few words, incomprehensible to Vereker, but apparently understood by its mother who said, 'Well, you can't. So shut up. See?' She came down the stairs and renewed her attack on Vereker.

'God? Is *He* still around, then? Does He get out much, or do you keep Him locked away in the church? I'll tell you one thing, for sure, *I'm* not coming to church; *He* can make a home visit. Maybe then He'd do something useful, like getting us rehoused. Even Dr. Leishner does a home visit sometimes, domiciliary he calls it, because he's a psychiatrist and "home visit" wouldn't sound important enough for him. How do I go about getting a domiciliary from God? Do I have to do it through you? That won't do me much good, you've already turned me out of the vicarage. What did He say when you reported that to Him? Well done, good and faithful, is that what He said? Well done, good and faithful, we don't want a load of rubbish like that at the vicarage!'

'Mrs. Peters....'

'Can He hear me? Will He strike me dead?'

'Mrs. Peters, God isn't....'

'It's what He bleeding well *is* that interests me.'

Vereker, who found this a difficult problem at the best of times, said feebly, 'God does hear you, Mrs. Peters.'

'So does the housing manager, but he doesn't do anything. We've got no lighting, no running water, and he tells me it's dangerous to use an oil stove. It's dangerous to live, mate, I told him. If God can sort out the housing manager, I'll come to church.'

At this point, rescue came in the form of Mr. Peters who walked down the row looking about him with an air compounded of surprise and condescension, as though he was coming to such things as fields, trees, cottages, for the first time and thought them well enough made. He almost overshot Mutton Row, but checked himself at the last minute and eased his way between Vereker and Mrs. Peters as though neither of them existed. Mrs. Peters grabbed his arm. 'What do you think you're going to do, then? Lie on that couch all day, like you did yesterday? Not in here, you're not! This isn't the national health.' He took no notice of her. He had a high-coloured, remarkably unlined face, and blue, unblinking eyes fringed with thick brown eyelashes; a scar ran from his left temple to the side of his mouth : it was a face like a cracked china doll. Vereker didn't think Mrs. Peters would ever get much change out of him. He had, however, diverted her attention and while she was fulminating against the health service, and Dr. Leishner in particular, Vereker turned away.

The Low Sunday attendances were better than usual, but Vereker was not encouraged. He had come badly out of his meeting with Mrs. Peters and this disturbed him. 'I should have accepted things as they are instead of meddling with people I don't understand,' he thought.

One day he spoke of this to Zoe Lindsay. She moved about the house so quietly during the mornings that he was seldom aware of her, but at eleven o'clock she always brought him a cup of coffee and two digestive biscuits.

'That coffee is a life-saver!' he said on this particular morning. 'I don't seem able to get going today.'

'Are you writing your sermon?'

'It would be truer to say I'm not writing my sermon. How can I preach to people I don't understand? What have I to offer them?'

'Jesus Christ.'

For a moment he thought she was swearing in a quiet, unemphatic way; then he realized she was answering his question.

'You know, people have odd ideas about Americans.' He was thoroughly irritated. 'They think we all belong to some crazy sect or other, hot gospellers, shakers, you name it, we belong! Well, I don't belong. I can't just stand up in front of people and offer them Jesus Christ as though He was this week's bargain buy!'

He wished he hadn't started this conversation and hoped

she would go away now, he had his sermon to finish and his coffee was getting cold. She remained, however, seated on the library stool, her expression meditative, faintly puzzled, as befits the seeker after knowledge. Vereker found her disturbing, the living embodiment of that depth which he found so black and incomprehensible.

'*Who* is He?' she said in that quiet, uninflected voice. 'I go to church every week and I take communion, but I don't meet Him.'

'Did you ever speak to Roberts about this?'

'He told me it would help if I kept repeating "I believe, help Thou my unbelief". But it hasn't really got anything to do with believing. It's a question of meeting. I don't ever meet Him.'

It was difficult, in her case, to know exactly what was meant by *meeting*. Vereker, with the nuns in mind, wondered how best he could elicit some information as to her state of mind. While he was deliberating she unfolded herself from the library stool and went quietly out of the room. Vereker drank his lukewarm coffee and reflected unhappily on the fact that it was not the people he did not understand, it was their questions. Then he thought : but why should I worry, since Zoe Lindsay is probably mad and Mrs. Peters is certainly disreputable; and, in any case, questions about the nature of God are best left to theologians. He picked up his notes and tried to concentrate on his sermon, but he was thinking : that other question, "Who say ye that I am?" is *that* to be left to the theologians?

How can a twentieth century priest answer that? he thought. There are no words with which to strike the image. What does it mean today to be a good shepherd, a true vine, to be "king", "master", "lord"? There are no archetypes today, only case histories.

That evening, he said to Donald Jarman, 'I'd like to have a meeting in the church hall, an open meeting, with a theme.'

'The role of the Christian in a secular society?' Jarman suggested, with a hint of weariness.

'I thought of something simpler than that – "Who is Jesus?".'

'People may find the "who is" a little disconcerting. It does rather suggest that this is an open-ended question.'

'If they think it's a closed question they can come and say so. Will they?'

'Yes, I think they probably will. Our folk wouldn't have come for Roberts; but you're an American and a bit of a novelty. The Pentecostals will come, expecting some kind of a revelation, again because you're an American and they believe revelation is your speciality.'

'How will people like Colonel Maitland react?'

'If you really want to do it, persuade the other chaps, Agnew at St. Luke's, and the Methodist and Baptist ministers. When they have agreed will be the time to tell the p.c.c.'

'What do you think yourself?'

Jarman thought for a moment, his strange, triangular eyes and thick jowls giving him the look of a mastiff anticipating some good red meat. 'I think it will be interesting.' Vereker wondered how the Roman Jarman would have viewed the circus.

Things worked out much as Jarman had predicted. The main objection came from an unexpected quarter. Nancy said, 'You'll never get the English working classes into church if *that's* what you're after. They fell for it once, they won't again.'

'How do you mean, they fell for it once?'

'Well, with John Wesley and people like that.'

'But Wesley did a lot for the working class, surely?'

'He made their lives tolerable by giving them an outlet for their emotions, and telling them they mattered to God. So they kept quiet and allowed themselves to be exploited. God lined up with the people who enslaved the working classes and the working classes aren't going to forget that in a hurry.'

Vereker was silent. Nancy said, 'I don't want to hurt you, but I think you ought to know that I don't believe in God. And if I *did* believe in him, he's so awful I wouldn't be able to worship him.'

She regarded him expectantly; she had come to a halt and looked to him to recharge her batteries. After a moment, he said, 'I couldn't worship that god, either.'

'Well, aren't you going to tell me about the God I *should* worship?' she challenged. 'Tell me about Him. Come on, I'm listening.'

76

But she wasn't listening; and it wasn't God she was ranting about, it was her earthly father, Matthew Vereker. She was growing away from him and this was the only way she could find of telling him. 'Here are the things that are precious to you, take them; they're not mine and they aren't of any value to me. What I want from you is my life; you've had it in your keeping too long.' That was what she was saying and it should have been said years ago. He just wished it didn't hurt so much.

When the hurt eased a little he was able to assure himself that he was a sensible parent who saw his daughter reasonably objectively and knew her weaknesses. Life could be dangerous; it wasn't safe for anyone as unprepared as Nan to go striding into it with such inadequate weapons. She ought to wait a little, sort herself out a bit, grow some more. He wondered whether he should talk to her about it, and it seemed that she would have welcomed this because he saw more of her than usual in the next few days and he guessed that she was frightened. She took every opportunity to pick a quarrel with him; but he could tell that rather than trying out new ideas on him, she was inviting him to reassert his authority. The main subject of her conversation was God, God Almighty, God the Father. Vereker listened to her, sometimes he asked questions, but he did not argue.

On the night of the meeting, she said, 'Don't expect *me* to come.'

'I'd rather you didn't come.' Vereker was short of patience.

'You don't want me?' she asked in surprise.

In truth, he did not want her this evening. He was nervous about the meeting and wished he hadn't called it. Nancy's presence would be an unnecessary complication. But he saw that he could not tell her this. Although she thought it natural that she should make a life of her own, she would be shocked at the idea that she could be excluded from any part of his life. He resorted to guile. 'I shouldn't come yet awhile, anyway. Only a few people may turn up and things probably won't get going for the first half hour.'

Word had got round, however, that some form of American "spectacular" was being given a trial run in All Hallows. By the time Nancy arrived the hall was full and several people, including Tudor, were standing at the back. Tudor was too far away for her to join him. She wondered why he had come. In the last row a girl with a pile of frizzed brown hair was saying to the man next to her, 'You have to be joking!'

'I tell you this is going to be good. I went to the Pentecostals last week. By the end of the evening the old daisy next to me was acting like she was transmitting the Fifth Gospel.'

'I don't care about the Fifth Gospel.' Her voice was a notch higher. 'I'm not going to spend the evening here.'

'Fuck off, then,' he said indifferently.

The platform in the hall was not in use and the chairs had been staggered in a semi-circle facing the long wall. Vereker had wanted the atmosphere to be informal and undevotional. He was seated out front beside a small table on which there was a large vase of spring flowers which he hoped he would not knock over. Miss Genevieve Draisey's golden retriever had elected to sit beside him and was surveying the assembly with the lofty benevolence of a high court judge.

Miss Draisey had wanted to sit at the door to make a note of the names and addresses of non-churchgoers, but Vereker had discouraged this so she had put herself in charge of the refreshments. Vereker had, however, agreed with some reluctance that Colonel Maitland and Donald Jarman should usher people into their seats. 'Left to themselves, they'll all sit in tight little groups,' Jarman had said. 'Especially the Baptists.' He had been right : to meet under the same roof appeared to be the limit to which even the most ecumenically-minded were prepared to go. Colonel Maitland, however, had been indefatigable, and as Vereker looked round the hall he could see the Baptist minister and two of his congregation penned in with giggling youngsters wearing jerseys with West Albion Football Club on their breasts and eating fish and chips from a carton. His own parishioners had shown no more inclination than the Baptists to spread themselves thinly, and Mrs. Hooper looked far from reconciled to her situation between a young man wearing a guitar as though it was an extra limb and a dishevelled old man with a severe list to port which continually brought his head down in the region of her bosom. A few people from the fairground area stood in the doorway sniffing the atmosphere. Colonel Maitland pounced on them before they could decide to turn away and nosed them firmly in the direction of the rector of St. Luke's; he stayed to bark some kind of introduction and then nosed after a couple from Virginia Close. The Virginia Close people wore tasteful casual clothes and quietly amused expressions and Colonel Maitland penned them with three hairy young men who might have stepped out of one of the Bible illustrations which adorned the Sunday School noticeboard. The Virginia Close people quizzed the other occupants of the hall, recognized acquaintances and exchanged rueful, must-enter-into-village-life-sometimes grimaces.

Mrs. Jarman came up to Vereker and said, 'The press are here,' as though she was announcing the arrival of the firing squad. She indicated a small, passive man sitting with hands folded docilely over a notebook. Behind him, the girl with frizzed brown hair was saying, 'You've got to be joking!' Her companion answered, 'We used to go to meetings like this when I was a kid. Honest! We used to sing a lot of fucking choruses. *"Wide, wide as the ocean. . . ."*' Mrs. Hooper turned to glare at him and he leant forward to speak to her. 'Do you sing that still, love? Do you still sing *"Wide, wide as the ocean"*? Christ!' He went off into a paroxysm of laughter. Mrs. Hooper turned away and the frizzy-haired girl bit her thumbnail.

Vereker looked at the clock which said five-past eight. Colonel Maitland, catching his eye, nodded. Vereker made a brief speech of welcome, apologized for sitting out front but said he thought that in a meeting of this size it was important to see that everyone had a chance to speak. Then he sat down and waited.

The golden retriever settled himself, nose on paws, and gave a deep sigh. The girl with the frizzed hair said to Mrs. Hooper, 'What's bothering you, then? Smell something bad, can you?'

Miss Draisey, who was now standing with her back to the kitchen door, said throatily, 'I am reminded of the words of St. John of the Cross:

> *"He Himself was the beginning*
> *So He had none, being one.*
> *What was born of the beginning*
> *Was the word we call the Son.*

79

> *Even so has God conceived Him*
> *And conceived Him always so,*
> *Ever giving Him the substance*
> *As He gave it long ago."*

I wonder how this strikes us today?'

It struck this particular assembly dumb, although the golden retriever loyally thumped his tail on the floor. The girl with the frizzed hair said incredulously to her companion, 'You're not going to listen to *this* all the evening?' Colonel Maitland moved quietly to the side of the hall and began a count of those present.

A young man got up. He had lank hair and a pale, pinched face and he was trembling as if he had just come out of a high dive and found the water colder than he had expected. 'Jesus is alive,' he said. 'He's here in this room with us.' People turned round, craning their necks to see the speaker; mostly, they looked anything but eager at his pronouncement. 'I'm not a g...g...good speaker,' the young man continued, miserable but undeterred by a snort from the chorus-singer, 'Some of you h...have a l...lot to say in other p . . . places. Let Him speak in you, n . . . now !' He sat down and there was a murmur of 'Well done, Jimmy !' 'Good lad !'

Jimmy had broken the ice. Old Miss Harmer, the Jarmans' daily help, was on her feet saying that they had all been shamed. Why were they silent? She told how she had nursed her sick mother and at times when her spirit failed her she had felt Jesus taking over. This had made her wonder how many other times in her life He would have acted in her if only she had been ready. She was a sincere and humble woman and she was listened to with respect. After she sat down, one or two people recalled similar experiences, words of comfort to the dying which came at a time when they themselves had no idea what to say, a sudden uncharacteristic braveness in the face of hooligans, the sense of a companion on a lonely night journey.

Then a bearded, middle-aged man got up and said he would like to know if Jesus had been Mary Magdalene's lover; he said he didn't want to give any offence because he personally would think all the more of Jesus if this was so.

The Methodist minister raised his eyes to the ceiling with the almost insupportable weariness of one hearing a question for the hundredth time and Vereker reflected that life among the Methodists must be very different these days. One of the Baptist youths told the bearded man that Jesus was the man for all men. The bearded man said in that case why was St. John singled out as the disciple whom Jesus loved? Miss Draisey said that it was Lazarus, not St. John, who was the disciple whom Jesus loved, and the bearded man said, 'Perhaps he loved them both?'

After that, the companion of the girl with frizzy hair sang *"Wide, wide as the ocean"*; but those around him had the sense to join in and he muttered, 'Oh, piss off!' and relapsed into silence. The golden retriever sat up and barked, then threw himself crossly under the table, endangering the stability of the vase of flowers. A young girl told how she went into pubs and asked people if they knew Jesus, and the landlords told her she was making a nuisance of herself, just as if she was a whore. A young man said that Jesus was in the factory, and the terraces at the football ground, and the parks where the meths drinkers slept. The bearded man shouted, 'What's He doing about it, then?'

How far Christianity had moved from its Founder! Vereker thought as he listened. No one was more to blame for this than the clergy who were as eager as any politician to respond to popular demand. You want a revolutionary Jesus, sir? He's yours. You'd like a comforter, grandma? We have him here; admittedly he wasn't comfortable company while He was on earth, but we've smoothed out the sharp edges. And you, young lady, you want to be turned on? We've got a very special Jesus for you. You want Him homosexual, heterosexual, bisexual, your local bishop can supply him : the all-purpose Jesus adapted to your particular preoccupation.

'This makes me want to puke! Yes, you'd better move away, dear, I might even do it.' Vereker looked up to see what spirit he had conjured up by his angry thoughts. It was Meg Jacobs. 'I came here because I thought maybe something was really stirring in this dump. But I ought to have saved my petrol. If you really care, you should be out *doing* something; there's plenty of work for you in this particular vineyard, every one of you, even the duchess in the pink hat. I'll sit at the door and you can enlist as you go out!'

She was well-known and people received her outburst with good-humour. Someone shouted, 'Good old Meg!' She hunched down in her chair, hands dangling loose between spread knees, head bent.

People looked expectantly at Vereker. He could see that on the whole they felt they had come out of it rather well; they had been abused, ridiculed and threatened, and they had kept their cool. Miss Draisey, at the kitchen door, was about to make an announcement when she was unexpectedly forestalled. Zoe Lindsay was standing up. Probably no one else in the hall could have made such an impact simply by getting to their feet. The little buzz of conversation dwindled and for the first time Vereker was aware of a tremor of unease, a primitive fear of things unseen; darkness pressed against the window panes and just for a moment it was in all their thoughts. Mrs. Hooper glanced over her shoulder as if to reassure herself that the horrible chorus-singing man was indeed behind her.

Zoe stood quite still, her hands resting lightly on the back of the chair in front of her; unlike Meg Jacobs, she was unaware of the attention centred on her and she looked at Vereker as if there was no one there but the two of them. Perhaps he was tired, or perhaps there was a voltage reduction, but it seemed to him that the lights in the hall had dimmed; he could see that there were a great many people in front of him, but they were blurred and formless, only Zoe stood out with a strange, frosty clarity. She said, 'What is Jesus Christ to you?' He had been given notice of this question : now he was called to account. But he was not ready and wished to be excused : whatever he said, he would say something different in a year's time because this was the question which it takes a lifetime to answer.

The relief in the hall was tangible. Now their patience would be rewarded with the love of God, the fellowship of the Holy Spirit, and a cup of coffee. Miss Draisey already had the kitchen door open and the golden retriever padded round to be first in the queue.

Vereker, lacking wisdom, could only speak out of his anger. 'T. S. Eliot put it pretty well, I think.'

They looked at him with polite unconcern as they fumbled

82

for gloves and handbags. Someone, eager to get it in first, said, ' "The wounded surgeon...." '

'No. "In the juvescence of the year came Christ the tiger...." '

Blankness. Eyes strayed towards the kitchen door. Donald Jarman looked at his watch.

'If you met a tiger in your path, you wouldn't be able to take it or leave it, would you? Well, my picture of Christ isn't a take-it-or-leave-it Christ.' Vereker was determined they were not going to enjoy their coffee. 'We have this enormous gift, this gift of Jesus Christ, and we're so mealy-mouthed about it, almost as if it wasn't quite decent. We tame Him, wrap Him up in jargon, make His teaching bland and easily assimilated, a pop-culture, media-image Christ with no sting left in Him. We'd be better off saying to ourselves, "Look, this isn't all that important to me and if it isn't all that important then I'm not really a Christian at all!" At least then we'd stand stripped of everything; we'd have to find something to clothe ourselves in, somewhere to go from there on. Perhaps that is when we really meet Him; when we've put aside all the comfortable, cosy, trivial things, including Him, if that's the kind of picture we have of Him. The Jesus of the pop group and West Albion Football Club : He's not much more than a mascot, is he? Throw him away. And gentle Jesus meek and mild, what about him? He doesn't have much to offer us today, does gentle Jesus meek and mild. Cast him out! Or is he a suffering Christ, anaemic, tortured, dying? He's even less use to us. Let him die !'

'But a tiger is savage !' an elderly lady protested.

'Sure, a tiger tears you apart. And I reckon that is how it seemed to those fishermen He told to leave everything and follow Him. And He *meant* that. He meant that their whole lives would be changed, not that they would give a bit more of themselves, try a little harder, lead a slightly better life. He meant *changed*. If you stand face to face with a tiger, you don't survive that encounter unchanged. Nor does your church. What is He saying to us today? Don't you think He might be telling us to tear down that medieval structure over there and set about the business of replacing it with something more meaningful for twentieth century man? He is the Christ of the living, not of the twelfth century.'

83

Zoe was still standing; she had a rapt expression on her face as though she had just heard an inspired rendering of the Hallelujah Chorus. This wasn't what those around her seemed to have heard; they looked like people who have made a modest request for coffee and been given a dose of quinine. For a few moments they were too aggrieved to move; then Nancy pushed her way to the door. Others began to move, the meeting broke up.

Nancy stumbled out into the cool darkness. It was dreadful! she thought. What had come over her father, bawling out like that? She was gooseflesh all over. She couldn't bear to meet anyone, so she walked towards the church and made her way round the side of it to where a footpath led across a field and eventually joined the footpath to Carrick Farm. As she passed the church she noticed that the side door was open, but she was too taken up with her own thoughts to wonder why. She had lost sight of Tudor and thought that perhaps he hadn't stayed until the end of the meeting. He would have gone home. She didn't want to talk to him now, but she thought that perhaps there would be a light on in the sitting-room and she would catch a glimpse of him.

Tudor, however, had remained in the hall. Much of the time he had found the proceedings vastly amusing. If only he had left before the end he would have felt unusually relaxed; but the end had spoilt it all. He turned into the graveyard, meaning to take the footpath across the fields. The moon was up and beyond the graveyard wall the flat fields and marshes were strange as a lunar landscape. The church hall with its lighted windows looked like some pathetic human capsule flung out into space. The sense of emptiness came to him when he was only half-way across the graveyard. There was something cold and hard in the pit of his stomach and he knew that one of his bad spells was coming on. He sat on the flat-topped tomb of the lords of the manor, Zoe's forebears. He had learnt a long time ago that it was better to put up no resistance to a bad spell, that way it was over quicker. It was the view beyond the graveyard wall that had brought this one on. He didn't like long views and uncharted territory; his weak, acquiescent parents had left him to wander about in uncharted territory all his childhood. He didn't like the words that went with this kind of territory, boundless, infinite, immeasurable . . . words that made him feel as if he was shrinking and shrinking until he was no bigger than a walnut. Why wasn't Zoe here? She was the only person who had ever shown him any understanding and she had decided to go mad, had deliberately steered herself round the bend in order to avoid her responsibility towards him. He looked at the lights of the church hall and shuddered as he thought of her standing there tonight, looking at Vereker in that strange way. The terror sharpened. He put his head on his knees and visualized his diary for tomorrow, the clients he had to see; he selected one of them and began to go through the case history details, date of birth, address, name of G.P., referred by, members of household. . . . Gradually, his breathing grew easier and by the time he had got to "family alignments", the terror had subsided. He rose shakily to his feet.

It was then, as he stood wondering whether it would be better to take the long way back to the farm, thus avoiding the marshes, that he noticed that the side door of the church was open. He walked softly across the grass, keeping clear of the gravel path, and entered the church. A shaft of moonlight slanted through the big rose window and fell across the altar and the chancel, and in this silver light Milo performed a dance of his own devising. He was naked and he danced rather well. The moonlight helped, of course.

Tudor moved slowly down the aisle until he had a good view. Milo's gestures were obviously obscene, but in the context Tudor thought that this was obscenity raised to the beautiful. There was a buried, crippled part of oneself that demanded to be released; even as he watched Milo, his own body throbbed for that release.

A breeze was getting up. It came in through the open door like a presence and ruffled through the church guides and sent a news sheet about Christian Aid skittering along the stone floor to Tudor's feet. Milo felt it. He stopped dancing and looked round, suddenly irresolute. Then he took one step and stood on the raised platform in front of the altar. He turned his head to one side and then to the other, looking at the heavy brass candlesticks, then he looked up at the cross. The breeze had passed and now all was quiet. The moon slanted its beam across the chancel. In the Lady Chapel a light burnt in a hanging lamp, the flame unflickering, still, eternal, perpetual. . . . The terror was coming back, only now it was worse than ever. Milo was standing still and it was coming down, folding itself around him, ineffable, undefinable, unimaginable, mind-bending evil, without form or dimension. . . . There was a big standing brass candlestick to Tudor's right; it was heavy, but he lifted it and rushing forward smashed it across the altar, then swung it at the stained glass window above the altar. He shouted to Milo, 'Get out of here! Get out!'

The substance of the boy seemed to have gone; in the dim light only two enormous eyes stared up at Tudor. 'It's not me you have to fear,' Tudor said. '*I* have saved you. Get out of this place.'

The eyes vanished and bare feet scampered over the stone-flagged floor. Tudor put down the candlestick and walked to the door. The night air brought the smell of wet grass and a rabbit scurried across the path at his feet. There was no other movement in the graveyard. Milo must have run as though the Devil was at his heels.

6

Dawn was full of false promise, that delicate rosy flush only too often was sweated out by rain within the hour. Dame Eleanor, who knew all about false promise, was awash already. She had one of the loveliest faces Zoe had ever seen, a little white oval on which the features had been lightly sketched, but to startling effect. The opal eyes solicited what the long nose with its prettily tilted tip and the light, frivolous mouth seemed already to have found; some slight irregularity – the eyes not quite level, the mouth a trifle lop-sided – set the seal of inconstancy. How blasphemous this little face must have seemed in this world of women! And how inexplicable that she should be condemned to live among them, a sad inconstant nymph with no place here where fidelity was at a premium. No wonder she cried! But would she have been happier in the world outside? She didn't look as though she would ever learn much about loving, she was as unthinking as a moth always flying into the flame. Dame Eleanor went very slightly out of focus.

Zoe rose from the tree stump on which she had been sitting and walked slowly through the ruined chancel. She was shocked by her treatment of Dame Eleanor, who was too frail for dissection. When Zoe glanced over her shoulder, Dame Eleanor showed distressing signs of disintegration; she seemed to have lost a dimension and had become a stencilled figure, lacking depth. Even her grief had no substance. But perhaps that was because Dame Eleanor's grief had somehow got itself mixed up with Nancy Vereker's grief, which definitely did have substance. Zoe could taste Nancy Vereker's grief in her mouth and it was strong and bitter.

Nancy had been standing on tiptoe peering in at the unlighted sitting-room window when Zoe returned from the meeting last night. Zoe remembered the father gazing in at that same window. What do they want of us, the Verekers, she asked herself? Demands frightened her and for a moment she contemplated creeping round the side of the house and letting herself in by the back door. But it was no use trying to escape; the Verekers and their need would still be here on Helmsley in the morning. Zoe walked across the lawn and said to Nancy, 'Won't you come in?'

Nancy was as agitated as if she had been about to break into the house only to be offered the key by the owner. 'I just had to go for a walk after that terrible meeting,' she gabbled. 'So I walked over here. You must think I'm very rude.'

Zoe knew how Nancy felt at this moment, just as she sometimes knew how Dame Eleanor felt; but Dame Eleanor was dead and Nancy was alive. Zoe put out her hand and touched Nancy's hand and felt how painful it was to be alive. 'Things aren't getting out of control, are they, Nancy?'

Nancy answered with guilty vehemence, 'Oh no, no!'

The grass and the shrubs were damp and Zoe could smell the rosemary. She said, 'As long as you know what you are doing,' and was surprised to hear herself utter these words, so well-worn with incommunicable love and concern.

'It's all right, really it is.' Nancy squeezed Zoe's hand, then she turned into the shrubbery, trying to find her way to the gate. Zoe followed her, smelling the rosemary more strongly as she pushed against it. At the gate, Nancy said, 'You won't say anything to Tudor about me being here, will you?'

'Not if you don't want me to.'

'I'd look so silly.' She sounded as if she couldn't conceive of anything worse than looking silly.

Zoe felt reluctant to let her go so unarmed into the darkness. 'I don't think you should go back alone, not at this hour.'

'I won't take the footpath. I'll go back through the village.' She seemed pleased to have someone fussing over her.

'I shall watch you set off, to make sure.'

'Oh, you're so nice!' Nancy said impulsively. 'You're the nicest person I've ever met.'

Zoe stood at the gate until the sound of Nancy's footsteps died away. It would be a lonely walk and a long one, but at least she wouldn't meet Tudor who would be certain to come back across the fields.

After this encounter Zoe had gone into the house. She made herself a cup of Oxo, ate a digestive biscuit and went up to her bedroom. Tudor would not intrude here. They had ceased to be lovers some time ago and he now had a West Indian girl on the mainland. No doubt he would like to have someone on the island as well; it would be more convenient and the West Indian girl wouldn't last, Tudor couldn't sustain a love affair for long.

It was not Tudor she thought of, however, as she prepared for bed. Her affair with Donald Jarman had been over for many years now. At the time some people had said it was touch and go whether he left his wife or not, but that wasn't true; Gwynneth was a determined, resilient woman and she had held fast and waited. Zoe was incidental to Donald Jarman's life, the whole affair was incidental. He had had to visit the house frequently when Zoe's mother was bedridden and obsessed with anxiety about her financial affairs. Mrs. Lindsay was a tiresome woman and Jarman would have given the work to one of the junior partners had he not discovered the daughter. The desire to play Prince to the Sleeping Beauty was irresistible. Unfortunately, the workaday world makes a muddle of fairy tales and in the end Beauty went to sleep and the Prince reverted a little sadly to the Beast. Donald Jarman had begun to draw Zoe together into a whole person, but he had gone away before the process was complete and what he had started, Tudor had destroyed. Ineradicably destroyed, it had seemed, until this encounter in the garden with Nancy.

The pain was out there; it had been waiting out there all these years for the moment of release. There were other feelings, harder to bear, that accompanied the pain. They were all out there, the garden was full of them, they pressed against the window pane; if they found the tiniest crack they would be in and she would never get them out of the house again. Even now, it might be too late. The faint smell of the rosemary was about her; she lifted her hand to her face and smelt it at her finger tips.

'Oh, Nancy, Nancy!' She turned away from the window and walked up and down the room. How can I warn her? There is only one person who can deal with experience and that is yourself; and once the experience has started, once the first symptoms appear, it is too late. There is no cure.

Moonlight reflected the tossing leaves of a tree on the wall above her bed. The wind stirred in the chimney and the leaves of honesty rustled together in the dried flower arrangement on the mantelpiece. It was too late.

She had slept and dreamt and forgotten her dream and had got up early. She had come out here to the ruined priory to assure herself that all was as before. But it wasn't as before, something had changed. And what it meant and what she was to do about it, she did not know.

By nine o'clock it was a dreary day, the rain pouring down the window pane in a way that made sense of that line of Swinburne "grief with a glass that ran". Vereker had a lot of grief. The fact that he had brought it on himself only made it harder to bear. It was the first of May. He had been here six weeks and as a result of his activities he had alienated half the congregation and the altar would probably have to be reconsecrated.

When he came down this morning he had found several letters on the door mat. One was from an old lady who had gone straight home and written to him "while your wicked words are still ringing in my ears." Another said that he had "betrayed his cloth", while another accused him of threatening the writer's peace of mind. If he had given hope or inspiration, he could only assume that the recipients were still sleeping soundly.

He buttered a piece of toast. Nan was still upstairs and he hoped she would not come down yet. The police would be coming soon to talk about the damage to the church which had been discovered late last night by a vigilant young constable. There was a knock on the front door. The police? Or perhaps the postman? At least the postman could not be the bearer of praise or blame, it would take the postal service some time to deliver itself of either. Vereker went to the door and found himself confronted by Mrs. Hooper, dressed in a black raincoat and sou'wester, and grim-visaged as the angel of death.

'I won't interrupt your breakfast.' She glared at the piece of toast in his hand as though it was proof, were proof needed, of his utter degeneration. 'Nor I won't come in. But there are things I have to say.' Vereker put the piece of toast down on the hall table, and wiped his fingers with a handkerchief; not, he realised, the happiest of gestures.

From the line of her attack, he gathered that she was as yet unaware of the damage to the altar. 'You upset a lot of people last night. And you know who you upset, don't you?

Not that foul-mouthed layabout who sat behind me; nor that bearded weirdy who made all those wicked suggestions. *They* went away laughing. It was the old folk you upset, the ones who come to church regularly in all weathers, and bear their afflictions bravely like we are told we should.'

Vereker put his handkerchief away in his pocket. He had a bad conscience where some of the old people were concerned, but this did not extend to Mrs. Hooper. It wasn't the old people she was talking about, it was herself; and as she talked it became apparent that she had God just where she wanted him, boxed up in her neat little house from which he must never be allowed to venture into a world where his dignity might be affronted by bearded weirdies, foul-mouthed layabouts and other mistakes of His creation. Vereker listened, his face expressionless. She didn't like him any the more for bearing his chastisement with composure. A dull mulberry mottled her cheeks and her little eyes grew hard with anger; her speech coarsened.

'We're told not to cast our pearls before swine, aren't we? That old man who sat next to me hadn't had a bath this side of Christmas. I never expected to find myself mixing with the scum of the island at All Hallows; I'd have joined the Salvation Army if I wanted to get down in the gutter.'

Vereker said, 'If you care to come into the church with me, we can talk about your feelings in this, and any other matter on which you have difficulty.' He had for the moment forgotten the damage, but the suggestion was, in any case, quite unacceptable to her.

'Talk! Difficulty!' She was outraged. 'I've never needed to have any "talks" with Mr. Roberts and I'm certainly not going to "talk" to you! *God* knows all there is to know about me.'

The telephone rang and Vereker turned to answer it. By the time he had dealt with the call, Mrs. Hooper had gone. No doubt when she discovered how swiftly God had visited retribution on All Hallows she would return much refreshed to the fight. He went into the study and read through the letters he had so far received. After a few minutes, Nan came in.

'Who was that on the telephone?' she asked.

'Someone from the local paper. Apparently Roberts used

to have a paragraph once a week. They've offered me a column. Isn't that nice?'

'It's more than you deserve. I thought you were dreadful last night. Whatever came over you?'

'I got rather cross.'

'Are all those about it?' she indicated the letters on the desk. 'What do they say?' She made no move to see for herself, but kept her distance like a frightened spectator at an accident.

'Some say one thing, some another. You know the way it is.'

'That was Mrs. Hooper at the door, wasn't it?' She searched his face anxiously. 'Was she foul?'

'She wasn't very pleasant. But I expect that was partly my fault. I don't like her and I daresay I showed it.'

Nan was silent for a few moments, then burst out, 'I think Helmsley Island is the most awful dump! And now it's started to rain as far as I'm concerned it can go right on until the whole island is underwater.' It was the nearest she could get to a gesture of solidarity with her father.

Vereker, touched, but aware how precariously the scales were tipped in his favour, said vaguely, 'It will all blow over, I expect.'

The knock on the front door was prompt to remind him of the untruth of this.

Nan said, 'Whatever it is, I don't want any part of it.' She scuttled out and Vereker waited until the kitchen door had closed behind her before he admitted the police.

Nancy had expected him to go straight to the door and the fact that he did not do so triggered an alarm bell in her system. The kitchen was too far from the front door, and the walls too solid, for her to hear what was said and this increased her uneasiness. She took a slice of toast and poured coffee. Perhaps it was the rural dean come to warn her father that unless he mended his ways he would be returned to America, labelled "unsuitable for export". Her father would never be able to defend himself. She tended to see her father as muddled, ineffectual, and vulnerable. She thought that most people over forty were vulnerable because they had staked their lives on so many mistaken beliefs that they were practically incapable of survival in the modern world.

She comforted herself by spreading butter thickly on the

toast, and while she was doing this, Zoe arrived. She was early because Tudor had brought her in the car.

'He promised to meet Meg Jacobs here to see how the Anguilos are settling down.' Zoe looked unsettled herself.

'They aren't going to move the Anguilos, I hope?' Nancy said.

Mrs. Anguilo had been pathetically grateful for the shelter offered her and desperately anxious not to cause any inconvenience. She never asked for help, but she would walk about the garden looking fraught. Nancy would watch her wandering distractedly round the lawn pretending to gaze at the flower beds, then she would go out and say, 'Tell me about it,' and Mrs. Anguilo would drop today's problem at her feet. Nancy had a lot to give Mrs. Anguilo, and there weren't many people of whom that could be said.

'It would be wicked to move the Anguilos!' she exclaimed.

'I don't suppose they will move them. After all, they haven't done any harm.'

Nancy poured coffee for Zoe. 'They don't do anything *I* would call harmful,' she said, 'but I happen to know that they ... well, take part in certain practices of which Mrs. Hooper, for one, wouldn't approve.'

'But I don't suppose Mrs. Hooper knows, otherwise we would have heard about it before now.'

'But you know!' Nancy exclaimed. 'Did Tudor tell you?'

'Tudor? He would consider it too silly and immature to discuss.'

'Don't you think it's immature?'

'What does it matter if it is?' Rags of colour streaked Zoe's cheeks and her low voice sounded unexpectedly rough, almost aggressive. 'It's something they *need*. Why don't people try to answer the need, instead of analysing it!' She had a finger hooked into the handle of the cup and as she jerked her hand she upset the coffee. 'Nancy, don't *you* ever look at yourself in the mirror and want to cry out, "I'm not like that"; or hear yourself speak and think, "this isn't me"?' She dabbed agitatedly at the spilt coffee with a tissue. 'We *are* the person in the mirror and the person who speaks, but there is *more* to us. We long for someone else to realize this; but it doesn't happen. We are left with so little, so very little.' She threw the sodden tissue aside as though its ineffectiveness was too much to be borne. 'And some people can't bear the littleness, so they undress and dance and make obscene gestures in the moonlight, and people call them immature; but they don't try to help them. They collect up the bits and pieces, not to make a person out of them, but a specimen.'

Nancy felt she was on the edge of a great truth; but at the same time she was irritated by the fact that the coffee was now dripping off the table onto the floor. She wanted to be like Zoe, unconcerned with triviality; nevertheless, she got up and fetched the floor cloth. 'I think you're so right,' she said as she mopped up the coffee. 'I feel an awful jumble myself.'

Impulsively, Zoe reached out a hand and patted Nancy's shoulder. '*You'll* be all right. I'm sorry; I shouldn't have spoken like that.'

Distress had changed her. Now that she had pulled out all her emotional pins she looked less remote, rather ordinary, in fact. Nancy went to the sink for the dish cloth; there was still a pool of coffee on the table. While she was standing at the sink, her father and two policemen walked past the window.

'They *are* going to turn them out!' Nancy exclaimed.

Zoe said, 'They mustn't do that.' Nancy put the dish cloth on the table to soak up the coffee and they both moved purposefully to the door.

In the basement Tudor was denouncing witch hunts while Mrs. Anguilo, quite unable to understand that he was angry for her, not with her, moaned, 'Oh no, no, no!' Meg Jacobs was surprised that Tudor should react so strenuously before the police had done anything naughty; Vereker was looking at the ground, his head to one side, listening intently; something seemed to be puzzling him. These people, and the two policemen, were standing in the centre of the room. Milo sat on a bench against the wall, slack, hunch-shouldered, like a player snatching a rest in the wings.

The elder of the two policemen, a sergeant, was as surprised as anyone by Tudor's vehemence. For all that had so far been said by the police, they might have come to make enquiries about a lost bicycle or a dead cat. The sergeant was a pleasant-looking, fresh-faced man with a gently amused manner, and shrewd enough to capitalize on these assets. The benign approach, in his experience, produced better results than bullying. He was, therefore, annoyed that a contentious atmosphere was being created before he had had time to set the tone of the proceedings. For this reason, he welcomed the diversion created by the arrival of the newcomers.

'Good morning, Miss Lindsay,' he greeted Zoe affably. 'And Miss Vereker, isn't it? I don't think we've met. I'm Sergeant Briskett and this is Constable Muldoon.' He noted that the two ladies looked rather hostile, but continued with impervious cheerfulness, 'You may not have heard that the altar and a stained glass window in the church were damaged last night? We are making a few enquiries. . . .'

'Which immediately led you down here.' Tudor could not let well alone.

'It's natural that we should start at the vicarage, isn't it? After all, the folk here are nearest to the church and therefore the most likely to have noticed anyone who might have been hanging about.'

'There was a meeting in the church hall last night after which close on a hundred people were hanging about,' Tudor retorted. 'Including everyone in this room with the exception of Milo.'

Milo shot him a quick, involuntary glance. It was the only time that he looked at Tudor during the whole interview.

'The key in my study is missing,' Vereker explained. He, like the sergeant, seemed content at this stage to behave as though this was an informal news conference.

'You've no idea when you had it last?' the sergeant asked.

'I'm afraid not. It was a spare key.'

'By far the most likely explanation is that the verger left the door open by mistake,' Tudor said.

'He says he didn't,' Vereker answered. 'I spoke to him this morning and he assured me. . . .'

'Of course he would assure you! After what has happened he'd be bound to say that he locked the door. He hardly knows one day from another, does poor old Morpeth, and he's afraid that if he were to admit to this costly piece of negligence, the church, with its usual record for compassionate dealings with its employees, would turn him out of his cottage.'

'That really is preposterous,' Vereker said quietly. 'Nevertheless he is forgetful. I suppose it's possible. . . .'

'We can go into the question of the key afterwards,' the sergeant said.

'After what, may one ask? After you have found a culprit and decided how the key can best be fitted into your theory?'

Zoe whispered, 'Oh, Tudor, don't! Please, please, don't!' She put her hands to her ears. It was not the adult Tudor whose voice she was trying to cut out; it was the child whose response to his own wrongdoing was to rage and strain so frantically that it seemed he must bring the framework of his small world crashing down, to prevent which his terrified parents would appropriate blame to themselves.

The sergeant, who was not seeking to blame Tudor for anything and most certainly did not see himself as in any way culpable, was irritated at the constant refusal of these people to play things cool. If they wanted it rough, he could play it that way. 'As I understand it, everyone here was at the meeting in the church hall, except for this lad.' He turned to Milo. 'Where were you yesterday evening?'

They all looked at Milo, except for Mrs. Anguilo who raised her eyes to the ceiling while tears streamed down her cheeks. Milo swallowed and flicked his tongue across his lips. 'I was in the church.' He was nervous, but it was the nervousness of the highly-strung artiste suffering a bad attack of stage-fright; it remained to be seen whether he had the resources and the courage to recover from a bad start. Certainly, he had no intention of letting his mother destroy his concentration, for he took no notice of her keening. He also resisted the temptation to talk compulsively and waited for the sergeant to say his lines. They were predictable.

'And what were you doing in the church?'

'I belong to . . .' He paused, and then corrected himself. 'I belonged to a group who call themselves the Ancient People.'

The sergeant made no comment. He had expected to have to tease this information out of Milo and was disconcerted at having it presented to him so early in the proceedings.

'We were supposed to be meeting yesterday evening,' Milo went on slowly and carefully, like someone controlling a stammer. 'But it was called off and I was bored. So I took off my clothes and went out onto the lawn. I decided I didn't need the others; in fact, I thought I might get on better without them. Some of them don't know the difference between abandonment and consummation.'

'And what is the difference?' the sergeant asked, poker-faced.

'You've got to concentrate if you are to achieve consummation.' Milo seemed surprised at the question. 'You must concentrate with every nerve and muscle, as if you were composed of threads that you were drawing together, closer and closer to the centre.'

The young constable seemed to be having trouble adjusting his weight-load to his feet. The sergeant said, 'And when you've done all that, what happens then?'

'Nothing, so far,' Milo admitted. 'I improvise a bit. Sometimes it's exciting, but it's always me exciting myself.'

'So you decided you'd have a go on your own?'

'Yes. But it didn't work any better.' Milo was master of his nerves now. 'I could see the lights on in the church hall and I wondered what was going on in there. So I went and listened outside one of the windows. Then I began to feel rather excited and I thought I would like to take part. I'd have gone in and danced for them in the hall, but I knew they wouldn't have let me in. One thing that really turns people on is nudity, and they don't think religion goes with being turned on. But I think they're wrong about that. So I went into the church. . . .'

He was in complete command now, pacing himself well, keeping something in reserve. He sensed that they were alive to him and he felt energy flowing out from him to meet their demand. There was only one black spot in the room which wouldn't come alive to him.

Vereker responded in spite of himself. He remembered that Gwynneth Jarman had said that Milo was a manipulator, but Vereker thought rather that he orchestrated his effects. Now, gradually, he was drawing together the ragged tempers of the people in the room and imposing on them his own order. It was chiefly the eyes which achieved this dominance; they seemed to hold the eyes of everyone in the room and to transmit an irresistible and totally irrational vivacity. Yet although the brilliant eyes compelled attention, Vereker thought that Milo himself was unaware of the nature of his gift; he could strike the chords he wanted from those around him, but he had little idea of how the trick was worked.

'So you went into the church and danced, did you?' the sergeant asked in a neutral tone.

Milo answered questions thoughtfully, and with enough hesitation to vary the tempo of his responses and to give an impressive integrity to his performance. It seemed to Vereker that he was witnessing an almost miraculous speeding-up of the process of growth; gradually, before his eyes, a mature person was emerging from this impudent young faun.

'And the key?' the sergeant asked.

For a moment, the miracle was suspended. Patches of colour glowed beneath Milo's eyes and slowly spread across his cheeks. Now he had difficulty in making the words come. 'I took it from the desk in the library.' He looked at Vereker. 'You said I could "make myself free of the books".' He was mortified by the pettiness of the act.

Vereker said, 'We can talk about that later.'

'So it was you who opened the door?' The sergeant fancied he saw weakness here. 'No one else could have known you were going to do it?'

Milo was relieved to turn his attention to the sergeant. 'No,' he agreed. 'It was all done on the spur of the moment.'

'So other people would have assumed that the church was closed?'

'I suppose so.'

Nancy was aware of the trap closing on Milo. She assumed he was guilty and she thought he would never be able to explain himself. How can you expect the people who have had all the good hands dealt to them to understand those who are left at the mercy of the joker, to a father who deserts them, to a loving God who strikes a mother down with an incurable disease and lets her die by inches over seven years? As these thoughts tumbled through her mind she became very angry. Gradually, the anger grew deeper and darker than anything she had ever known.

'You say you didn't touch anything on the altar?'

'No.'

'You didn't pick up the candlestick?'

'No.'

'And you didn't see anyone else?'

'The church was dark.'

The anger was darkening the room. Tudor was standing beside Nancy and she put out a hand and laid it on his arm. She felt the darkness pressing against her temples, on her eyelids; the other people in the room were sliding away, already out of focus. She looked at Tudor and saw that he was suffering much more acutely than she. The darkness was in him, it was pushing against the bone frame of his thin, tormented face. She eased close to him; his unrelaxed body was tense as though pain had got at him long ago when he was a child and worked its way into the very marrow of his bones. It frightened her to see him suffering like this.

The sergeant said, 'You saw no one as you left the church?'

'I was very excited; I wasn't aware of what went on around me.'

'And when you left the church, the altar and the window were undamaged? You would have noticed that, surely?'

Milo hesitated. He had hesitated before, refusing to be hurried, choosing his words carefully; but he looked tired now and the skin, pale beneath the red hair, had a transparent quality. Nancy knew that something terrible was about to happen; the darkness was taut as a drum.

'Come,' the sergeant said, 'either the damage was done before you left or not.'

Nancy said, 'Everything was perfectly all right after Milo left.'

Something snapped; she could feel a twanging in the air.

'I was making my way to the footpath and I noticed the door was open,' she said. 'Milo came out while I was wondering what to do. He ran off and I went in to see what he had been up to. But nothing seemed to have happened. So I came away.'

The young constable was looking at her in fascination, as though he had seen a few things in his time, but nothing as perverse as her. The sergeant said, 'What a pity you didn't say this in the first place, Miss.' He looked at her speculatively. She could tell that he did not believe her. 'And when you left the church, did you shut the door?'

'No . . . I suppose I was a bit put out and so. . . .'

'It wasn't automatic, to shut the door behind you?'

'No . . . I . . . I went out quickly.'

'And you didn't attempt to attract Milo's attention when you saw him? Ask him what he was up to?'

'He wasn't dressed,' Nancy said primly.

Tudor gave a sour little bark of laughter and turned away, jangling keys in his pocket. Milo was hunched forward, his eyes closed; he held one hand to his side as though he was winded. The others seemed temporarily stunned, as though someone who was tone deaf had suddenly taken control of an orchestra; then Mrs. Anguilo sat down on a packing case and began to cry, 'He didn't do it! He didn't do it!' She sounded intensely relieved and not a little surprised. Meg Jacobs moved across to Nancy and said, 'Bully for you, my girl!'

The sergeant, realizing that there was little chance of turning this day's defeat into victory, comforted himself with the thought that he who fights and runs away lives to fight another day. He would, he said for the benefit of anyone who might be listening, make further enquiries and return to take statements.

In the quiet that followed the departure of the two policemen, Vereker looked across the room and met Zoe Lindsay's troubled eyes. He thought, 'She really does see things the rest of us don't see.'

'They're a rum lot,' the constable said to the sergeant. They were in the church waiting for the photographer to finish his work.

'Mmh. What did you make of the Reverend?' the sergeant asked.

'He took it all very calmly, I thought.'

'He did, indeed. Even this.' The sergeant looked up the nave at the smashed altar; there was something more than a decent disgust in his face. He wasn't a religious man but he believed that there are some things which are better not tampered with, and a primitive fear stirred in him when he thought of what might come of this clash between the holy and the unholy.

7

After the rain had stopped, Vereker and Nancy worked in the garden.

Nancy said, 'Well, I'm glad that silly business is over and done with!' She looked expectantly at her father.

The wallflowers, battered by the rain, were bowed across the path and Vereker bent down to examine them. 'I'll have to tie these back. Could you run and get string and a pair of scissors?' She did not move and he looked up at her, surprising panic in her face. He said, 'There's string in the box under the pantry shelf.'

When she came back, they worked together in silence. He waited for her to tell him that she had lied about seeing Milo leave the church, but she said nothing. He wanted to hug her and make her his little girl again, to take this burden from her. Surely parents have a duty to protect their children? Love isn't something that can be switched off when a child reaches a certain age. It was, however, the very word "love" which held him back : to love is not to guide, to persuade, to advise, love is letting be. He said nothing and let Nan be.

Vereker had a sleepless night and Nancy dreamed that her father had died and woke weeping for him.

In the morning, Vereker looked forward eagerly to Zoe's arrival. She was sympathetic to Nan and he had decided he would talk to her, in a general way, about the problems of girls of Nan's age. Now that he knew Zoe better he was no longer daunted by her beauty; he noted the details of her face but seldom saw it as a whole. They talked together easily. This morning, however, she was late arriving. He had to see Donald Jarman, and by a quarter to ten he decided he could not wait any longer. He would be back at the vicarage before she left and they could talk then.

The Jarmans stayed late in bed on Saturday mornings. When Vereker called, Barbara, colourful in cherry sweater and slacks, was the only member of the family who was fully dressed. Her crisp bronze hair shone in the sunlight, her hazel eyes were clear, her mouth was moist and red, the small teeth incisive. Her father, blue-jowled and pouch-eyed, seemed jaded by so much resounding good health and Mrs. Jarman was less ebullient than usual.

Vereker, having refused food and drink, sat by the window. Although he was not tempted by the food, he found the smells appetising. Barbara and her parents were arguing, but this was not unpleasant. The Jarmans rounded up their problems and disagreements and gave them a good airing every day; there was no impression in this house of grievances left to fester, or of pain anaesthetized.

Somewhere out of sight a robin was singing and there was a rustling in the eaves where martins had nested. The air was soft and seemed to combine with the smell of bacon and coffee to promise a warm, lazy day. The slight breeze hadn't the energy to lift the curtains. Impending change was proclaimed in a way that was less dramatic than the manner in which weather changes were apt to be announced in Coopers Town; yet, though subtle, this was more profound. One was made aware that this shift of wind direction, the rise in temperature, increase in the pollen count, were elements of a myth; the earth was stirring.

Mrs. Jarman was conscious only of the squirrel attacking the barrel of nuts hung out for the birds. 'Excuse me!' She leant across Vereker and aimed a dry crust at the squirrel. Jeremy came into the room in pyjamas, moving like a sleep-walker. Barbara picked up the threads of argument where the squirrel had broken them.

'It's typical, isn't it? All this talk about compassion and caring, and the first time anyone puts a foot wrong, OUT!'

Jeremy said, 'I think I'll take a tray up to bed if this is going on.'

Mrs. Jarman said to Barbara, 'That statement is about as full of inaccuracies as it could be, my love. "Anyone" is not yet *out*; it certainly isn't the first wrong; and no one, certainly not your father or I, is talking about caring and compassion!'

Barbara pushed back her chair. 'I'll leave you to your witch-hunt.'

She went into the kitchen, and Jeremy, having piled a tray with eggs and bacon, marmalade, toast and coffee, headed towards the stairs. As her offspring withdrew, Mrs. Jarman said, 'Well, why can't we get rid of the Anguilos? Devil-worship is as sound a reason for a witch-hunt as any that is likely to come to hand.'

'You are only making him more interesting to her,' Mr. Jarman said.

Mrs. Jarman swivelled round in her chair and said to Vereker, 'Our daughter is smitten by this awful Milo.'

'She, of course, denies it,' Donald Jarman said. 'But my wife is doing her best to bring her round to our way of thinking.'

It was obvious that, as far as the Jarmans were concerned, the Anguilos' continued stay at the vicarage rested on whether or not it was deemed to be in their daughter's best interests.

'And anyway,' Donald Jarman continued, 'we can't drum them off the island. Not a second time. So surely the vicarage is as good a place as anywhere for them to be, right under our good vicar's nose.' He looked at Vereker slyly.

'A second time?' Vereker asked.

'Mrs. Anguilo has previous connections with the island,' Jarman said, but before he could explain his wife interrupted.

'A lot of people will be very angry if they stay. That stained glass window. . . .'

'I doubt if that was damaged by Milo,' Vereker interjected. 'I'm taller than he is, and I couldn't have reached across the altar to that window – and certainly not wielding a candlestick as heavy as the one that was used.'

The Jarmans thought about this. Donald saw the point at once, but Gwynneth was more reluctant. 'He must know who did it, anyway,' she objected.

'Not according to Nancy's evidence.' Vereker braced himself for their reaction.

Donald said, 'You have your difficulties, too, haven't you?'

'I can't understand what they see in him, can you?' Gwynneth wondered.

They assumed that Nancy was lying and it comforted them to think that she, too, was infatuated by Milo. Vereker did not think that this was so, but then he was not perceptive where his daughter's sexuality was concerned.

Donald Jarman lifted the coffee pot; only a trickle of coffee remained. Gwynneth said, 'There's more on the stove.' When his wife had departed, Jarman said, 'I must confess to being very shocked about this. It made me feel quite sick when I saw the damage.'

Vereker said, 'Yes, I can understand that.'

Jarman pushed at a few crumbs with a forefinger. 'I get the impression that you are rather less than outraged.'

'I was very upset when I saw it. But what matters most is the person who did it. A person who is self-mutilating. *That* is the real blasphemy. Or so I believe.'

'Do you know that before you came here we had just finished repairing the roof?' Jarman spoke in a level voice, but he was angry. 'And before that it was the organ, and before that it was the west wall. Over the years since I have been churchwarden we have had to raise something over thirty thousand pounds in this small parish with very limited resources. And you are saying that the hooligan that got in there the other night is more important than the damage to that stained glass window! The altar's not so badly damaged, and it's of no architectural merit, anyway. But that was an early fourteenth century window!'

The two men stared into each other's eyes. Vereker thought : it is law and order with which this man is really concerned. Jarman said, 'You've got your priorities wrong, Vicar. In my view, that is.' He helped himself to marmalade and when Gwynneth returned they discussed details of an emergency meeting of the parochial church council.

It was a quarter to eleven when Vereker left the Jarmans. When he got back to the house, Zoe would be there and they would talk about girls of Nan's age. He quickened his pace. In Virginia Close men were washing their cars. One or two stopped to call out a cheerful good-day, and a woman supervising her husband paused long enough to issue an invitation to a wine and cheese party. He was a part of their landscape now, an odd feature to be pointed out to house guests from more sophisticated places. 'There goes our mad American vicar. Don't think we don't have any curiosities in Helmsley!' Vereker wasn't worried what they thought of him. He had more important worries.

The first thing he noticed when he entered the vicarage was the quiet; not the murmuring peace of early summer, but a quiet without resonance as though the current of life had been switched off. He went to the foot of the stairs and called out

'Miss Lindsay'. No answer. He went up one or two steps and paused, looking up at the bedroom doors. He remembered doing the same thing a week after Alma's death, seeing the door to her room ajar and a shaft of sunlight falling obliquely across the carpet. He called louder, 'Miss Lindsay! Miss Lindsay!'

The telephone began to ring. Of course! Something had delayed her and while he was out she had probably telephoned several times to explain. He hurried into the library and picked up the receiver.

'. . . not excessive . . . could have been much worse. . . .' It took Vereker a moment or two to realise that Colonel Maitland was talking about the damage to the church. 'Pity you said that about tearing down the medieval structure, though.'

Vereker said, 'Yes, stupid of me. . . .'

'I understood what you were getting at, of course, but I don't suppose many of the rest of them did.' Vereker looked about the room, noting that nothing had been disturbed by vacuum cleaner or duster. He felt scared as a lost child, abandoned in this house that was not his house, in this country that was not his country.

'We used to have open air services when I was in Burma.' Colonel Maitland was saying. 'Splendid. Never felt the same inside a building. I went to hear Billy Graham for that reason. You know him, I expect?'

Her role, though unspectacular, was more important than he had realized. That mid-morning cup of coffee to which he looked forward eagerly was not just a welcome stimulant; it was a reassurance that someone had given thought for his comfort.

'A well-meaning man, but emotional. We had one or two of his converts here for a time; came expecting a revelation a day. A church can't maintain that kind of emotional temperature, so they drifted off.'

The tactful handling of a telephone call on his behalf not only saved him time, it was a gesture of sympathy. The wild flowers in the bowl on his desk gave him good cheer each morning.

'But the army services were different. I had a talk with Slim about it once. Fine fellah, Slim. Much more sound than Montgomery.'

105

The dusting, the hoovering, the polishing brought this dead house to life. These simple activities were her gift to him. Once given, a gift can't be withdrawn. Can it?

'I've got both of them,' Colonel Maitland said. 'I'll lend them to you if you like.'

Vereker said 'Thank you' and Colonel Maitland rang off.

Vereker picked up the receiver and dialled Zoe's number. When she answered, she said, 'Oh hullo,' as though she had been expecting him to ring her, but hadn't wanted it. There was an awkward pause. 'Oh dear!' She sounded annoyed. 'I was going to write to you. But now . . . I suppose. . . . Well, I'm afraid it's just that I don't think I can manage to come again.'

'I see.'

'Anyway, I will write.'

'No, no, you mustn't bother. I'm afraid we must have been a lot of trouble to you.'

'No, you weren't.'

There was another pause, and then Vereker said, 'Well, thank you for letting me know.'

She said she was sorry and he said she mustn't be sorry. He did not know which of them put the receiver down first.

He was busy preparing his sermons for the rest of the day and on Sunday he was busy all day. At supper on Monday, Nancy said, 'Zoe hasn't been for a couple of days. Perhaps she isn't well. Shouldn't you call on her?'

'I don't think that would be appropriate,' he answered.

The next morning he set out to call on her. The damp meadow was threaded with wild flowers, but it was not the slender grace of Ragged Robin, or the modest charm of Scarlet Pimpernel with which he was concerned as he hurried along the footpath. He was thinking that her decision not to come to the vicarage any more had been made after that scene with the police. She had realized something, he had seen it in her eyes.

He did not pause to look through windows; he went to the front door, lifted the heavy knocker and banged it down hard. It was only then that he asked himself what he would say if it was Tudor Lindsay who answered the door. In fact, no one came to the door. For the first time, Vereker wondered what had happened when the two cousins returned to the house after the scene with the police. He hammered on the door more urgently. Nothing stirred. He was by now a little alarmed, and he was about to turn away with some wild idea of trying to find an open window, when he heard the creaking of the stairboards. He waited, his heart beating fast. Footsteps crossed the hall, the heavy latch was lifted, and there was Zoe Lindsay, dressed in faded blue slacks and an old pullover with sleeves rolled up to the elbows.

He said foolishly, 'You're all right, then?'

She looked startled and not entirely pleased. 'You'd better come in.' She stood aside for him to cross the threshold and then shut the door. They stood close by the door. She looked at him speculatively, as though considering what to do with him now she had let him in. After a moment, he saw in her eyes that she had made a decision. He felt it was important, but he had no idea what it was. 'I'm working upstairs.' She turned towards the stairs and he followed her. 'That's why I took some time to answer the door.' Her manner towards him had changed, but it was difficult to say in what way.

They walked down a long corridor with doors on one side and windows on the other overlooking the orchard. The apple trees were heavy with blossom and their sweet scent hung faintly in the air. At the end of the corridor four narrow steps led to an attic room; he had a glimpse of sloping ceilings before she pushed the door wide open. It was a larger room than he had anticipated, running the width of the house, with windows at each end. It was sparsely furnished with a cane armchair, a day-bed with paintings propped on it, work-tables and easels. There were books on the floor, some arranged neatly against the skirting board, while others, propped open, were scattered haphazard over the floor.

'I'm an illustrator,' she said. 'Mostly children's books.'

He looked round the room. 'Is this why you stayed away? Because you had work to do here?'

'No. I haven't done any professional work for some time. I stayed away because I thought you were better off without the Lindsays.'

'That's absurd.' He was a little apprehensive as to what was to come. He could still smell the apple blossom and he wished she had taken him out in the garden instead of bringing him up here.

In the basement, when the police were questioning Milo, she had seen something that no one else had seen and she had been shocked. He was quite prepared to talk to her about that, if she chose to confide in him; but for that to suffice he should have come sooner. Since then, shock had had repercussions. Things moved fast in Helmsley; he was always a little behind events, bewildered and unprepared. He felt like a middle-aged Alice.

'Why don't you do any professional work now?' he asked to gain time. 'Is it hard to come by? I don't know much about the book trade.'

'I'd better tell you about myself,' she answered abruptly. 'Tudor and I were lovers, you knew that? He couldn't bear to be excluded from anything I was doing. He said it was bad for me to work here on my own. Whenever he was at home, he came up here with me; he would study my drawings and tell me what they revealed about my subconscious. Loathsome things!' Her face puckered in disgust. 'Gradually, I found I couldn't draw; as soon as I started I was afraid of what I was revealing about myself. I suppose I could have locked him out of the room; but it would have destroyed my pride in my work if I had had to do it behind locked doors like a pornographer. So I stopped. That was why Genevieve Draisey suggested I should help at the vicarage. She thought I ought to be occupied.'

Vereker looked down at his shoes and saw that they were caked with mud. 'From my point of view, you were very usefully occupied.'

'I am odd. Haven't you noticed? I see the nuns, Tudor deduces from my sketches that I live on the borders of insanity.' She spoke fiercely.

'You may see the nuns,' Vereker turned his left shoe to the side, wondering if he had muddied all her carpets, 'but I'm sure you are not insane.'

'Make *me* sure. I want you to tell me what you think of my sketches.'

'I don't know anything about art,' he protested.

'I don't want an artistic judgement,' she said impatiently. 'My work is good, I know that.'

He was the last person who should be asked for this kind of assessment, he thought wretchedly; he was always so conscious of other people's separateness, their right to their own solution. He turned reluctantly towards the long table which was cluttered with line drawings, artist's proofs, water colours; she must have decided to give herself a retrospective exhibition.

He began to study the exhibits, afraid of what he might find; he could not bear the thought that there were maggots in this woman's mind. Almost without exception they were illustrations of myths and fairy stories; and they did indeed reveal the topography of the artist's mind, so that the observer could trace the recurrent themes and the contours in which they were contained. The landscape of Zoe Lindsay's world was dark, a landscape seen through a gauze of mist or in a shaft of moonlight. There was a multitude of little creatures, gnomes, elves, pixies, who dwelt on the fringes of this landscape and formed a decorative frieze around many of the pictures. In the heart of the pictures, bounded by this frieze of half-malign, half-benevolent creatures, there were prisoners – children, maidens, princesses. Only the young men rode proudly across the distant golden fields. The prisoners all looked outward; hopefully waiting for release, they peeped from between the slats of log cabins, through the bars of a castle window, from a cave on a mountainside. All, that is, except the sleeping beauty, who must lie immobilized on her bed until one of the young men comes to give her life. There was a series of sketches of her, lying with hair streaming about the submerged dreamer's face, while outside the window one after another of the young men rode indifferently by. There was not, Vereker noted, a picture of the beauty being woken in the accepted manner. He wondered how the particular story she was illustrating had ended.

Another theme that was interwoven with that of the Prisoner was the Quest. But this was not the quest for the Grail, there were no knights here. This was the quest of the children for the key to a locked door, a path through a wood, a star to follow. It was the quest of the maidens who seemed always to be gazing into mirrors. Even the Wicked Queen, staring into her mirror, was taking part in the quest: her eyes demanded something more from the mirror than the assurance that she was fairest of them all.

There was one drawing which was different from all the

others. There was no landscape with mountains, no valleys, no frieze of Little People, no distant golden boys. In the foreground, there was a shadowy figure of a woman, back view, dark hair merging into the drifting cloak which enveloped her. In the centre, a pair of hands held a great crystal in which was reflected the face of the woman. But whereas the figure that gazed into the crystal was only a suggestion of a woman, a tentative idea, half-formed, incidental, the face in the crystal, brought into being by a few bold strokes, had above all qualities, clarity; neither beauty nor personality, passion or repose, but clarity. She was neither dark nor fair, for only the essential features were there, eyes, nose, mouth; it was like a face drawn on a smooth white stone, made radiant by refracted light. Vereker noticed that the hands which held the bowl did not seem to be holding it aloft so much as presenting it to the woman. He wondered what Tudor had made of this picture. But perhaps Tudor had not seen it; some sticky substance, glue probably, had caused it to adhere to one of the sleeping beauty series, and Vereker himself might have missed it had he not picked up the last of the series to see whether the name of the book might be written on the back. Whatever Tudor might have made of it, it gave Vereker satisfaction. When he looked at it, he did not have the feeling that he was peeping into a private world. He was puzzled, and he wasn't sure that he understood its meaning, but he liked it because it was assured and affirmative and he felt it could stand on its own, independent of its creator.

He had come to the end now. He had not attempted to think what he would say to her; he had simply allowed the pictures to happen to him. Now, however, he went back to the beginning and studied them all again. This took some time. She had seated herself by the window, looking into the garden. She did not stir or turn her head; she might have been asleep for all he could tell. When he had finished, he went to her and touched her gently on the shoulder. 'May I make my report now?'

'Come and sit beside me. I must see your face.'

He was disconcerted, and as a result he spoke at first with defensive asperity, like a schoolmaster who has been pinned down by a too-demanding pupil. 'I have to confess that I have never been at ease in the fairy story world and these drawings of yours seem to me very disturbing because they are all about people who are on the outside of life trying to get in.' He spoke slowly, ordering his thoughts. 'But if I wanted to indulge in a little amateur psychology, one of the things to which I would call attention would be the liveliness of the figures, which look to me as if they would like to bust right out of their dream world.' He was pleased about that, perhaps after all, he was acquitting himself rather well. He decided not to mention the face in the crystal, since he was not sure that he had been meant to see it, and went on. 'The other thing I particularly noticed, was the strength of the composition, which suggested to me that the person who executed the work is more firmly in control of her mind than she herself imagines.'

There was a pause. In the garden a thrush trilled unconcernedly and the sound of a car in the lane set a dog barking. Zoe roused herself and said, 'Thank you.' He realized that she had not been attending to what he was saying. How extraordinary women are! They beseech you for advice as though you were Solomon himself, and as soon as you start to speak their minds wander to other things. He wondered what she had been thinking about. Whatever it was, it seemed to have made her happy.

Somewhere near at hand a car door slammed. Zoe started up. 'That's Tudor! I wasn't expecting him.' She moved towards the door. 'Do you mind? I don't want him to come up here.' As they went down the stairs, she said, 'When we got back yesterday morning the telephone was ringing; it was the police about one of his cases on the mainland. He was away for the night. I thought he would probably spend the week-end in Portsmouth; there's a woman there he sometimes stays with.'

Tudor was closing the garage doors when Zoe and Vereker came into the garden. As he came towards them, Vereker said idly, 'You've got a pile of logs up against the fence. I should like to have a fire in the vicarage sitting-room. There's an electric fire there now.'

'You'd have to get the chimney swept,' Tudor said. 'I can give you the name of a sweep.'

'And logs?'

'Do you want them sent to you? Or do you want to gather your own kindling?'

111

'Oh, gather it myself, I think, don't you? The complete ritual.'

Zoe said, 'We can tell you where to go for logs in the autumn.'

They had been strolling across the lawn and had now reached the gate into the field. Zoe said to Tudor, 'I forgot to go to the vicarage this morning and Mr. Vereker came across to see if I was all right.'

Tudor said, 'How very kind of him.'

As Vereker walked away, Zoe called after him, 'I will come to the vicarage as usual tomorrow.'

Tudor demanded, 'Why did he really come?'

'I told you.'

'That was a pretext. He was trying to find something out, wasn't he?'

'What is there for him to find out?'

The sun was bright and he turned his eyes away from its glare. 'I've been up half the night trying to find a J.P. to sign a care order. I'm too tired to think.'

'Why don't you go to bed? I'll bring you soup.'

He dragged a hand across his mouth in a gesture of irreso-lution. 'Perhaps I will. Don't bother with soup. It's sleep I need.'

They went into the house. Tudor looked up the stairs as though measuring the distance to his room.

Zoe said, 'Can you manage?'

'Yes.' He went up the stairs slowly, holding the banister rail, while Zoe watched from the hall. He drove himself hard at his work and had had sudden collapses before; but it seemed to her that at this moment he was like a person suffer-ing from shock rather than overwork.

When Tudor was in bed, Zoe returned to the studio and cleared away the drawings and paintings. She sorted them into three separate piles and put them away in the drawers of a map chest. The only one which gave her pause was the drawing of the woman gazing into the crystal; she looked at this in surprise, then shrugged her shoulders and put it in the top drawer of the chest.

She sat on the window seat and looked around in satis-faction at the bare tables and easels. All those pictures, she thought, all about me! Always *me* searching for *my*self! And then, quite suddenly, today, here in front of me, there is a human face. I can see it still. How lovely it is, this face with the eyes so bent to their task, the mouth so honestly wrestling with words to give to me. He has one hand to his brow and the fingers, resting lightly on the bridge of the nose, draw the whole man together, summoning, in spite of tiredness and disinclination, all his power of perception, penetration and compassion, to my service. How humble I should feel! But what I am really feeling is pure joy at the discovery of this marvel of creation. How far it exceeds the aesthetic pleasure of gazing at works of art shut away in museums! What work of art can produce so humorous and so serious a face, at once so errant and so dedicated, such a combination of weakness and strength, a face so still yet alive to its nerve ends? I don't want to commit this face to paper, I don't even want to listen to what he is saying. I simply want gratefully to accept this moment of actually *seeing* him.

8

Dandelions had taken over from daffodils on the vicarage lawn. The air was warm from early in the morning and the sun had shone for eight days in succession which seemed to be a record. Vereker had several calls to make. Old Miss Harmer who did housework for the Jarmans had had a heart attack, and there were other sick persons to visit. Nancy got up early and cooked him bacon and egg and fried bread. She was particularly tender to him because she had let him die again in her dreams.

Soon after Vereker had gone, Tudor arrived. 'I came to see Milo,' he said to Nancy. 'But he isn't in the basement.'

'He was half an hour ago. I asked him why he wasn't at school and he said he was studying on his own.'

Tudor looked annoyed.

'He's not very sociable lately,' Nancy said. 'In fact, he has hardly spoken to me since I said I saw him leaving the church. . . .'

'Did you expect him to be grateful?'

'I didn't think he'd act as if I'd done him a mischief.' She wondered if this was the time to confess; she had to confess to someone soon.

'Let's forget about Milo, shall we?' He turned towards the gate. 'What about coming with me? I've got to see several clients on the island today.'

Miss Draisey had called at the vicarage earlier in the hope of seeing Vereker and, finding he was out, had remained to hinder Zoe. They were on the upstairs landing while Tudor and Nancy were talking in the garden. Miss Draisey was standing by the window and Zoe was polishing a pair of brass candlesticks.

Miss Draisey was surprised at the difference a few weeks had made in Nancy Vereker. 'That little creature is coming into bud,' she said, 'and when she flowers she'll make her presence felt. So *thrusting*, like all young Americans.' As Nancy talked to Tudor, gazing up at him one moment, the

114

next turning her head away in a confusion of emotion, Miss Draisey could see her working out the mathematics of male-female equations. Miss Draisey had observed this in one or two of her girls. It had been a rarity, for Miss Draisey's girls had not been encouraged to develop this particular facility quickly, if they developed it at all; but she remembered the few who had done so, and one in particular. She could imagine Nancy Vereker looking at herself in the mirror as day by day these things happened to her, thinking in wonder, 'I am a woman!' Miss Draisey wasn't quite sure *what* things happened because there had never been a moment when she had said to herself, 'I am a woman!' She had always supposed it was the kind of thing that happened to only a few very emotional adolescents, like being saved : one could be a Christian without knowing the exact moment one was saved, and so, she had presumed, one could become a woman without actually being aware of it. She said to Zoe, 'I hope your cousin can teach that young woman some sense, for her father's sake, if not for her own.'

Zoe watched Nancy and Tudor walking towards his car and made no comment.

Miss Draisey sighed. 'Most of the good men I've known have been quite intolerable. But Matthew Vereker really does restore my faith. I think it's because he's so droll that one can accept his goodness.' Miss Draisey watched Nancy getting into Tudor's car, wriggling about in her dress like a puppy who hasn't yet filled out all the folds of skin. She wondered whether, if she married Matthew Vereker, she would be able to tolerate his daughter.

Zoe, who had finished polishing the candlesticks, said, 'The material of that dress she's wearing reminds me of voile. You never see voile now, do you?'

'Or shantung!' Miss Draisey accepted this diversion with enthusiasm. 'I used to love shantung, I thought the word was so seductive. Satin was better, of course, but I knew that satin was sinful and only women like Jean Harlow and Lillian Tashman, who were up to no good, could wear it. Films were so marvellous then, weren't they? All those veiled moments when you hadn't the slightest idea what was going on because you imagined that there were some really unspeakable sins and not just the dreary ones we all know about. It's dreadfully dull now that it's all so explicit.'

Zoe nodded. 'Mysteries should never be explained, should they?'

Miss Draisey placed her hand on Zoe's arm. 'My dear, of course you are right!' Zoe had always seemed to her to be a rather blurred person, but now she had moved sharply into focus. Miss Draisey ached with longing when she contemplated Zoe's beauty. This always seemed to happen to her. No sooner did she find a man whom she could love than she was confronted by a woman with whom she could live (the thought of loving a woman was quite abhorrent to her). She had spent the best years of her life trying to decide whether to marry a man or live with a woman and soon it would be too late to do either.

Zoe moved away from the window, uneasy as she often was in Miss Draisey's company. The grandfather clock in the hall was wheezily gathering itself to strike eleven o'clock. Perhaps the best way of getting rid of Miss Draisey without hurting her feelings would be to have coffee. Mrs. Anguilo was using the washing machine in the kitchen, and Zoe knew that Miss Draisey would not stay long in Mrs. Anguilo's company.

As they turned towards the stairs, Miss Draisey exclaimed, 'I think there is someone in the study. Has Matthew come back?'

'No; that will be Milo.'

'Milo!' Miss Draisey's surprised disapproval was worthy of Lady Bracknell; it was obvious that she thought Milo's presence in the study about as appropriate as the infant John Worthing's in a handbag.

'He's taking A-level religious knowledge and Matthew has said he can use the library.'

'A-level! Even if he had the brains, he wouldn't have the application.'

'You mustn't condemn him because of the past,' Zoe said gently.

'You have only to look at him!'

'But you never do look at him.'

Zoe led the way into the kitchen before Miss Draisey could answer. Mrs. Anguilo was taking her washing out of the spin dryer. Miss Draisey watched her smoothing the wrinkled arm of a shirt before folding it across the front in such a way as to make it more creased than ever. She did this without actually looking at Mrs. Anguilo herself. Mrs. Anguilo smiled ingratiatingly as she accepted Zoe's offer of coffee; she was obviously acutely aware that she was not wanted and determined to stay. It was a relief when Milo came in; he had books under one arm and was heading purposefully for the back door when Miss Draisey challenged him. 'Don't you have religious instruction in school?' She stared at him boldly, her eyes wide open. He had his back to the light and she saw him as a dark outline with no detail.

'The Reverend Binns comes from Portsmouth especially to give us religious instruction.' His tone implied a wasted journey on the Reverend Binns' part. 'We spend all our time discussing such issues as whether the Red Sea really parted for the Children of Israel.'

'Of course it did!' Mrs. Anguilo stopped smoothing a pair of pyjamas and directed an agonized glance at Miss Draisey.

'When you go down there,' Milo pointed out of the window in the general direction of the coast, 'and look at the stretch of water between the island and the mainland, does it ever occur to you that the water might fold itself up on either side for you to walk through on dry land?'

'Not for me, it wouldn't.'

'For anyone!' Milo made a graceful gesture which embraced Zoe and Miss Draisey. 'Can you imagine it happening to anyone?'

'It was a miracle,' Mrs. Anguilo pointed out.

'Shit!'

Miss Draisey thought it time to intervene. 'What, in particular, are you reading?' she demanded.

'I'm reading the Bible from cover to cover.'

'And what do you expect to get out of it?' Miss Draisey asked in the amused tone she would have adopted had she come across one of her girls searching for salacious passages in *Lady Chatterley's Lover.*

'Jesus.'

'Jesus wasn't *born* then.' Mrs. Anguilo was embarrassed. 'Not at the time the Children of Israel crossed the Red Sea. That was hundreds of thousands of years before. I don't know what they teach you at that school.' She looked at Miss

Draisey hoping for an indication that she had acquitted herself honourably as a parent. Miss Draisey ignored her .

Milo held up the copy of the Bible and said, '*This* is all Jesus. Jesus was the Word made flesh.'

Miss Draisey said, '*I* understand what that means, of course, but I very much doubt whether you do.'

'The Word was there before Jesus was born and. . . .'

'I think you should talk to the vicar about this.' Miss Draisey was at her most magisterially dismissive.

'Yes, I shall have to do that in the course of events.' Milo departed with the air of one who has tarried too long in the presence of fools. Mrs. Anguilo began to cry.

'What did he mean "in the course of events" in that apocalyptic tone?' Miss Draisey demanded.

Mrs. Anguilo folded the last garment. 'God has told him to found his own church.' She balanced the washing basket on her hip and went out weeping.

'Well, I doubt if *that* need concern us !' Miss Draisey said to Zoe. 'What I really came to see Matthew about was the church fête. We really must do something different this year. . . .'

Tudor and Nancy were by this time driving along the road that skirted the farming area which Vereker had visited several weeks earlier. Nancy was still anxious to confess. She had been trying for weeks to make her father accuse her, but without success. She could not carry the secret around on her own much longer.

'There's something I want to tell you,' she began.

'I don't want to talk about the church affair, if that's what you have in mind.'

'It's rather important. . . .'

'To you and your father, perhaps; but it doesn't affect me in the slightest. To me, the blasphemy is the Church itself. Can we leave it at that?' He stopped the car at the gate of a large, ramshackle house. 'You can meditate on your trouble while I visit mine.'

'That looked like a goat at one of the windows,' Nancy said when he returned.

'It was a goat. Lady Piers Monceaux, who must be all of one-hundred-and-ten, lives in a caravan and the goats have the house. She won't see me, but I pay a token visit whenever I come this way and we make faces at each other through the window.'

'How awful to live like that!'

'Pointless and unprofitable, certainly. If it was left to me, I'd have her put down along with her goats.'

'She must have problems, poor old thing.'

'You think so? For myself, I think that if the upper classes want to stick to their privileges they will have to relinquish the right to have problems.'

Nancy liked the way he sounded when he said this kind of thing, so sharp-edged and hard. This was the way he looked, too. There was nothing to spare in face or body, he was lean and hard and driven. It was this quality of being driven which made him so compulsively attractive; he lived every moment as if it was crucial and this intensity harrowed his face in a way which was very exciting.

Tudor stopped the car outside a row of dilapidated farm cottages.

'Does one of your problem families live here?' Nancy asked.

'It's the problem family your father turfed out. Remember? They came with the Anguilos.'

'The dark, shrewish woman and the long-haired men?' Memory brought the woman sharply to mind.

'The same.'

'And now they live here?'

'One of the men, Mrs. Peters' brother, is in prison. The rest of the family is squatting in the end cottage.'

There was another car parked outside the last cottage and Meg Jacobs was standing at the front door talking to Mrs. Peters. Tudor said to Nancy, 'You'd better stay in the car.'

It was hot and Nancy had the window wound down, so she could hear Meg Jacobs quite clearly; she was telling Mrs. Peters that there had been reports that the children were left alone in the house at night without access to a telephone.

'We don't have a telephone and they'd only break it if we had,' Mrs. Peters said as though this disposed of the matter.

The front entrance led straight into the living-room and Nancy could see two small children grubbing about on the uncarpeted floor; neither looked old enough to make use of a telephone. There was a settee against the wall and a bearded man was sitting cross-legged on it, the palms of his hands resting on the soles of his feet.

'Who's been on about them being left alone? That old tabby in Number Four? She's probably listening now.' Mrs. Peters thumped the wall and shouted, 'Can you hear all right, Mrs. Nye?'

A shower of crumbling plaster was the only response to this attack on the wall.

'It's not the noise they make,' Meg Jacobs held to her course stoutly. 'They're a bit young to be left alone. . . .'

One of the children crawled onto the doorstep. 'I've got to go to the pub. How would I get another job these days?' Mrs. Peters yanked the toddler up by the scruff of its neck and tossed it negligently, but without apparent malice, into the road, where Tudor fielded it. The other, a few years older, made its own way without maternal aid.

While Meg Jacobs talked to Mrs. Peters, Tudor took the opportunity to examine the children. Tommy had a bruised arm and a scab on his nose, but neither seemed of recent origin; the toddler, Cylla, was filthy as usual but apparently without bruises, breaks or scars. Tudor called out to Nancy, 'There's something for them in the back of the car. Can you keep them occupied for a minute or two? I want to talk to Eddie Peters.' Mrs. Peters was a sharp, manipulative woman, the kind who knows what she is doing even in her sleep; Tudor thought she probably thumped the children from time to time, but he didn't think she ever lost control. It was the father he was not happy about.

Meg Jacobs was leaving and Mrs. Peters accompanied her to her car in order to tell her the kind of accommodation which would be acceptable to the Peters family. Nancy watched the two women while Cylla and Tommy squabbled on the back seat of the car. Mrs. Peters, in spite of her misfortunes, seemed a very formidable person. Meg Jacobs, for all her pugnacity, would be much more easily put down; she would fight for others but had never learnt to fight for herself. Nancy liked Meg and thought that she was a good person.

In the living-room, Eddie Peters was still sitting on the settee. He appeared not to register what was going on, but as soon as Tudor came into the room, he said in a soft un-expectedly cultured voice. 'I kept my appointment with Dr. Leishner.'

'Good.'

Eddie reached up to smooth the long, dark hair on either side of its neat central parting. 'I don't seem able to establish a rapport with Dr. Leishner.' He looked steadfastly at Tudor; he had eyes like brown lollipops with a slight glaze on them.

'Psychiatrists vary,' Tudor answered easily. 'Dr. Leishner believes in a more formal approach than some. It doesn't mean he isn't interested.'

'Yes, I realize this is true.' After contemplating this truth for a few moments, Peters went on, 'It's just that I need someone to warm to me. I don't seem able to take in what people are saying if they're not sympathetic to me.'

'How are things going here?' Tudor changed the subject, since he could not change Dr. Leishner.

'Oh, fine,' Peters nodded his head to emphasize this. 'I really am surprised at the difference I see in myself. You know, I never really *liked* children, I can see that, looking back on my life. But now I find I *do* like them. I take their hands when we walk along the beach and I find the feel of their flesh pleasant. And when I see a woman with a baby in a pram I go and ask if I can look at it and I'm fascinated by its little fat hands and the pleats in the flesh at the wrist; and I notice how lovely the colouring is, not all pink, but with traces of blue, particularly under the eyes. I get a lot of pleasure from children now, visual and tactile.' He might have been describing a shell he had picked up on the beach.

'Do you play games with them in here?' Tudor looked round the bare room.

Something closed down behind the eyes. 'I take them for walks on the beach, like I told you. I'm one of those people who ought to live in the open; I don't like having things on top of me. I try to explain that to Dr. Leishner, but it's very difficult to judge whether he gets the point.'

The children came scrambling back and stopped in the open doorway. Tudor said, 'Hullo, Tommy.'

The child said, "'Lo' and edged into the room, his eyes on Peters' face; he put his hand in Tudor's. Peters stared in front of him as though he had not noticed the arrival of the children. Mrs. Peters returned, full of complaints about the unsuitability of the accommodation.

Outside, Nancy and Meg Jacobs had strolled along the road and were now leaning over a farm gate.

'How is it with our Tudor?' Meg asked. 'I haven't liked the look of the lad recently. Been overdoing things again, has he?'

'He really identifies with people, and I guess that's a bit wearing.'

'He identifies, I grant you that! But I'd have said he identified people with his convictions, and I'm not sure that's good for them.'

'In what way can it be bad for them?' Nancy asked.

Meg turned her head to one side to get a cigarette going before she answered. Her fingers were stained with nicotine and so was her upper lip. The cigarette bobbed about as she talked.

'Tudor can't see that a few small adjustments might meet their needs quite as well as a revolution.'

'You don't believe in revolution?'

'My God, yes! I'll be there at the barricades when it happens. But I get worried about the inadequate; they can't cope with day-to-day living, let alone a revolution.' She gave a deep sigh, caught her breath and spluttered. 'I always have a nasty feeling that the same sort of people are going to come to the top after the revolution, like they always say the bright pupils win out whatever system of education you have.' She stopped talking to cough in earnest. She looked very depressed; it was obvious she had little confidence in herself. When she had got her breath back, she began to revise her previous statements. 'Don't think I don't admire Tudor. I know some of the other social workers think he's unprofessional, but I think he's worth a dozen of them. I just don't have his guts, that's my trouble.' Tudor was coming towards them. When he joined them, she said, 'What are we going to do about that little lot?'

'If there was a better health service he'd get to see a psychiatrist more often than once in six weeks.' He put his hands on the top bar of the gate, which was padlocked, and rattled it to and fro as though this locking of the gate was the final demand on his patience.

'You can't send *her* to a psychiatrist.'

'The children won't come to much harm from her.'

'They'll come to harm left on their own. Can't you get a care order?'

'On what evidence? The old woman next door? She'd turn milk sour by looking at it. We'd need something more than her unsupported testimony, and the G.P. won't co-operate.' His hands moved restlessly, fingers examining the padlock. 'What we need is a commune for problem families, supervized by resident social workers.'

'Mmh, I like that.' Meg tended to quick enthusiasm, but even she could see drawbacks. 'Where would you find the money? More important, where would you find a site on this tight little island?'

'There's the priory site.'

'You wouldn't have a prayer, Tudor!' Meg hooted. She was pleased to be noticed by Tudor but reacted to him in a gauche way. 'Problem families have a very bad rating in the charts. If you suggested giving some of this island's precious open space over to them, you'd be lynched!'

'Maybe.'

'And, what is more, my dear boy, that old priory is part of our heritage. And it's no use making rude noises, because if anyone threatens that heap of rubble, you're going to hear a lot more about our wonderful heritage; the priory site may be neglected now, but just breathe the word "development" and the archaeologists and conservationists will spring up everywhere like buttercups and daisies.'

She turned away to her car, pausing before getting into it to shout, 'But if you want to stick your neck out, *"I'll be there, I'll be there, and the creed and the colour and the name won't matter . . .".*'

'What a woman!' Tudor said disdainfully.

'Are you going to stick your neck out?' Nancy asked.

'I'm going to have lunch. Are you coming? The woman at the farmhouse does a nice line in bacon and eggs.'

'Super!'

'What an enthusiastic creature you are. If I'd suggested dry bread and stale cheese you would still have said "super".'

Nancy did not answer and he bent down to look in her face. 'I'm sorry.' He picked her up and sat her on the gate. 'You look very nice today, did I tell you that? My idea of the all-

American small-town girl, young and eager and wholesome.'
He clambered over the gate and lifted her down. They began
to stroll round the side of the field. His arm was round her
waist and she wanted to stroll in silence, bumping against
him, getting the feel of him; but he kept throwing out in-
consequential remarks in a nervy, staccato manner.

'What are American small-town boys like?'

'Not so formal as English boys.'

'I always think of Americans as being rather stereotyped.
Particularly the women. I imagine salons everywhere that will
rid you of your individuality and turn you into the all-
American matron.'

'Maybe you'll be like that over here one day,' she answered.
'When Wales and Scotland and Cornwall and Yorkshire have
their own state government, you'll find it's necessary to have
something in common, to prove you're one people, and then
you'll start trying to *look* British instead of being it in your
bones.'

'Very penetrating.' He had a way of cutting her down to
size with a sardonic comment. She decided not to say anything
more until they were settled over the meal.

The meal was simple but good. Unfortunately, the farmer's
wife was lonely and welcomed any chance to talk to people;
she did not leave them alone for longer than it took her to
clear the dishes and fetch butter and cheese.

When they left the farmhouse, Tudor said, 'I feel sleepy. I
shouldn't have eaten so much. Usually, I have a sandwich on
my way from one place to another.'

'Isn't that bad for you?'

'It's even worse if I don't get round to seeing all my urgent
clients.'

'You're too conscientious.'

'The day you're a little less conscientious, something blows
up.'

They walked round the back of an outhouse; there was a
bundle of straw on the ground outside disused stables. It was
very quiet, even the farm dog was too sleepy to do more than
raise a dusty nose from its paws. Tudor said, 'I'm going to
have five minutes' sleep. Be my alarm clock.' He was asleep
almost before he touched the straw. Nancy sat beside him,
wondering how long she should let him sleep. She did not

think that less than half an hour would do him any good. The outhouses were not overlooked by the farmhouse and there was no sight or sound of human activity. She supposed that she and Tudor could probably stay here undisturbed for the afternoon. Even so, she felt guilty as if there were notices flashing "forbidden" all round the yard : very earthy places, farmyards, all right for animals but rather rugged for humans. She looked down at Tudor. He looked very fierce, even in sleep.

After half an hour, she shook his shoulder gently, but he only groaned and turned his head away. She tickled his nose with a straw and he sneezed. 'What's the time?' He looked up at the sky, startled, and then turned his head to one side, blinking his eyes at the stable wall.

'Two o'clock. You've been asleep half an hour. Do you feel better?'

'God, no!' He hunched himself up and rested his head on his knees. It was obvious that the sleep had not done him any good. He had wound himself up for the day and this short rest had interfered with some vital piece of the mechanism that kept him going; he wasn't sure he could get himself started again.

'Lie down,' Nancy commanded. 'Have a few minutes just lying and breathing deeply.'

He did as he was bidden. She put a hand on his ribs. 'You're so uptight you can't even take a deep breath,' she accused him.

'Never mind about that.' He drew her down against his chest and said, 'Just stay with me.' For a few minutes, he seemed to labour for breath, then, when it came more easily, he began to talk. 'I live in a straitjacket, a damned straitjacket!'

'Tudor, why?' She raised herself to look at him, but he pulled her down.

'No, don't leave me.'

'I won't ever leave you.'

'The only way I can function is to conform, to obey the laws even if they are bad laws; I have to consent to be lamed and limited.' He sounded as if he was working a problem out aloud rather than confiding in her. 'I accept all this so that I can do my social work. I don't push beyond the limits because if I did I would be locked up, in prison, or a mental home. And what use would I be then?'

'You're much more use where you are, doing. . . .'

He held her tighter, crushing her to silence while he went on, 'But sometimes I cannot stand it any more. I can feel it closing in on me. I try to smash it; but it doesn't work. You can't smash evil, you only release it and then it has you cornered.'

Nancy thought he was not as much in command of himself as usual. Poor Tudor! He was like a child who has had a nightmare and she had the responsibility of comforting him. She was unused to responsibility and unsure how to exercise it.

Tudor said, 'I broke that window in the church.' He spoke quietly. 'I am proud of it. It was the most magnificent thing I have ever done.' He was silent for a moment, and then he said, 'I wanted to tell you,' as though he was giving her a present.

His words weighed on Nancy, demanding a response so urgently that she had no time to examine what exactly it was that he had said. She was sure that there had never been a moment in the whole of her life when so much depended on finding the right words. She took Tudor's hand and twined her fingers between his to give him some comfort; in spite of this talk of magnificence, she thought that he must be very disturbed by what he had done. She prayed for the right words to come, but they did not come. She never had believed those stories about God giving you the words when you really need to comfort others. The truth was out of the bag now : you damned well have to find your own words! She said, 'I love you, Tudor. But I'm not very experienced, and you've been too unhappy to love. So we'll have to take things slowly. We'll grow into love together.' She lifted his hand to her lips and kissed his fingers. He did not answer and his hand was heavy. She looked at him timidly, hoping he wasn't disappointed in her. He was fast asleep.

9

At a certain stage in the meeting of the South Wessex District Council's planning committee the chairman, prompted by his clerk, announced that the committee had now to discuss matters which, in the public interest, must remain confidential. It would, therefore, he said, glancing towards the slightly raised tier at the back of the chamber, be necessary to ask the public to leave. The few members of the public present began to shuffle about and while they did this the chairman shuffled a few of his papers. When all this shuffling seemed to be over, the chairman said, 'Now, item six, use of the Priory site on Helmsley Island. . . .' The clerk leant forward and hissed in the chairman's ear. A small, docile-looking man was still seated in the public gallery. He was requested to leave, but he appeared to be deaf as well as docile, so the clerk went in search of the policeman on duty.

When the policeman arrived, the small man followed him meekly out of the chamber. It seemed incredible that the same man could have written the piece which so upset Miss Draisey when the *Herald* was delivered to her house.

'Read that!' she commanded Vereker who had called on her to discuss her suggestions for the fête. She had the appearance of having dressed in some confusion, her frilly blouse had been pulled over her head leaving the sausage curls crumpled and the zip of her skirt had not been fastened. Her face was heavily made up and lipstick was smudged across her teeth. As though in explanation of her disarray, she said, 'This is very distressing. And now the worst has happened!' She buttoned up her mouth and breathed heavily. Vereker assumed that he was to read first and hear the worst later. He read :

"The ghosts of Helmsley priory have taken on a more sinister aspect. Their activities have become so menacing that in the islanders' interest it was necessary to clear the public gallery before the members of the planning committee could bring themselves to discuss the latest happenings connected with the priory site.

"Of the several ways of despatching ghosts, exorcism is currently the most favoured. Could it be that last Thursday evening the members of our dauntless planning committee sat in secret concourse to devise their own brand of exorcism? It is rumoured, and rumour, on Helmsley Island, has a way of turning into fact, that the nuns of Helmsley priory may shortly be seen wandering the corridors of a luxury hotel when they are not dining in one of its three restaurants, contemplating its swimming pool, or meditating on its squash courts. The chairman of the planning committee, when asked to comment on this on the telephone, said that he had never heard such nonsense. But then in 1968, the chairman, who is a senior partner in the firm of Engels, Biggs and Sullyman, estate agents, said that he had never heard such nonsense as the suggestion that the old market was to be closed in order to make way for a multi-storey car park."

Vereker let his eyes travel over the printed words, but even on a second reading his mind refused to come to terms with the matter of the use of the priory grounds. It had been a hot week, exceptional, so he was informed, for early June; and it was indeed exceptionally hot in Miss Draisey's sitting-room. The house was Edwardian and solidly built; there was neither crack nor crevice through which air could come if the owner chose not to open a window. The chairs and settee were upholstered in a dark, oppressive brown corded velvet; there were brown velvet curtains at the window which, together with a jungle of pot plants, kept the sun in its place and allowed only a faint light to filter through. The upholstery, the curtains and Miss Draisey herself were impregnated with the smell of stale cigarette smoke and the more recently released fumes of whisky. Vereker remembered that he had been told never to call on Miss Draisey without warning, but he had not understood the reason until now. He wished he had spared her this.

Miss Draisey sat opposite Vereker. A little sweat pricked through the thick coating of powder and she dabbed at her face with a paper tissue. Henry, who was leaning heavily against Vereker's thigh, contributed his own smell, a mixture of leather, powdered dog biscuits, and exhaust fumes.

'He's taken a great liking to you,' Miss Draisey said. She

seemed momentarily to have forgotten about the newspaper report.

Vereker tickled Henry behind the ear and looked at a photograph of the pupils and staff at Creighton Manor School.

'Do you go back to the school often?' he asked.

'Never! It's a great mistake to think one can ever go back.' Vereker was conscious of a great loneliness which Henry had failed to assuage. Henry, however, had not been made aware of this, for he had an air of enormous self-confidence.

'You can't trust them at all.' Miss Draisey was not, it seemed, speaking of the unreliability of golden retrievers, but of the happenings since the newspaper report was written. 'They've got a bulldozer out in Hammetts Lane. Gwynneth Jarman telephoned, she's going to sit in front of it and wanted me to go with her. But I can't go down to that place. Of course, she wouldn't understand that; she's so insensitive.' She looked at Vereker, protruding eyes inviting him to assuage a grief she could not put into words.

Vereker had been promised tea but so far it was not forthcoming although there was an occasional clatter from somewhere in the rear of the house. He felt acutely uncomfortable, but he was resolved not to leave before tea was served. He sensed that only too often people had backed away from this woman and he told himself that, however inadequately, he would sit this out.

Miss Draisey sighed and patted her cheeks again with the tissue. 'Do you believe in evil?' she asked unexpectedly.

'As an independent force?' Vereker was cautious.

'I don't know about that,' she said crossly. 'You clergymen are no better than lawyers, never give a straight answer to anything.'

Vereker, at a loss to understand the turn which the conversation had taken, chucked Henry under the chin. Miss Draisey said, 'He doesn't behave like that for everyone,' as Henry lifted an ecstatic head.

'You were talking earlier about Hammetts Lane,' Vereker said, glad to have escaped the subject of evil. 'I don't know where that is.'

'It runs past Carrick Farm to the priory grounds. That's where the bulldozer is now.'

All conversational routes seemed to lead to the priory. Vereker asked, 'Who owns the priory site?'

'It *was* owned by the Pendrells who lived at Bookers Farm. When old Mr. Pendrell died it went to a nephew. A terrible man called Wenfield who has "interests in the city". When he inherited, he said, "All I want to do here is to continue what has been done for hundreds of years – to farm the land well." Which was nonsense, anyway, because it isn't good farming land.' Here spoke a crisper, more authoritative Miss Draisey. 'I said at the time, "I give him three months." And I was quite right. In less than three months he had put in an application for planning permission to build a hotel on the priory site. The site is one of the few remaining open spaces on the island; and, of course, the ruins are part of the island's history. The Friends of Helmsley Island, of which I am Vice-President, opposed the application and I'm glad to say we won. But now it looks as if he's trying to take the law into his own hands.'

At this moment, an old woman in carpet slippers backed into the room carrying a tray. 'You want a window open in here,' she shouted as she put the tray down on an occasional table.

'No, I don't,' Miss Draisey snapped.

'Suit yourself. You'll have a bad head again. Do you want me to pour?'

'I am perfectly capable of pouring myself.'

The old woman looked at Henry and said, 'Come on! OUT!'

'He's all right,' Miss Draisey said.

'No, he's not. He's smelly. He hasn't been out since first thing this morning.'

Henry, with great good nature, prevented any further altercation by following the old woman out of the room. Miss Draisey looked at the tray as though not quite sure what to do with it. Confusion made her depressed. 'When I was a child there was nothing beyond this house but green fields. Even as late as the war I could see the priory ruins from this house.' She sighed. 'I fight, of course; we all fight. But it's too late. It was too late after the first bungalow estate went up. I said to them at the time,' she rallied at the memory and lifted the teapot, ' "Once you have paid the Danegeld, you never get

130

rid of the Dane".' The spout of the teapot wavered above the cups, 'And the evidence of Danegeld is not far to see anywhere you look on Helmsley Island.' Powered by the strength of her own rightness, she held the pot steady and poured tea into the cups without spilling any in either of the saucers. Vereker rose in salute of this performance. As she handed him his cup, she said : 'I ought to go down there and join Gwynneth, but the place upsets me. You can't exorcise ghosts.'

He looked at her in surprise, he had not thought her a superstitious person. Her eyes were like dark bruises in the powder-caked face. She bent her head and flicked fastidiously at a tealeaf in her cup. 'It was about the fête that you came, was it?'

'Zoe Lindsay told me you called about it the other day. I should be very interested to know your ideas.' Whatever was at the root of Miss Draisey's trouble, it was plain that she needed compensation : the arrangements for the fête were hers for the asking.

Miss Draisey took a small cream bun, popped it in her mouth and swallowed it as if it was an oyster. She wanted, it seemed, to revive the medieval fair which had at one time been held on the island and which had lasted for a week. While she told Vereker about this she swallowed three more cream buns. Vereker promised to think about the medieval fair.

He was glad to get out of the house. It was very hot in the street, but at least the air was fresh and there was a slight breeze coming up from the sea. The tide must be on the turn; he knew quite a bit about the tides now. He met Donald Jarman outside his office and they talked for a few minutes.

Nancy was in the kitchen when Vereker returned to the vicarage. 'I'm glad you're back,' she said. 'I'm going to make us real, dainty cucumber sandwiches for tea and you can cut the bread.'

'That'll be nice.' She was easily discouraged and he hadn't the heart to tell her he had already had tea.

'Mrs. Anguilo wants to see you.' She passed the breadboard and knife to him. 'But I made it fairly clear you weren't going to be available until we had had tea.'

Nancy was protective. This was becoming a habit with her; if she wasn't careful she was going to get addicted to it. Ever since Tudor had told her his secret, she had felt that he needed her protection. And now, here was her father looking harassed and instead of yelling at him that she had her own troubles, she was being protective and talking cheerfully when she did not feel at all cheerful. Only two months ago, it would never have occurred to her to hide her feelings from him.

'Mrs. Anguilo is worried about Milo.' She picked up a serrated-edged knife and began to slice the cucumber. 'But I told her there's no need for her to worry. He's a reformed character.'

Milo came to church sometimes now and Vereker saw his face, beautifully carved as a Michelangelo sculpture, gazing out from the blur of the congregation, brilliant, sensitive to the point of unbalance, yet with a certain toughness which suggested that the will to survive was strong.

'He may be a reformed character, but I'm not sure that means there is nothing to worry about.' He paused to count the slices of bread and then asked, 'You understand him better than I do; how do you feel about him?'

Nancy thought about Milo as she sprinkled salt on the cucumber. 'Meg Jacobs says Mrs. Anguilo is a stone around his neck. But I don't see Milo drowning. If you ask me, the one bit of scripture Milo has assimilated is the bit about hating your father and mother and being about your own business.'

Vereker looked at her, his head a little to one side as if some unfamiliar note had sounded in his ear. His smile was droll, half-way between gladness and sadness, which was probably the effect she had on him at this time. Nancy began to butter the slices of bread. Panic fluttered in her stomach. She wanted to fling her arms around him and off-load these wretched secrets so that he could take the burden from her; but when she stole another look at him he was concentrating on cutting the bread very fine, his dear face intent, and she knew she could not hurt him by telling him. She had always been able to hurt him before, and now that she could not do it any more they were slipping apart, which was even more hurtful. It didn't make sense. Even so, she changed the subject and asked him if he had had a good day.

He finished the sandwiches and brought the teapot to the table before he answered. 'I went to see Miss Draisey. She has some plans about a fair.'

'Good?'

'I think so. I met Jarman on my way home and had a chat with him about it. He isn't enthusiastic; but he's going to let me play with the idea because he hopes it will keep me quiet and prevent me from doing anything irresponsible.'

Nancy poured tea. 'But why should he think you irresponsible?'

'I don't know.' He thought about it, his eyes narrowed as though he saw something in the grain of the wooden table that did not entirely please him. Nancy looked at him, studying his face as she might have studied the face of a stranger. The features were not arranged in the regular pattern which constituted her idea of masculine good looks; in fact, the nose which fluted out above the wide quirk of the mouth had always seemed to her to be quite disastrous. But she saw now that the features, though regrettably unorthodox, were nevertheless finely, almost fastidiously, wrought; and over the years, while she hadn't been paying attention, they had grown together to form a face that would not easily yield up its deepest truths. But then, what truths could he have stored away out of her, his beloved daughter's, reach?'

'Why?' she persisted, 'Why irresponsible?'

'I get the feeling he thinks I'm a little mad.'

'You were never mad in Coopers Town.'

'No, well, there you are . . . I seem to be mad in Helmsley. Something to do with priorities, perhaps.' Like letting Miss Draisey organize the fair, even if it wasn't a financial success, because Miss Draisey needed resurrection more than All Hallows needed money.

'Perhaps we're both mad,' Nancy said.

He looked at her, waiting for her to go on, while she waited for him to prompt her. The gas whined under the kettle and the cheap little clock on the shelf ticked noisily. Nancy took another cucumber sandwich and said, 'Did you remember to send a postcard to old Annie Schultz?'

'No, I forgot. I'll do it after tea.'

When Vereker went into the library, he did not look for the postcards they had bought to send to people in Coopers Town. He sat at the desk with one hand shielding his eyes from the sunlight, his face tired. Nan was growing further away from him each day and he was frightened for her. It was not the question of the damage to the church that mattered; the police now had doubts as to whether Milo could have done it, and it looked like remaining one of those unsolved crimes. But it was unlike Nan not to off-load her troubles and he realized that for the first time she was trying to pick her own way through a problem. Once she had done this, however badly, she would not retrace her steps. But where would she go from there on? He wished he felt more hopeful for her. What distressed him was that she didn't seem to have the right instincts, let alone common sense; without thought for herself or others, including Milo, she had jumped in the dark and jumped the wrong way. He hoped she wasn't fundamentally incapable of judgement. He prayed that she might not come to any harm; although this was the kind of prayer which he did not advocate when advising others. 'God,' he had been wont to say, 'has hazarded His creation and we are all subject to the chances of life; it is our response to what befalls us that matters.' He still believed this to be true, but it was immeasurably harder to accept when applied to one's own child.

The telephone rang and Nan went to answer it. Soon, the door opened and a glowing face looked at him. 'You're not writing that card even now!' she accused him gaily. 'I'm going for a swim with the youth club folk. We'll probably go on somewhere afterwards, so don't wait up for me.'

She looked so happy that he thought perhaps he had been foolish to be so worried about her. He raked through the drawer, found the postcards, and began to write, 'We are having beautiful summer weather....' He felt better when the cards were written. It was indeed a beautiful evening and he sat in a deck chair on the paved area outside the french windows and watched the sun going down behind the distant trees in a splendour of rose and saffron. Gradually, the shadows lengthened and he was beginning to feel some refreshment of spirit when the nearer shadows wavered and took more definite shape.

'I'm worried about Milo,' Mrs. Anguilo said in the soft, helpless voice with which she was wont to inform him that the kitchen sink was stopped up or the lavatory pan cracked.

Vereker stared at the ground between his knees. Perhaps Mrs. Anguilo thought he was gathering his forces to offer comfort, in which case she was mistaken. He wanted a rest from worry, his own and other people's. 'I'm so worried about him, I don't know what to do, Father.'

As far as Vereker knew, Mrs. Anguilo was not high church, she just called him Father whenever she wanted to remind him of his duty. Vereker said crossly :

'What seems to be the trouble?'

'He's changing, Father. He's so moody and he goes off for long walks on his own.'

'I can't see that that is any reason for you to be troubled about him.'

'He's had a vision.'

Vereker digested this in silence for a moment or two; he did not look as though he found it very palatable. 'Has he come home yet?' he asked eventually.

'No.'

Vereker eased himself wearily out of his chair. 'Don't worry. I think I know where he is. I'll go and find him.'

'And please talk some sense into him, Father, and make him come back here.'

Vereker took the footpath from the churchyard. He guessed that Milo had joined in the battle of the bulldozer and was soon proved right. The battle was over and most of the combatants had departed. The main casualty appeared to be the bulldozer itself; it had come to grief just inside the priory grounds, its nose buried in a fairly considerable cavity. Two cows were examining it curiously, and Milo and Zoe were gazing into the cavity.

'You've missed the excitement,' Milo told Vereker. 'There must be an underground tunnel here.'

'It may just be the cellars.' Zoe had a sketch pad with her and she had drawn some objects which had been laid out on the grass.

'What are these?' Vereker bent down and picked up what looked like a rudimentary knife. 'It's very clumsy, isn't it, even for those days?'

'That wouldn't have been used by the nuns,' Zoe said. 'There were people here before they came.'

'Iron age man,' Milo said.

'Later than that,' she protested.

'There was a settlement here long before the nuns came.'

135

Milo spoke with certainty. They were both, Vereker noted, possessive about their forebears.

'At any rate, this will put a stop to Wenfield's activities,' Zoe said. 'The archaeologists will put up a stronger fight than the Friends of Helmsley Island.'

'How long would they have had a settlement here?' Milo wondered. 'Hundreds of years? Then the English came and drove them out. A new people with a new religion. . . .'

'We don't know any of this,' she protested.

Milo leaned against the bulldozer and wiped his hands on his thighs. He was pale and there were smudges beneath his eyes; either the excitement or the heat had exhausted him. He looked at Vereker and said, 'I had a vision about the nuns.'

Vereker said, 'You have upset your mother with this talk of visions.'

'My mother wants me to be a schoolteacher. She says they have long holidays and good pensions.'

Vereker looked away across the fields; he smelt the freshness of the evening air and the tang of salt on the incoming tide. Milo waited until eventually Vereker said, 'What is all this about a vision?'

'The Word of God came to me in your church.'

'Did it?' Vereker was neither incredulous nor very impressed. Zoe said, 'Tell us about it, Milo.'

Milo, too, looked beyond the priory ruins to where the field dissolved in the evening greyness of the marshes. Perhaps it was just that his timing was very good; or perhaps he was trying to absorb himself in this hour when all colour has been thinned out of the day and the drama of the night has not yet taken its place. He spoke quietly, when eventually he began. 'Do you remember that meeting you had in the church hall? I listened outside one of the windows and I heard you talk about Christ the tiger.'

'I was angry,' Vereker said, 'I wanted. . . .'

'Let him tell it his way.' Zoe sat on the ground looking up at Milo.

The two cows were still observing the bulldozer from a distance of about four feet and a pale honey-coloured cow was leading the rest of the herd towards them. Vereker stared at the cows, biting his lip, finding it difficult to control his irritation.

Milo was saying, 'I thought you were splendid. Most preachers nowadays talk about Jesus apologetically as if he was a little man they had to defend. You made him challenging. It was all a bit loony, too; I liked the looniness. I wanted to do something to celebrate how I felt so I took off my clothes and went into the church. I felt the Church had got it all wrong and I wanted to show how little I cared for it; I danced about and made obscene gestures. Then something went wrong. I felt deflated and a bit sick; I seemed to be standing outside myself, watching, and I thought, "Oh, you silly bugger!" I stood there in front of the altar, thinking I'd have to grow up. It was very quiet. . . .'

Vereker spread out his hand in front of him in the twilight; he ran a finger of the other hand soothingly across the outstretched palm. Zoe plaited stems of grass, head bowed.

'That was when this other person came rushing in.' Milo was silent for a moment, remembering. It had been a shattering experience and he had run out of the church; he had put on his clothes and gone down to the priory grounds almost without knowing what he was doing. 'I sat against that pillar over there, where the valerian is growing.' He pointed and they turned to look. The pillar was tall and hooked at the top.

Although he knew the person who had come into the church, at the time it seemed as though it was a spirit he had conjured up; his first real success in necromancy and he had not liked it. He was the more horrified because for a moment, standing in front of the altar, he had felt something like peace descending upon him – at least, he supposed it was peace, he hadn't much experience of peace and before he could get the feel of it this dreadful thing had happened.

As he sat beneath the pillar, shaken by this first encounter with the forces of darkness, he realized how much more shattering it must have been for the nuns when they came to this place. Hitherto, he had been too uninterested in the nuns to bother about whether their "appearances" were real or not. But now he saw quite clearly this group of women riding into a wild, unfriendly country where a new priory had been built and where they would spend the rest of their lives. It was a dark, alien place and the old gods watched and waited their moment. He saw the nuns over the years making painful inroads into superstition and barbarism, being driven back so often that it seemed that for every step forward they were forced to take two backwards. The nuns died and others took their place. It was never easy; always there was fear, danger and suspicion. Then, when at last they seemed to have established their presence, there arose a new kind of barbarism with the coming of Thomas Cromwell and the sacking of the monasteries. How bitter it must have been for them! No wonder they haunted this place, waiting the time when the long defeat should be turned into victory.

Suddenly, he saw that victory, as though he was there after the event. 'It was so beautiful it stopped my heart,' he said. 'Quite literally, stopped my heart. I don't know for how long; but when I was myself again, I knew that I was the one who would bring about that victory.'

Vereker rubbed at the palm of his hand in silence and Zoe poked at the earth with one of the iron age implements.

'God told me to found my own church,' Milo said.

As simple as that! Vereker said, 'I can't see, from anything you have told us so far, why that should be necessary.'

'Because the established churches have failed.' Milo was surprised at the question. 'They haven't anything to offer because they don't really believe any more. Wasn't that what you were saying the other night?'

Vereker wanted to say, 'And who are *you* that you should be singled out in this way?' But he bit back the words. The prophets had been awkward, unlikely people; he had always been afraid he might have been one of those who stoned them.

Zoe had no such inhibitions. She stood up and shook the grass out of her skirt. 'You had a bad shock in the church,' she said, 'and then you came down here and your imagination did the rest.'

Seldom could Milo's magic so totally have failed to work. He took it well. Perhaps he welcomed his first taste of incredulity. He said, as though acknowledging a reasonable response, 'I know this is going to be hard to accept and it will take time.'

'You're being very self-indulgent, relating everything to yourself.' She was as angry as though the nuns could still be hurt. 'Do you really think that for centuries they have been waiting around for *you*?'

138

'What do *you* think they have been doing?' He looked at her, his head a little on one side; he seemed to enjoy provoking anger.

'The ones that we see are prisoners. They are the ones who never managed to live, so it's hardly surprising they couldn't cope with their dying, either.'

'You think all that time ago they were on to that crap about being unrealized, or unfulfilled or whatever? Now, I think only a very self-indulgent person could see them that way.'

She appeared to think about this, then she said, 'How ruthless you are, Milo. You'll go far.'

Vereker said uneasily, 'It's getting chilly. I think we should go.'

'Yes, I'm late as it is. I promised to call on old Miss Harmer.' She walked away without making her farewells to either of them. Vereker watched her disappearing in the twilight; he wondered whether he should go after her, but had the impression she might not want him cluttering up her exit.

Milo, who had also been watching her, said, 'She's tougher than I thought.'

'You meant to hurt, did you?'

Milo said, 'It's unavoidable sometimes, surely?'

Vereker looked at him thoughtfully. There wasn't much humility in Milo's face; but possibly there hadn't been much of that in the face of Saul of Tarsus. Compassion was a different matter, though, and it was his lack of compassion which made Vereker uneasy about Milo.

It was getting dark now; the hooked pillar was silhouetted against the sky like a letter in an unfamiliar alphabet. Vereker said brusquely to Milo, 'Your mother will be wondering where you are.'

They fell into step together. After a few moments, Milo said, 'I had hoped for more.'

'For more what?' Vereker did not try to keep the asperity out of his voice. 'One vision will probably have to suffice you a lifetime.'

'More from you.'

'You mean you wanted me to authenticate your experience? I can't do that for you.'

'But you don't doubt it?'

He sounded so hushed, as though doubt was the sin against the Holy Ghost, that Vereker laughed and gave his shoulder a shake. 'Milo, the deepest things in our lives are the things we can't be certain about. The things we don't doubt, that the ground we are walking on is composed of certain chemicals, for example, are the things that don't trouble our hearts and minds much anyway.'

'What does all that mean?'

'Sometimes I doubt God.'

They did not say much after that, but when they parted, Milo said, 'I'd like to talk to you about my vocation from time to time.'

'I don't know that I'll be of much help to you.'

'You'll be more help than anyone else around here.'

As soon as he was in the house Vereker went up to the study. He spent the rest of the evening browsing through the books, intending to tone up his intellectual muscle. Roberts' choice of book tended towards the purely devotional, but a certain John Penn, who wrote his name on flyleaves with a bold young flourish, had contributed much of a more controversial nature to the library. It was not one of the names included on the list of vicars of the parish. A curate, perhaps?

Nancy was not in by the time he was ready for bed; no doubt she was enjoying herself with the members of the youth club. He stood at the front door for a few minutes. What a strange evening it had been. Milo's story was, of course, the strangest thing of all; yet it was not of Milo that he was thinking, but of Zoe. He strolled down the garden path. The breeze had whipped away the petrol fumes which so often pervaded the island in the summer and the air smelt of shrubs and cooling earth. Milo had been right about one thing : she was tougher than she had at first seemed.

It was a bright night and he thought how wonderful the stars were, like pure, benign intelligences looking down on the human tangle. He thought of Alma, not as his wife, but as a person loved but imperfectly known as all our knowing is imperfect. When she had died, he had been freed of the responsibility for her; but it was only now that he knew that she was at last released from his demands. He left the front door unbolted and went to bed.

10

B_y mid-July there had been no rain for seven weeks. Water rationing was threatened if householders did not practise voluntary economies. The word "voluntary" aroused the dying embers of past greatness; all over the island bath water was scooped into buckets, or piped onto lawns by means of ingenious devices fixed to waste pipes; washing-up water was carried from kitchens, the contents of tooth mugs emptied over pot plants. The spirit of Dunkirk stirred in their bones.

Alas, in spite of ingenuity and self-denial, the hills on the mainland daily grew browner, while the leaves of the hydrangeas in Virginia Close turned yellow and curled at the edges; roses bloomed prodigiously but did not last long; great cracks appeared in the parched fields, and it was rumoured that the island's fruit crop had failed.

Vereker grieved over the lawn. Nancy said there were more weeds than there was grass anyway, so what did it matter? But apparently watering an English clover lawn was something he had always wanted to do. The other thing he had always wanted to do was to have a real old English fire in a real old English hearth.

'And what about the chimney?' she asked.

'Zoe Lindsay knows of a sweep.'

'She *does*? That's dandy, isn't it? And logs?'

'Zoe knows a place where we can go for logs in the autumn.'

She suspected him of being a bit devious about Zoe; but as she liked Zoe and thought she could be trusted to deal gently with her father, she decided to let him go ahead and make a fool of himself. She had troubles of her own. Tudor was her lover now. Sometimes she wanted to shout it out loud, not so much for joy as to get a reaction which would make it real for her. She had gone swimming with Tudor and the youth club, and when the members of the youth club had gone home, she and Tudor had swum alone. It was all there, the warm June night, the moonlight, the hushed whisper of the waves on the sand, the little caressing breeze; there hadn't seemed any choice but to make love afterwards, there wasn't any other way to conclude the evening. If they had been playing tennis, they would have gone into the pavilion and downed beer; but as it was, they were alone on a moon-lit beach, so they made love.

Afterwards, she didn't feel as though it had happened. Once again she had been through all the necessary motions, and she was still on the outside. She wondered if this happened to other women. One day when they were working on costumes for the fair, she blurted out to Zoe:

'I've been reading John Donne.' John Penn, the curate, had left something behind for her as well as for her father. 'But I don't feel that way about love.' She was on the verge of tears. 'I never get to feeling the things other people feel.'

'What *do* other people feel?' Zoe asked. 'Sexual achieve-ment has become a standard measure of success, and it's all so dishonest, because how many people *are* really success-ful?'

'I don't think I can bear it if it doesn't come good for me.' Nancy was in despair. Life was slipping out of her grasp; she felt it happening now, some process was taking place within her which if it wasn't halted would soon become irrevocable. She would grow up like all those women in Coopers Town; adequate, busy, comfortable, but dulled.

'It doesn't have to be you that's at fault,' Zoe was saying. 'It could be that whoever he is, he doesn't have much to offer any woman. There are men like that.'

But not Tudor! That was too hideous to contemplate because if it was true, it could not be changed; whereas she could and would and must change herself!

Zoe watched her during these days, not knowing what to do for the best. She was sure that Matthew was unaware that Nancy was having an affair with Tudor and equally sure that no good would come of telling him about it. It was not the outcome of the affair that worried her, Tudor's affairs never lasted long; what worried her was the fear that Nancy might drift from one unsatisfactory man to another. She recognized some aspects of herself in Nancy. There is a certain kind of woman who will only dare to love in a situation

142

where, either because the man is married, or flawed, the future is blocked. It came as a surprise to Zoe to realize that up to now she had been afraid of marriage.

About this time, the shadowy figures who had kept Zoe company for so long began to withdraw. Sometimes on her early morning walks in the priory fields she was aware that if she turned her head sharply she would glimpse Dame Alice or Dame Eleanor and she felt pity welling up within her. But she walked briskly through their poor shadows and concerned herself with the world of the living. She worked at the vicarage in the mornings and in the afternoons she supervized the preparation of costumes for the fair.

In previous years the fête had been held in the vicarage garden at the beginning of June. Miss Draisey, however, had long been advocating a fair to be held in August, lasting for a week instead of one day. In medieval times, she insisted, the island had been famous for its August fair and she painted a vivid picture of the roads of southern England thronged with travellers and strolling players on their way to Helmsley Fair. The travellers, as she pointed out, were still coming, the exhaust fumes of their cars were there to prove it; local school children could take the place of the strolling players and perform miracle plays. After some hard bargaining with the teachers, many of whom, according to Miss Draisey, were as heathen as Hottentots, an agreed programme was drawn up. In addition to the performance of the miracle plays, stalls were to be set up in the vicarage garden and members of the congregation had offered to display their talents, which included Morris dancing, acrobatics, juggling and running a Punch and Judy show. Colonel Maitland, whose historical sense was keen, was arranging for some of the men to police the gathering and keep an eye on those thought most likely to practise the less acceptable activities of medieval fairs.

Gwynneth Jarman had her doubts about the enterprize. 'Have you been down to the beach to see the kind of traveller who comes to Helmsley Island during August?' she asked Vereker. 'The only people who will come to the miracle plays will be the kids' parents and the teachers. And *they* won't support the other activities.'

'Perhaps if the youngsters put on something of a more secular nature, as well as the miracle plays. . . .'

143

'If they performed fertility rites in the nude you wouldn't drag people up from the beach in this weather.'

'Yes, I do see that,' Vereker mused. 'Perhaps *we* should go down to the beach to perform?'

'We'd have to get permission to hold a Punch and Judy show, and to put up my fortune teller's booth. But it's worth a try.' She looked at him quizzically. 'Are you going to preside over all this in your dog collar?'

'I think that would spoil the carnival atmosphere, don't you? I thought of myself as something quite humble – the juggler's assistant, perhaps.'

The fair project had attracted those members of the congregation with a taste for pageantry and they supported with enthusiasm Vereker's suggestion that the fair should be taken to the people. Colonel Maitland, schooled in military parades and bush warfare, also lent his support, spurred on by his wife's reproving, 'You're not in Burma now.' Donald Jarman, however, was not happy about it.

'You may be able to picket the vicarage garden,' he said to Colonel Maitland, 'but you can't keep the whole island under surveillance. You haven't got enough troops.'

'We've had hymn singing on the beach before now,' Colonel Maitland pointed out.

'And one of the choir girls got into trouble then!'

Colonel Maitland made a gesture with his hand that indicated that soldiers will be soldiers the world over and for all he knew this applied to choir girls as well. Jarman did not press the point, but he told his wife that he would offer up private prayers for rain.

In fact, it grew hotter and hotter. The heat made Tudor irritable and demanding. He kept talking to Nancy about his attack on the altar and the stained glass window. 'I can't "confess",' he would explain. 'If I were to confess it would mean that I was trying to come to terms with that great confidence trickster who demands that, in the hope of eternal life, we should live this life haunted by fear and guilt. You do see that, don't you?'

Nancy said, 'Yes'; what she did not see was why he had confessed to her. It seemed that she was being burdened by fear and guilt even if he wasn't.

144

'I'm not making excuses,' he assured her. 'I am proud of what I did. I want you to understand that.'

But he could not make her understand because what had happened was so very strange. He had confronted God with his rage and God had been forced to acknowledge him. At least, in the moments of release that followed, that was how it had seemed. But how could he possibly make such a claim when to do so was to admit God? He could only speak about the magnificence of his act, leaving it to Nancy to make the great leap for him.

Nancy failed him miserably, there was a yawning gap between his expectation and her understanding of his need. No fumbling, well-meaning response would do for him, no hint of condonation or justification would be tolerated, and the slightest suggestion of comfort was enough to make him threaten to break off their relationship. 'You are too superficial to waste breath on!' he told her in one agonized moment. She winced and bowed her head. But it was he who was the greatest sufferer. He could not hold on to the validity of that confrontation and gradually his expert mind set to work questioning, analysing, reducing; just as he had tried to diminish Zoe, so now he tried to diminish himself. She had found a way of escape : there was no escape for him.

'You are totally insensitive and quite lacking in subtlety,' he raged at Nancy.

She accepted all this meekly and comforted herself with the knowledge that Tudor was one of those complex, tortured characters to whom only a Dostoevsky could do justice. How could homely Nancy Vereker ever hope to understand the intricate thought processes of the iconoclast, the outsider, the anti-Christ? But, at times, when she was half-awake in the morning and had not yet grappled with consciousness, the thought came to her mind, slovenly with sleep, that he was just a misguided man who had defaced an altar and taken a swipe at a stained-glass window.

Life grew more feverish as the temperature rose daily. In the vicarage garden Morris dancers practised, tumblers tumbled, and Vereker, timing his mischances to a nicety, threatened to steal the act from the juggler. The vicarage was full of long wooden poles, cut-out cardboard monsters, half-painted wooden boxes, strips of material, shawls, old evening dresses, drums, cymbals, fans and cast-off jewellery. Even Nancy, who had started by being sceptical, became interested and agreed to help Zoe in the wardrobe department. Mrs. Anguilo was supposed to be doing the actual needlework, although in fact she delegated the greater part of this to her two daughters. Milo had not committed himself to taking part in any particular event : Vereker had the impression that Milo was waiting the chance (or inspiration as he no doubt would see it) to make a take-over bid for the fair. Miss Draisey unaware that she might be one who prepares the way for a greater yet to come, roamed the vicarage garden booming instructions through a loud-hailer.

After the first week of preparations, they stopped saying they hoped it would not rain and began to take precautions against fire.

Grass and bracken were tinder dry and there had been one or two bad fires in thatched cottages. On the beaches the sand was blistering to the feet and mid-day saw only the hardiest of sun-worshippers exposing their bodies. Dustbins and drains were smelling. Milk had turned sour before it was taken from the doorstep. Cases of sunstroke vied with sufferers from sickness and diarrhoea in doctors' surgeries. In the evenings, the air was choked with exhaust fumes as the cars queued to get off the island.

It was in this temper-testing weather that Mrs. Hooper awoke to the full evils of the fair. She was at a time in life when she was subject to bouts of depression which made her lethargic and deeply pessimistic. In this state, she had welcomed the fair as yet another proof that she lived in an age of wickedness – in fact, in that very age of wickedness which as a child she had been led by a zealous school mistress to believe would herald another divine intervention. During the period of her depression, she was sufficiently unbalanced to look forward each day to the Second Coming. But when one morning she found herself in better health she saw things connected with the fair rather differently. She saw a lot of people working very hard, and, worse still, enjoying themselves, in preparation for what she could only regard as a pagan festival; and she was not comforted by any sign that divine intervention was imminent. God, as He tended more and more to do as Mrs. Hooper grew older, was leaving the matter in the hands of the faithful here on earth. Mrs. Hooper, weary but indomitable, accordingly mustered her forces in the form of her dog, Billy, an assertive Jack Russell, and set out to do battle.

The enemy, she saw clearly, was not Vereker, whom she regarded as morally weak and possibly weak in the head, too : the enemy was Genevieve Draisey. Mrs. Hooper disapproved of Miss Draisey because she was "one of those", and she disliked her because she was vulgar, slovenly, sometimes uncouth in her speech, tactless, irreverent, and self-indulgent to a degree about such things as whisky and cream cakes. All Mrs. Hooper's life people of Miss Draisey's kind, eminently unsuited to have a place in the Kingdom, had nevertheless, by means of their social position in this world, exercised authority over Mrs. Hooper.

The day that she decided to do battle with Miss Draisey was the first day the temperature on the island went up to ninety in the shade. In the basement at the vicarage, Miss Draisey was inspecting costumes with Zoe and Mrs. Anguilo. The Anguilo girls were winding wool. Vereker and Milo were examining cracks which had lately appeared in the wall and around the windows, and as Mrs. Hooper came in Vereker was saying, 'You ought to get some of that stuff down.' He indicated a wall cupboard, the shelves of which were so cluttered with Mrs. Anguilo's bargain buys that she had had to range other items on top of the cupboard.

Barbara and Jeremy Jarman and Nancy were making music with an assortment of instruments, tambourine, flute, pennywhistle and mouth organ, which had been donated by various parishioners. Jeremy said, 'This is a good flute !' and Barbara said sharply, 'Don't put it in your mouth ! You don't know where it's been.'

'There are three of the choir boys out on the lawn jumping about like frogs on sticks and making a noise I could hear half-way down Virginia Close,' Mrs. Hooper said.

'They are riding hobby horses,' Barbara told her, rattling the tambourine.

'Hobby horses !' Mrs. Hooper took a step forward and put her foot through a paper hoop.

'I don't think we can have you jumping through hoops, Maud,' Miss Draisey guffawed as she came to the rescue. She frequently called Mrs. Hooper "Maud", although Mrs. Hooper had never felt free to call her "Genevieve". 'But what about your Billy? Do you think we could train him to do it? He's about the right size, unlike my poor Henry, who is too fat and I'm afraid too lazy as well.'

Henry, who was sitting under the window, thumped his tail at the mention of his name. Mrs. Hooper's Billy, who found the heat irritating, trotted over to Henry and nipped his ear. Miss Draisey said, 'Naughty, naughty, Billy!' and put the broken hoop over Billy's head. 'There you are! Just like a Punch and Judy dog.' She found this vastly amusing and so did Henry.

Jeremy, who had the tambourine, began to sing, ' "I like that old time religion. . . ." '

'Can you tell me what all this has to do with the Church?' Mrs. Hooper shouted at Miss Draisey.

'Oh, my dear! What has a church fête to do with the Church? A genteel affair of scones and tea, guessing games about weights of cakes, and the exchange of all the useless nick-knacks picked up at the previous year's fête. No, no, my dear! We positively can't do *that* again. It's my turn for that awful puce tea-cosy sicked over with sequins.' She laughed uproariously at her own joke, caught her breath and was seized by a racking smoker's cough.

' "It was good for old Jonah. . . ." ' Jeremy sang. The Anguilo girls were clapping their hands and Milo was beating out the rhythm on a drum. ' "It was good for old Jonah. . . ." '

'And you think *this* is going to be better than a church fête, do you?' Mrs. Hooper snatched what looked like a bathing costume made of patchwork from Zoe's hands.

'That's part of Merry Andrew's costume,' Zoe said mildly.

Mrs. Hooper flung the costume across the room and Henry obligingly snapped it up. Billy, maddened by his ruff, pounced upon it and the two proceeded to lurch about, Henry dragging the smaller but no less determined Billy across the room. Miss Draisey, still whooping for breath, signalled frantically to Vereker who made a half-hearted attempt to persuade Henry, whose teeth seemed the less sharp, to loosen his hold.

' "It was good for old Jonah and it's good enough for me!" ' Jeremy sang. Barbara had now joined in on the penny whistle.

'That was a very stupid thing to do,' Miss Draisey whispered hoarsely to Mrs. Hooper.

'Merry Andrew!' Mrs. Hooper picked up a pair of tights one leg of which had been dyed blue and the other pink. She was by now feeling rather flustered and could not think how to get out of this situation. She decided to throw a few more articles about until she could think of something to say which would enable her to retire without ignominy. Miss Draisey, however, grabbed hold of the tights and for a moment it seemed as though the mistresses were about to emulate the performance of their dogs.

It was at this point, while Miss Draisey and Mrs. Hooper measured up to each other, that the rudimentary fixture which held the wall-cupboard to the wall gave way. The cupboard itself did not fall far into the room, but the jars, bottles and plastic containers which Mrs. Anguilo had stacked on top of it tipped forward. The first to fall was an enormous jar which the Reverend Roberts and his wife had bought when they were first married. 'We went into a sweet shop and asked for old jars,' Roberts would say when showing this treasured enormity to friends. Vereker, not realizing its sentimental value, had loaned it to Mrs. Anguilo who had filled it with Swiss breakfast cereal. The jar now disgorged its contents over Miss Draisey and Mrs. Hooper. This would not have mattered much, since the cereal would have brushed off easily, had it not been for the fact that its fall was closely followed by that of a large plastic bottle of cooking oil which glued the cereal down and provided a wet surface for a cascade of castor sugar.

In the ensuing confusion, Billy bit one of the Anguilo girls on the ankle. Henry, no doubt under the impression that the whole building was coming down, rushed up the basement steps followed by Mrs. Anguilo. Henry remained at the top of the stairs, peering down and whining piteously, while Mrs. Anguilo raced towards the vicarage screaming 'Help, police!' Billy remained to defend his mistress and to impede the efforts of Zoe and the Verekers to assist the two victims.

The choir boys joined Henry at the top of the stairs. As the casualties were guided towards them, their excited chatter died away and silence seemed to fall over the land.

'I don't think I'd want to excavate an Egyptian tomb,'

Jeremy said as he watched Miss Draisey and Mrs. Hooper emerge into the daylight.

They began to clean up the room, sometimes stopping to laugh hysterically.

'What did your mother want with all this cereal?' Barbara asked the Anguilo girls.

'It was a bargain buy. So was the oil.'

'A pity the lids weren't screwed down properly.'

'We don't have lids!' Milo exclaimed. 'At least, not ones that fit.'

A few minutes later, Nancy returned. Her face was scarlet, eyes bulging with incredulous horror; her hand went to her mouth and she gave a nervous whimper of laughter. 'Do you know what? It's the water board . . . they've turned off the water!'

When at last they stopped laughing, Milo said, 'Let's have another go at that hymn.'

They were quite uninhibited now and sang so joyfully that the choir boys left their hobby horses and joined in, one of them managing very well on the mouth organ.

' "*It was good for old Jonah,*" the tambourine rattled.

"*It was good for old Jonah,*" piped the penny whistle.

"*It was good for old Jonah,*" the mouth organ proclaimed.

"And it's good enough for me!" ' they yelled.

The Anguilo girls were so happy at being included that they cried as they clapped their hands.

'Again!' Milo said and began to drum out the rhythm. The rhythm held them together and they felt they were one person as they raised their voices. Even Nancy, who had considered she had outgrown this kind of thing, forgot all about her problems as she sent the words throbbing out into the drowsy air. Something was happening she had always wanted to happen and as she looked at the group of youngsters around her she thought that at last she belonged to a big family and she loved, and was loved by, each member of it.

The heat grew more intense and towards the end of July temperatures of a hundred were recorded. There was no water during the afternoons, and there was a talk of stand pipes being brought into use. All too often dark plumes of smoke rose into the cloudless sky. A spark would set a hedge alight in a flash and given the slightest breeze the flames would race away out of control. Fire had a fascination for people; it was the awesome sound of its roaring as much as the sight of it which drew them like a magnet, sometimes making them foolish enough to stop their cars and get out to watch. People who knew the speed of light had little idea of the speed of leaping fire.

There was smoke in the sky when Tudor drove past the house where the old woman lived with her goats. He had always been frightened of fire, so he stopped the car at once. He could hear the flames crackling and popping and he knew the fire must be near; it had not yet, however, gained a hold, that moment of breakthrough when the flames would roar their triumph was still to come. He drove forward slowly. The road bent to the right and he saw the farm cottages. The end one, where the Peters lived, was on fire. There was a little group of people huddled in the field at the side of the cottage. Tudor thought, 'They are such stupid people, none of them will have called a fire engine and that is what I must do.' But something about the way they were gesticulating told him that there were people in there for whom the fire engine would arrive too late. He had got out of his car and was running towards the cottage while his mind was still working this out. As he joined the spectators, a woman said to him, 'He just walked out, the sod!' She pointed to Peters who was leaning against a parked van, blank-faced with shock. 'The children are in there.' A flame licked over the sill of the first floor window, like a tongue running round the palate, savouring the taste of the morsel offered to it. The van driver and a postman had broken down the door, but the stairs were ablaze and they were driven back.

There was a westerly breeze which meant that the other cottages would stand little chance and the woman next door had dashed into the street carrying a budgerigar in a cage and leaving the front door open. Tudor ran through her living-room; the partition walls were only lath and plaster and he could hear the fire crackling. 'I won't go any further than is safe,' he promised himself. The cottage was full of black smoke and the heat was intense. He went to the foot of the stairs which led out of the living-room wondering whether it was feasible to break down the bedroom wall or whether that was the last thing one should do. Above him, some obstruction

151

shifted and slithered and now the fire had made its break-through. For a moment, he remained quite still, listening in fascinated horror as the fire spoke with jubilant tongues. Then he saw the flames, no longer tasting, but consuming. He ran into the scullery and turned on the tap over the sink : there was no water. On the gas stove, however, there was a saucepan filled with water and he doused his handkerchief in it before going into the backyard; he was not quite sure why he did this. An old man was already in the yard, struggling with a ladder. Somewhere above a child was screaming. The fire must have started at the front of the house and although smoke was billowing from the window of the back bedroom no flames were yet visible. 'I told them to jump,' the old man said, 'but they won't.' Tudor helped him to place the ladder against the wall. He could see Tommy crouched at the bedroom window; his mouth was wide open but he seemed to have stopped screaming. Tudor shouted, 'Jump, Tommy!' The boy shook his head in a prim, inappropriate way. Flames licked out between the tiles in the roof. Tommy hung above Tudor, tan-talisingly out of reach, like forbidden fruit. 'You hold the ladder steady while I go up,' Tudor said to the old man. He shouted encouragement to the boy; then he tied the wet hand-kerchief across the lower part of his face because he had once been told at a lecture that this prevents the heat from searing the lungs. He had been to several fire lectures because he was afraid he would panic in a fire, but now everything happened so fast, like a speeded-up film, that terror lagged behind and common sense was out of the running altogether.

When he reached Tommy the flames were eating away the far wall of the little room and the blast of heat almost knocked him back. He grabbed the boy who wriggled about like a frightened animal, making it difficult to carry him. The van driver was coming up the ladder; he shouted, 'Give him to me, you get the other one.' Above the noise of the fire there sounded the wail of a siren. What would the firemen do with-out water? They must have something else, foam wasn't it? He was going up the ladder again instead of following the van driver down. Didn't horses do that, head straight into a fire? He reached the sill and toppled himself hands foremost into the furnace. Fire reached out and singed his hair. Smoke blinded his eyes. He would never have found the child had

152

he not accidentally stumbled over her huddled body. The room was ablaze now. He could no longer see, but he crawled along the skirting board, holding his light burden under one arm, and reaching up with the other to feel for the window sill. Something had been said in a lecture about getting down on the floor where there might still be some air. There didn't seem to be any air but the smoke was not so bad. It was a small room and he came to the window quickly. He managed to get out onto the ladder, but by this time there was no way down : the fire was blazing below. They were trapped at the top of the ladder and the fire raced towards them.

People were shouting. The next door cottage was ablaze, too. He swayed and caught at the window sill; it was red hot. But he had changed his position slightly and was now looking to his left into the field. Blurred figures were gesticulating to him. He was beyond reading signals, but there was only one way to go now, so with his last remaining strength he edged the ladder further and further to the left. When he was a child he had been taken by his parents to a film in which a witch had been burnt, not at a stake, but tied to a ladder which was toppled so that she crashed down face forwards into the bonfire. The old woman's face floated before his eyes, a terrible, terrible face. He could not topple the ladder; however much they shouted to him, he could not topple the ladder. The child was growing heavy; he tried to hold her tighter and in doing so his weight shifted and the ladder keeled over. He dived into his worst nightmare.

11

The municipal graveyard was on a sloping site which over-looked the sea. It had wide green walks cut between the rows of graves and there were pine trees in clusters and smaller, individual trees which provided shade for the old people who came and sat there during the day because it was so peaceful. Most of the old people agreed they would be happy for their bones to rest there.

The bones of Cylla Peters who had died in the fire, before Tudor Lindsay ever got to her, were not allowed to rest. Her grave was disturbed every night by someone who wanted to make a gesture about Mrs. Peters, because she wasn't there when the cottage caught fire, or about Mr. Peters because he abandoned the children, or about Tudor Lindsay because he did something but too late, or about the Housing Manager because he hadn't housed the Peters family, or about Vereker because he had turned the Peters family out of the vicarage : against one, or all of these people, some demented person had a grudge which could only be satisfied by digging up the child's grave night after night.

'Does Mrs. Peters know about this?' Vereker asked Zoe as he stood with her by the grave one evening a week after the burial.

'Those flowers were put there by her. She comes each morning with fresh flowers.'

Vereker looked around him unhappily. He and Zoe were alone. The graveyard had been locked for the night when they walked past it on their way from a meeting at Miss Draisey's house. Vereker had seen the gap where the palings had been broken. 'Anyone could get in here,' he had said and had eased his way through to prove it. There had seemed no harm in strolling down the broad central path. But this had brought them all too soon to Cylla's grave.

It was getting dark. The flowers in the glass jam jar were fading and in this heat the night air would not restore them.

'Where does she get the flowers?' Vereker asked.

'She takes some from the church,' Zoe said. 'I caught her doing it. She said the church owed them to her.'

'Do you think I was to blame?'

'No. But I can see that she has to think so; if she's not to blame herself, she must have others to blame.'

'It was a terrible thing. How has your cousin taken it?'

'For the first few days the doctors said he wasn't to be told. But one of his colleagues went to see him yesterday and told him. He said he had an idea Tudor knew already.'

'He was very brave.'

'Yes, he was.' She did not sound interested.

'How long will he be in hospital?'

'Quite a time, because of his leg being in traction.'

'You must feel. . . .' He lost conviction in what he was about to say and left her to finish the sentence if she wanted to. She did not want to.

The rooks cawed in the trees, a harsh, pitiless sound. Zoe was kneeling down, pulling aside bits of straw, paper bags, bus tickets which had blown over the grave during the day. A breeze parted her hair at the nape of her neck. Vereker wondered how she felt about the dead child, and immediately found himself wondering how she felt about child-bearing. The thoughts went in and out of his mind, elusive, dismaying.

He walked down the path, examining the gravestones. 'I wouldn't want another child,' he thought. 'That wouldn't be fair to Nan. Would it?' The older graves were in the churchyards; this graveyard had only been established at the beginning of the century when the churches ran out of space and people ran out of faith. He stopped by one gravestone and bent down to examine it more carefully. He went back to Zoe who was still tidying Cylla's grave.

'Would that John Penn be the curate at All Hallows?'

'That's right. He was killed in the war. Poor John Penn.' Something in her tone, a suggestion that it was the frailty of man, rather than his inhumanity, which John Penn's death evoked, made Vereker ask:

'How did he die?'

'Some say he was bewitched. Miss Draisey had two girls from her school staying with her; it was the school holidays and the girls couldn't go home because of the blitz on London.

155

John Penn had an affair with one of them. They used to meet in the priory grounds at night.

'Apparently he fancied himself as a rock climber. The girl said afterwards that he climbed the great arch which was still standing then (there is only a part of it standing now, that strange hooked pillar). There had been an air raid over London and a German bomber jettisoned its load on Helmsley on its way back. The bombs came down near the priory and the blast brought down part of the arch, and John Penn with it. He broke his neck.'

'Not much witchcraft in that!'

'My mother said the girl was a scheming baggage. When she was asked why he should have been so foolish as to climb the arch she said he was showing off; but a lot of people thought she dared him to do it. Miss Draisey was very upset. People said Miss Draisey was too fond of her.' Zoe looked between the rows of graves which seemed to be drawing closer together in the gloom; she might have been trying to discern the forms of those people who had disappeared from the island soon after she was born. 'Her name was Delphina. She was pregnant and she was expelled from the school.' She looked up at Vereker. 'No one has seen her since, but her daughter came to the island a few years ago. Mrs. Anguilo.'

'I see.' Vereker nodded his head, remembering remarks and reactions which had puzzled him. 'Why did she come back? Has she relatives here?'

'No, but she may have had a forlorn hope that there might be something to which she could lay claim because she is John Penn's daughter.'

'Is there any proof that John Penn was her father?'

'Milo, perhaps? They say red hair skips a generation. John Penn had a flaming thatch, by all accounts.'

She stood up and looked around for a waste bin. It was almost dark now and they had no right to be here. It had only been dusk when they eased through the palings.

Vereker had not thought of it as trespassing. The heat had broken down barriers on the island and during the day front doors stood open to any wandering cat and the rude inspection of passers-by. At night, the people came out like glow-worms, some stood in front gardens talking to neighbours; while others strolled up and down the streets as though they lived in one of those southern towns which comes alive at night. It had been a mistake, though, to come here, making a way where there should have been no way.

'People thought a lot of John Penn,' Zoe said. 'Old Colonel Maitland was particularly distressed and you'd think he'd seen enough that was good go to waste in his time, wouldn't you?' They began to walk slowly down the broad central walk. 'Do you think anything ever goes to waste?' she asked, thinking of Cylla and the pain that had brought her into the world and taken her out of it with so little time in between for there to seem much purpose in the exercise.

Vereker was looking for the way out. Even in daylight, his sense of direction was not good. He wished he had not intruded here. The past should be left alone, neat, well-ordered, out of the reach of well-intentioned meddlers. Yet every step one took was a step out of the past; if one looked over one's shoulder for so much as a second . . . And here he did look over his shoulder. Something moved between the gravestones, crouching low.

'Whatever it is, let it be.' Zoe grabbed his arm. 'If you drive it out of here it will only do more harm elsewhere.'

She had understood more than he, her intuition outdistanced his slower reason. But he thought there was something crouched by the grave that he must challenge and he ran down the path without any sense that he was tackling a person who, however depraved, still needed understanding. Zoe cried, 'Let it alone!' A brick, hurled with some force but less precision, grazed his temple. He lurched to one side and tripped over the base of one of the more ornamental tombs. He lay full length on the tomb with his face resting on a mossy bed of flowers which had a peppery smell. He was much sobered.

Zoe came running to his rescue. She picked up the brick and hurled it at the same time shouting, 'Get out! Go on, get out! Go back where you belong.' She threw a handful of pebbles which she had scrabbled up from the path. 'Get out! Get out!' The long grass at the back of a tombstone parted as a startled rabbit scurried for shelter. There was no other response to her furious activity.

A wind which sprang out of nowhere caught the tops of the pine trees; it filled the graveyard with a strange, ominous roaring and then whirled away as quickly as it had come. On the ground all was still, not a blade of grass moved.

Zoe knelt beside Vereker, 'Your head is bleeding.'

'It's only a graze. Just give me a moment to get my breath back.'

'We'll go to the farm. It's nearer.'

'I'm all right now.' He stood up to demonstrate the fact. She put a hand on his arm to steady him and he allowed her to lead him down the path.

'Should we go to the police?' he asked.

'We haven't anything to tell the police, have we? Did you see who it was?'

'I didn't see anything except those flowers up against my nose.' In spite of all that had happened he felt surprisingly cheerful and he was talkative on their way to the farm. It was only when they entered the sitting-room and Zoe had made him comfortable on the sofa that a wave of desolation engulfed him; he was wet and shivering as well as infinitely sad and he buried his face in his hands and said, 'Oh dear, oh dear, oh dear' over and over again.

Zoe said, 'It's quite all right.' It might have been his mother speaking; she had sounded just like that when he or one of his brothers had been sick – matter-of-fact, good-humoured, comforting. He did not feel that he deserved to be comforted.

'Drink it while it's hot.' She was pressing a cup into his hands. He took a sip of the tea which was scalding and very sweet. 'Why couldn't I do more? I just walked away and left the Devil in possession.'

'It's shock.' She laid her hand over his and raised the cup to his lips. 'You went down with an awful bang, as well as getting that blow on the head.'

'I can't cast out devils.' He took more sips of the tea to please her. When he had finished the tea and she was bathing his forehead, he said, 'I've always thought that God didn't expect spectacular things of me. But do you know what Milo said? He said, "You should go about among people as though you were branded!" and he struck his forehead when he said it.'

'How very dramatic!'

'But mayn't he be right? Shouldn't something mark a priest out from other people? Tonight, in the graveyard, there was a creature crying out for help and I had nothing to give. I've always tried to accept my limitations, but I would like to feel that just once in a way I could do something extraordinary. Milo thinks he's extraordinary, and if it turns out he's right, I shall find it very painful.'

Zoe put the bowl of water aside and took his hand in both of hers. 'How can *you* tell what you may have done for another person, Matthew? Perhaps you *have* cast out devils and never known it.'

He looked down at his hand in hers. He felt confused and rather ashamed of himself. 'Have I been talking a lot of nonsense?'

She smiled at him. Their relationship had changed recently. Sometimes she would enter into conversations with him gingerly, like a person feeling the temperature of the water with a toe; at other times, she would talk and laugh unguardedly. Yet, whatever her mood, he had the feeling of something tremendous happening just below the surface of her skin. He had the feeling very strongly at this moment.

'And now I am going to get us something to eat,' she said.

When she had gone, he sat and looked at the big brick fireplace. He remembered that when he first came here and gazed through the window into this room he had seen firelight leaping on a wall. He was beginning to feel more comfortable and a little drowsy. When we are young, he thought, we rage because our parents have such simple remedies for our great pains – a hot drink, a good night's rest in a warm bed will put the whole world to rights. How we sneer at such simplicity! But when we are older we learn the value of even the humblest offering of warmth and comfort. In the ordinary, everyday acts of caring, Christ changes our water into wine.

Oh, to be cared for again! When Zoe came in with bread and butter, home-made scones, jam and cake, and other symbols of caring, the longing was almost too much to be borne. She bent forward to place the tray on the table near the sofa. When she was older, she would be one of those gaunt women who, seen in a certain light, will suddenly make a man catch his breath, realizing how she must have looked when her beauty was fleshed; but that man would never be able to imagine quite how lovely she was at this particular time when, so late she had ceased to expect it, she found life pricking at her finger tips. Longing was drowned in a surge of desire such as Vereker had not experienced for a long time.

'This is strawberry jam,' she was saying. 'And that is damson. We have to make the most of our jam today; it won't be so good next year because of the drought.'

He took a slice of bread and helped himself to strawberry jam. His mouth was dry and his mind refused to present him with any small talk. He could not look at her, so he looked around the room. She had propped a few recent sketches on top of the bookcase. They were village scenes : there was the fishmonger hooking a pole to the blind with something of the swagger of one who might if he chose swing himself up onto the blind instead of taking it down; and there was the interior of a draper's shop with two old women sitting behind the counter and, standing in a pool of sunlight in the doorway, a hovering child to whom the shop with its silk threads, its coloured ribbons, its lace and velvet and satin, was as magical as Aladdin's cave. The sketches troubled him. The one which troubled him most was of little stick-like children dancing in the village street; the figures were more like a cascade of quavers and crochets than children and they had a surprising vivacity.

Zoe said, 'They are of the old village. I was surprised how much I remembered.'

But these sketches were more than a recreation of things remembered : the faces of the people, the very smells they evoked must have come to her instantly, as though they had been released from a capsule. The capsule had contained something else too : the joy of being alive on a summer's day.

'What are you thinking?' she asked.

'I was thinking how good they are.' The praise was grudgingly given; in his heart he begrudged her her joy because he feared he might have no part in it.

'I think you are tired,' she said kindly. Then she suggested that he should stay the night at which he protested so vigorously as to make the proposal seem improper. She offered to drive him back to the vicarage, but he said he preferred to walk, that the night air would clear his head. He sounded as if he could not get out of the house fast enough. It was not

160

the way he wanted to sound. Nothing was going the way he
wanted it to go, or the way she wanted it to go, either. They
said goodnight to each other in mutual confusion and
disappointment.

Vereker walked slowly. His head was aching and he felt
sick. When he came to the priory grounds he sat beneath the
pillar where the valerian grew, the same pillar beneath which
Milo had had his vision, perhaps the same from which John
Penn had fallen. He felt oppressed by the sense of the past
and he thought how hard it must have been for the nuns,
living here at a time when the skin of civilization was so thin.
It was very hot even at this late hour and the air was heavy
and had a rank smell; even in the daytime a vapour seemed
to rise from the ground so that one had the impression of a
fine gauze net having been thrown over the area, while at
night the darkness pressed on the eyelids. He could see the
blurred outline of trees which had been hacked down, while
around him the ruins had been worn away into grotesque
shapes; even after the passage of centuries there was no sense
of reconciliation, only of mutilation. The stones cried out for
release from some intolerable strain that had been placed on
them; every blade of grass proclaimed a need for clean, fresh
air and the healing clarity of light. It wasn't a sane place.
He had a very strong feeling of being in a place where
Christianity had failed to shake itself free of the web of superstition. He was glad Zoe seemed to be ridding herself of the
influence the place had had on her.

The idea of Zoe's freedom did not, however, raise his
spirits. What would she do when she could move freely in the
here and now of life? He had seen himself as her rescuer, but
how would she see him? Not every woman who is set free
marries her rescuer : in real life, the right to be ungrateful is
a condition of freedom.

He got up and continued on his way to the vicarage. How
unfair life was! How cruel that he should be awakened to
hope only to face the possibility that nothing might come of it.
But wasn't that always the risk of loving? Not the second
time round, he complained angrily; the second time round we
should be spared all uncertainty, our love affairs should be
comfortable and cosy like a romantic novel, only the young
have the stamina for literature. For the middle-aged all should

slot conveniently into place with as little fuss and bother as possible. Dear God, there must be *some* concessions for the middle-aged, the young have so much going for them as it is!

When he got back to the vicarage Nan was making orange juice. She said the heat had got her down and she was going to bed.

'What have you done to your head?' she asked with half-hearted concern.

'I fell over.'

She looked surprised. For a moment it seemed as though she might demand more details; then, as he looked at her, he saw her eyes reckoning how much this would cost her in terms of energy expended. Her resources were obviously low, she looked tired and miserable.

'Perhaps you'd better go to bed early as well; you look a bit rough,' she said. 'There is enough orange juice for you to have a drink, too.'

12

On the first day of the fair, Barbara said to her mother, 'You can't sit in that tent looking like that, you'll be drummed out of the Brownies.' Barbara had always demanded standards of her parents and recently these demands had become more exacting. 'You can't show your navel at your age.'

'My stomach's as flat as yours.' Gwynneth slapped her stomach appreciatively.

'It isn't a question of having a flat stomach. Your skin is all scratched and flaked like old leather.' Barbara turned away and looked out at the parched brown grass beyond the sitting-room window. Mother and daughter were close at this moment, very near to understanding what the other was doing and why.

Gwynneth gathered up the red silk skirt which hung from her hips and came to stand beside her daughter. 'It's not my fortune teller's outfit that is upsetting you. What is it?'

Barbara turned her head away and answered through clenched teeth. 'It's the heat.'

Gwynneth studied her daughter thoughtfully. 'You should have taken a dose of liver salts this morning.'

'I can't stand you yap, yap, yapping at me!' Barbara kicked the french window further open and went out into the afternoon heat. Gwynneth watched her for a few moments before she turned away to pack her effects into a zip bag. She wondered why, if Barbara felt so strongly about Milo, she didn't have sex with him and put them all out of their suspense. Barbara deflowered would still have been her Barbara and none the less lovable for being vulnerable, whereas this self-controlled, rather calculating little person was someone she neither knew nor liked. It would be sad if Barbara were to grow up into one of those people who are not prepared to run the risk of making a mistake.

Barbara skulked in the garden, waiting for her mother to go down to the beach. It would all be happening on the beach : there would be Miss Draisey, who seemed to have unstoppered

163

something more lethal than a whisky bottle, co-ordinating the saturnalia with about as much restraint as a whirling Dervish; Mrs. Hooper, watching from a distance, knotted up with envy because her principles had such a firm grip on her she could not join in anything although she was a natural joiner (she'd even managed to see the nuns, hadn't she?); and Mother, sitting in her booth, telling fortunes and imagining how it would be if she was a travelling woman with no roots, no ties, and most important, no morals. That was one thing they had in common, Barbara thought; they were all respectable, but deep inside they would like to be wicked. There was something about these women that frightened Barbara. Men displayed their weaknesses and vices as naively as if they carried placards; but women were subterranean creatures in whose depths primeval impulses stirred. What a stupid man Matthew Vereker was, letting these harpies loose!

The fair got off to a good start in spite of the fact that one of the Morris dancers had a stroke on the first night and Gwynneth failed to recognize the chief constable and warned him that the law would catch up with him if he didn't choose his associates more carefully. 'You'll put me out of business,' Donald Jarman told her. He made this an excuse to stay away from the fair, but his real reason was that he sensed there was a mischievous, disruptive element abroad he did not much like.

Barbara followed her father's example for the first two days. But on the third day, at eight o'clock, having failed to settle herself peacefully in the garden, she decided to go for a walk. It was very hot, the temperature seemed hardly to have fallen as evening came. The cars were packed tight on the pebble beach, sizzling like eggs on a grid. A policeman with a loud-hailer was advising motorists not to leave yet as there had been an accident and the causeway was blocked. In the distance ambulance and police sirens wailed in support of his plea. There were long queues for the ice-cream vans; a young man with shoulders burnt a smarting crimson was shouting at a snivelling child, 'If you don't make up your mind you're just going to have a cornet.' Gangs of teenagers loafed around, pummelling each other occasionally, but without much zest; pop music pounded from transistors; a youth sat astride a motor bike absently revving the engine and looking as though he didn't know where to go if he did start it up.

The sea was a long way off, like a wrinkled crêpe border; there weren't many swimmers because at low tide you had to wade so far out before the water was deep enough to swim. People sat in deck chairs too heat-dazed to move. And even if they did move, where were they to go when they had been everywhere and done everything during the day? It was a good time for the fair to begin. In spite of herself, Barbara found that she was walking towards The Strand. The Strand was little different from any other beach on the island, but, as Miss Draisey had pointed out, the hotels were "nicer" and there was the additional advantage that it was some distance from the fairground which presented the only rival attraction.

The Morris dancers were performing in the park adjacent to the putting green; Barbara could see them in the distance, lolloping about in slow motion because they didn't want any more of their number to end up in hospital. Her mother had set up her booth not far from the Morris dancers and two people were waiting outside it. As Barbara walked past the park she could hear intermittent shrieks from the children who were watching the Punch and Judy show. This apart, there wasn't much excitement being generated.

She went on walking. The sand was hot in her sandals and, although there wasn't any wind, sand found its way into her armpits and the hollows at the backs of her legs. It was beginning to get dark. There were a few pale stars and behind her the fairground lights had come on. She could hear music in the distance now, not the jingle of the fairground, and she thought, 'That's Jeremy and his group; they'll be playing choruses or something awful.' As she walked it seemed to her that gradually the zombies came to life, rose from deck chairs, got up from shelters, abandoned the ice-cream van, left their cars, their newspapers, their bickering and their castles in the sand, and moved towards the music. She heard the creak of deck chairs being folded, the clink of bucket on spade, the yelp of dogs, the "hurry, hurry!" of children; and in the distance pebbles were slipping and slithering and nearer there was the stealthy padding of feet on sand. It's all come alive, she thought, feeling light-headed in the hot, taut air; all these squeaks and grunts, this scurrying and jostling, just as though the Pied Piper was calling the tune!

There was a crowd round the group already and at the

back children had been hoisted on their father's shoulders. How extraordinary that people should behave like that, lifting children up to see Jeremy and his grotty friends! Barbara could not swallow properly and there were tears in her eyes. It was not that she cared all that much for Jeremy, it was that she *wanted* to cry, every nerve and muscle in her body had apparently been aching for this release of stupid, meaningless tears. 'I must be in a very run-down state,' she told herself as tears trickled scalding down the side of her nose. Jeremy and his group had been playing one of the Beatles' numbers when she came towards them, but now they started belting out *"The Lord who walked on the water"*; Milo was holding up a big placard with the words on it, but there seemed to be plenty of people who knew the words, anyway. They sang loudly, some of them linked arms and swayed from side to side, little children clapped, watching their parents to make sure they got the rhythm right, strangers smiled at one another as though they weren't strangers at all; they were all one, it was something they had wanted for a long time and the yearning to belong seemed to swell up from the sand beneath their feet.

This is it, Barbara thought, this is where we really take off, go over the top, all the things my generation has never had a chance to do. She felt tremendously excited. But at the same moment she was conscious of something that made her look over her shoulder. Out of the happy, sunburnt blur, a face exploded. As she looked at Mrs. Peters, Barbara's head seemed to vibrate and shock fizzed up her nose. Mrs. Peters was not alone : there was a small, compact group of men with her, men who weren't holiday-makers, or weirdies, or drop-outs, men who had come here with a purpose that had nothing to do with singing *"The Lord who walked on the water"*. They were flashily but shabbily dressed; one or two wore dark suits, several had shirts rolled up to the elbows and forearms tattooed and smeared with grease from machines. 'It's the fairground folk!' Barbara thought in panic. 'They're going to wreck this!' She looked round for somewhere to run, but there wasn't anywhere, she was too far into the crowd.

Mrs. Peters' shrill voice rose above the noise of the singing, 'Where was Jesus when my Cylla was burnt to death, where was he then, tell me that? He didn't walk on no water then, did he?' People edged away; the crowd parted like the Red

Sea for Mrs. Peters and the fairground men went along with her. Jeremy and his group continued to play but the singing had stopped. The fairground men leant on the platform while Mrs. Peters hectored at close quarters. 'Where was Jesus when me and my kids was turned out of the vicarage?' One of Jeremy's group lost his balance and fell off the platform, another lost his head and poked one of the fairground men with a trumpet. 'He didn't want to know, did he? He doesn't give a fig for the likes of us, your fucking Jesus,' Mrs. Peters screamed. The people at the front of the crowd now became anxious to go home quietly while the ones at the back were curious to find out what was happening. Altercations arose.

Milo grabbed the drumsticks from Jeremy's drummer and beat a tremendous roll on the drum. For a moment, it had its effect; people paused, expectant, as over the centuries they have heeded the message of the drum. Into the sudden silence, Milo shouted, 'Mrs. Peters, GOD WANTS YOU ! HE WANTS YOUR SOUL !' He pointed his finger at Mrs. Peters. At this moment, he believed in himself with every particle of his being; energy charged through him to the very tip of that pointing finger and Mrs. Peters, receiving the full shock of it, lost her impetus so that there was the slightest but most impressive of hesitations, before her jeering laughter rang out. 'You hear that?' She looked from side to side, inviting sympathetic laughter. But the holiday-makers had suddenly become very fastidious. The surge of emotion evoked by *"The Lord who walked on the water"* had in no way prepared them for a God who demands a woman's soul – and the soul of a woman none of them would have wanted to associate with at that ! They did their best, in the cramped space afforded to them, to behave as though Mrs. Peters was invisible. 'You won't get what you need from them, Mrs. Peters,' Milo shouted. She began to circle the platform, snarling and spitting at him. He bent down and taunted her, 'Where were *you* when your child was burnt to death, that's the question you are really asking isn't it, Mrs. Peters? Where were *you*, where were *you*? Only God can help you to stop asking yourself that.'

The fairground people had not come to help Mrs. Peters discover God; they had come to make a reasonable protest about the effect the church fair was having on their trade, and they now set about doing this. The flimsy platform was breaking up and the holiday-makers were breaking apart in panic. Barbara saw Milo pulled down. 'Milo!' she screamed. It was as if a cord attaching her to the ground had snapped; she was over the top now, way above this jostling mass, soaring so high she could see exactly what to do and had all the time in the world to do it. She grabbed an abandoned bucket and a folding canvas chair. 'What's the matter with you all?' she shouted to the stampeding holiday-makers. 'You've got weapons, too. Use them!' And she demonstrated on the nearest of the fairground operators, ramming the bucket down over his ears; then she drove the chair between the legs of another man.

The fairground folk, who had their living to think about, had scrupulously avoided bringing any really offensive weapons with them. No bicycle chains, no steeel combs, no broken bottles; it wasn't going to be that kind of a party, they had virtuously agreed. If only the initiative had been left to them, they would have seen to it that the whole affair was conducted as decorously as a children's tea-party. The trouble was, the crowd wouldn't *trust* them. These "innocent holiday-makers", as the local paper subsequently dubbed them, had no idea of the limits within which little local disagreements must be worked out in order to avoid unpleasant complications, such as police intervention. It was beyond belief, the passions that were unleashed just by a bit of shoving and the tossing about of a few beer cans! As for the girl who urged them on, it made a man's blood run cold to see what a she-devil is produced when a female is brought up without benefit of correction and chastisement.

None of this, of course, was acceptable to the police. As far as the police were concerned anyone who owned a bucket and spade was a peaceful, law-abiding member of society who had come down to the beach to dig sand-castles.

The sergeant on duty greeted Vereker cheerfully on his arrival at the police station. 'I don't think we'll be bringing charges against any of your parishioners, sir. It was the fairground gang that started all this.'

'They are my parishioners, too.' The bright scarlet paint on Vereker's cheeks and mouth had smeared; he had forgotten to take off his false nose. 'Times are bad without having the church stealing your trade. I should have thought of that.'

'Well, we can all be wise after the event, can't we, sir? But I'm not sure about your stealing their trade. If you ask me, it was Mrs. Peters stirred things up.'

'You won't be charging her, I hope?'

'Not this time.' The sergeant was as relieved as Vereker about this, they both knew a potential martyr when they saw one. 'It seems she didn't actually assault anyone; so she's got away with it this time. But she'll try again, if I know anything about her. You want to keep an eye on things; particularly on those young people of yours.'

'I'll do my best.' Vereker fingered the elastic at the back of his head and realized he was still wearing the false nose. He took it off. The sergeant thought that his appearance was more grotesque without it; he didn't look like a clown now, just someone who had been involved in a ghastly accident.

'A couple of our chaps have taken Jarman's daughter home,' he told Vereker. 'Between you and me, I think she asked for all she got; she really turned the heat on the fairground mob by all accounts. Young Milo is still here making a statement. You might like to walk back with him; keep the lad out of mischief for one night, at least.'

Milo walked with a limp, but he was not one to be discouraged by a little local violence. 'The fairground people were just concerned about their trade,' he told Vereker as they walked along Marine Parade. 'It would have been all one to them if we'd been the National Front or the Whole Earth. But Mrs. Peters was really out to get *us*. She was great. It seems crazy for all that energy and expertize to go to waste. I mean to work on Mrs. Peters.'

'If I were you, I should leave her alone.'

'How can I leave her alone?' Undoubtedly Milo felt that this was one matter on which he and Vereker could scarcely fail to agree and he was pained by the older man's lack of evangelical fervour. 'How can we ever leave any human being alone? That would be to give up on them.'

'Because *we* have to give up on someone, that doesn't mean they stand condemned,' Vereker retorted. 'God doesn't necessarily fail when we fail.'

This silenced Milo for the time being, but Vereker was under no illusion about his determination to go to work on Mrs. Peters.

'You might have been killed,' Barbara's mother said when the heroine of the battle of The Strand arrived home with a black eye and a badly swollen nose. Barbara succumbed to her parent's ministrations, holding to herself the knowledge that the greatest danger of all had been that *she* might have killed someone and that, just for a few minutes down there on the beach, she would not have cared if she had.

The details of the battle were conveyed to Tudor Lindsay by various visitors. People in hospital gradually sink below the horizon of everyday life and so it was with Tudor who was not interested in the activities of his visitors but was none the less irritated by their barely concealed anxiety to get away as soon as possible. 'I don't want to tire you,' they would keep insisting, 'you must say when you get tired'; and all the time they had one ear strained for the sound of the tea trolley, or the arrival of Sister with a reminder that visiting time was up. The battle of the beach was a godsend to them. 'Although strangely enough,' Tudor said to Zoe, 'the one person who didn't avail himself of it was our Reverend friend. We had an interesting little chat about solar heating. I suppose if you visit hospitals as often as he does you develop a technique for dealing with difficult patients.'

Zoe was standing by the window at the side of his bed, looking at the lime trees which bordered the lawn. Tudor watched her.

'At least you're in the shade here,' she said. 'It was ninety-three yesterday in the garden.'

She moved away to the right where he could not see her and he felt very frightened. He heard her talking to the man in the next bed. In spite of his progressive views, at heart Tudor nursed certain old-fashioned and rather romantic conceptions of human behaviour. He had imagined that the drama of the fire, and the realization that she might have lost him, would be the climactic shock which would bring Zoe back to him; that in future she would be lover, sister, comforter and constant companion, asking nothing better than to devote herself entirely to him. As the days went by, he realized that something quite different was happening. She was concerned about him but she seemed further from him than she had ever been; and gradually, as he made good progress, so even her concern slipped away and she made few enquiries when she visited him, contenting herself with seeing to his laundry, making lists of items he needed, and changing his library books.

Now, she had moved away from the other man's bed and was at the window again, reluctant, it seemed, to turn from her contemplation of the lime trees. Her gaze was intense, as though she was trying to conjure something out of the deep green shade of the trees; only "conjure" was not the right word, it was too persuasive, too patient. She had come to the end of her patience and was about to make demands. He wanted to say to her '*What* are you demanding?' but he was afraid that the answer might present him with a situation with which he could not cope. Always, it came back to himself, all his forays into other people had always led back to himself.

'Do you mind being alone in the house?' The question came into his mind unbidden.

'It seemed strange at first.' She smiled, but not for him. He had known her since childhood so that there seemed never to have been a time when she was not familiar to him; yet today she was a distinct person, in the way that only strangers, like Sister or the trolley lady, were distinct.

'I'll be back soon, I expect,' he said.

She moved from the window and began to sort through the clutter on top of the cabinet at the side of his bed. 'I thought your leg had to stay in traction for at least six weeks.'

'I'm going to ask them to amputate it. Anything is better than being strung up like something in a butcher's shop in this heat. I'm sure I could manage quite effectively with one leg. After all, the Good Book tells us in its practical way that if our hand offends us we are to cut it off, and I daresay the same goes for the leg.'

'Yes.' She screwed up a few unused envelopes and put them in the waste-paper bin. 'It must be miserable for you in this heat.' Her absent-mindedly soothing tone was quite inappropriate.

'You have always been tone deaf to humour,' he told her.

'Have I?'

She had moved away from him again. He twisted his head round, trying to see what she was doing; he could not adjust the position of his body and it maddened him that she should take advantage of this to move out of his limited field of vision.

'Tell me all the interesting things that are happening in your world,' he said. 'Are they still having a carve-up on the beach every night?'

'They are using the priory grounds for the hymn singing now. Wenfield made the offer – some say to improve his image.'

'The priory? So we have the nuns' chorus, do we?'

She did not answer and he waited for her to come into view again, hoping to see that little flush on her neck that indicated that she was agitated. But when she reappeared, holding a pair of scissors, it was difficult to tell whether she had even heard what he had said.

'I've been thinking while I've been lying here,' he told her. 'You really ought to get some professional advice. I blame myself, I should have taken this trouble of yours more seriously.'

'I don't need professional advice, Tudor.' She picked up the local paper. 'Do you want me to cut out the report on the inquest?'

'No. The coroner didn't make any sensible recommendations.'

'He was very nice about you.' She looked at him directly for the first time that afternoon. 'You were very brave.' She sounded surprised, as though it was something that did not entirely please her. She did not want, at this stage, to find new qualities in him. This, more than anything else that had happened, made him realize that she intended to finish with him, perhaps even thought she had already done so.

'What do you mean, you don't want professional advice?' This was the area in which he had always had his successes with her. He was still effective. The cutting edge to his voice made the old man opposite reach for the glass jar in which he kept his teeth; he was, Tudor had noticed, in some confusion as to the respective uses of his teeth and his hearing aid. 'Do you think you have had some kind of miracle cure?' he asked, while the old man was still fumbling for the jar.

'Hush,' she rebuked. 'People will wonder what's wrong.'

'You must count me among them. I wonder very much what is wrong. I have noticed quite a change in you; I didn't

172

want to say anything about it because you always get so upset if we try to talk through your problems.'

'What change have you noticed?' In the past, when he started to attack, she ran away; now she no longer seemed to be afraid. 'Please tell me, I shan't be upset.'

The man in the next bed hunched over on his side the better to hear. Visitors further down the ward glanced in Tudor's direction, grateful for any diversion which took the conversational load off their shoulders.

'I think you have had a little while on your own and found that you managed rather better than you had expected. So now you imagine you are a new person and can go out into life and . . . well, I don't know the particular fantasies you may have indulged in. . . .'

'I do feel that I am, if not a new person, then a person who can "go out into life". Is that so very terrible?'

'It's terrible for you because you can't do it, my dear.' The wireless had been turned down. Tudor felt handicapped by having so large an audience. Zoe was looking at him expectantly and he seemed to have nothing in reserve with which to shock her. 'You looked after your mother because that provided you with a reason for *not* going out into a world in which you couldn't compete; you had a love affair with a married man who was unlikely to leave his wife. . . .' He had told her these things before, there must be something new to say. 'And these were limits which you unconsciously set yourself because you needed to protect yourself. You were being wise in your way. . . .'

'But there was always something I wanted, something I was searching for.'

'You talk absolute rubbish!' In spite of himself he began to shout. 'Stupid, sentimental, rubbish, as though life was some kind of a treasure hunt. . . .'

'Not for you, it wouldn't be a treasure hunt! You'd soon have the treasure under the microscope and discover a flaw in it.'

She spoke with a quiet venom that winded him. For years she had been gentle, unargumentative and ultimately, he had believed, on his side. Now, when he was injured and helpless, she released this little poisoned dart which must always have been hidden, waiting the time to use it. Only a woman could

173

be so cowardly, so lacking in any moral scruple. The old man in the bed opposite had paused with his teeth half-way to his mouth. Tudor felt sick. Sister was walking briskly down the ward. To his dismay, she plucked Zoe away before any more words had passed between them.

'Where is my cousin?' he demanded when Sister reappeared. 'There is something we must settle. . . .'

'What you have to do now is settle down for your rest and let everyone else do the same,' she told him grimly.

When she had finished fussing around he lay back against the pillows, too weak to resist the awfulness of what had happened to him. He had lost Zoe. In their long battle he had driven her back and back and back, but she had never capitulated. Now, the fortunes of war had changed and she was prepared to challenge him; he knew that she would win, she was the stronger and ultimately the more ruthless. He wished he had died in the fire, that would have been the only way to hold on to her.

Zoe, in fact, had moved beyond any thought of conflict with Tudor. Even as she walked down to the car park, she had forgotten what had passed between them although she felt ruffled by Sister's strictures. 'They shouldn't have been listening,' she had answered when Sister said that she had disturbed all the other patients. In spite of her quiet manner, she had never accepted correction willingly. Also, she had never been able to contend with more than one emotion at a time. So now, she soon ceased to think about what had happened at the hospital, and as she drove between the parched fields she was saying 'Matthew, Matthew, oh Matthew!' She knew that he was on the way to loving her, but how to bring him safely to her side? She drummed a fist on the steering wheel, sounding the horn by accident and annoying an elderly cyclist who had been riding well to the side of the road. Some women know intuitively all the short cuts to lovers' meetings, but she did not.

For years, she had waited for someone to unlock the door to her personality; but once the door was unlocked, she had immediately forgotten what all the anxious questioning had been about. Even if the answers to all the questions she had ever asked had now been vouchsafed to her, she would not have been interested. She only knew that her fulfilment de-

pended on one other person; and no striving for self-know-
ledge, no orgy of liberation, would be the slightest help to her
while she waited for him to come to her. So, she thumped on
the horn, and wondered how she could struggle through the
days of helpless, agonized longing that lay ahead.

Nancy came to see Tudor in the evening. She was first through
the door when visitors were admitted. He turned his head and
watched her walking towards him, bouncing up and down as
though to make up for her smallness.

'You're about the most buoyant person I know,' he said.
'You must be made of cork.'

She pushed towards him some useless thing she had bought
in the hope of pleasing him.

'Do I have to guess what it is?' he asked. 'It feels like a
time-bomb.' It turned out to be a pineapple. 'Oh, I shall
enjoy that.' He made a small effort for her benefit and because
he really did like pineapple. He lay for a moment or two,
pressing the pineapple to see how ripe it was and getting a
faint smell of it. As he did this he experienced a gush of
feeling. 'Here put it down somewhere.' He thrust it at her and
turned his head away, trying to gain control of his features.
She let the pineapple roll onto the floor and took his hand in
both of hers.

'Oh, Tudor, it must be wretched for you! I thought of you
this afternoon when it was so unbearably hot.' The occupants
of the other beds looked at them expectantly; she was as unaware of their attention as Zoe had been, but her behaviour
corresponded more to what is acceptable in hospital visitors
and gradually they lost interest and turned to their own rela-
tions and friends.

Tudor, on the contrary, found Nancy more interesting than
before. 'Tell me what you have been doing,' he said huskily,
watching her eager little face as she talked.

She had been to a party. The parents of Mike Hanley, one
of Jeremy's group, had given their house over to the young
for the night. It was a Queen Anne house, and it had a
terrace with steps leading down to the garden. As she talked
he could imagine the hot evening, the youngsters spilling down
the terrace steps like flowers; some of them would have
stayed in the garden all night and emerged the next morning,

blinking stars out of their eyes, making their farewells and saying it had been a nice party.

'How long did you stay?' he asked.

'Until just after midnight. Then I got so desperate for you that I couldn't bear it any longer and I went back to the vicarage.'

'When I'm better,' he said, 'we will hire an entire Queen Anne house so that we can spend one night together in the garden.'

She laughed, but after he had said it he thought that there was some legendary quality that the picture conjured up which had unpleasant associations. *Hassan*, perhaps; hadn't the lovers been offered the choice of parting, or accepting abominable torture and death as the price of one paradisial night together?

'You *will* be out of here soon, Tudor.' She squeezed his hand, mistaking the reason for his despondency. She was like a little cork, he thought, bobbing along on the surface of life; but instead of being angered by her superficiality, he suffered an attack of what, for want of a better word, he could only call conscience.

'Pick up my pineapple,' he commanded. 'Hospitals are the last places where you want to eat food that's come off the floor.'

As soon as Nancy had gone, he experienced again the feeling of terror he had had when Zoe left him in the afternoon. He was very uncomfortable and he could not move about to ease himself; he was convinced that he would be crippled throughout his life. Nancy had changed, he thought; she was still rather silly, but not so childish as she had been when he first met her. It was possible that they might work something out together, but experience made him wary. When he had first become Zoe's lover he had been wildly happy, but he had lost his nerve and drawn back; he had deliberately behaved badly in order to see how much weight their relationship would bear and he had found fault with everything she did until they drifted apart. How was he to be sure that Nancy would be any more reliable than Zoe? It was not just on his own account that he was so cautious; the business of hurting another person is pretty traumatic and not to be undertaken lightly. If there was one thing about Nancy that was not in

176

doubt, it was that she was eminently easy to hurt. There were things she should know about him so that she did not get completely unrealistic ideas as to the kind of relationship which they could sustain.

'Did I tell you I had a West Indian girl on the mainland?' he asked her, after she had kissed him when she arrived the next evening.

'No, but Barbara Jarman told me.'

'And a school teacher in Portsmouth? Very sensible and matter-of-fact – a bit chilling, but thaws out in bed.'

'And no one on the island?' She was obviously determined to be cheerful and resilient and this worried him.

'I am incapable of forming stable relationships.'

'Poor Tudor!'

'And even those relationships which I do form don't last. I soon come to the end of people.'

'Perhaps it's just that you haven't met the right person for you.'

'Oh, my God, I was waiting for something like that! You're not planning to redeem me by your love, are you?'

'I'll have you as you are.' She meant to redeem him, he could tell it by the serenity of her expression.

'Because I'm not the redemptive kind. That is something you will have to accept about me.'

'Oh, I accept, Tudor.'

Their hands touched. It was madness, he could not believe he had allowed himself to get into this position; but now he was clinging to her hand, holding it against his cheek, telling her how much he needed her and begging her not to ask too much of him because he always failed; he was behaving like a terrified child afraid it has been cast out of the world of love permanently. Now she was smoothing the hair back from his brow, teasing away a frown. She was assuring him it was going to be all right, there had been a takeover and from now on she was in charge and there was nothing he would ever go in need of again. The prospect of such abundance of caring was horrifying.

He had a relapse the next day. There was a report in the local paper that a further application had been made for the development of the priory site. This had roused predictable passions : the Wessex Archaeological Trust, which normally slept sounder than King Arthur, had roused itself to announce that it was planning a major dig on the site of what, readers were reminded, was not only a priory but probably an Iron Age settlement as well, and conservationists protested that the last green acres on the island must be preserved at all costs. In the meantime, it seemed there had been a great upsurge of religious feeling and the site was being used for community singing of unusual fervour.

Tudor was in a fervour by the time Nancy arrived. He pointed to the item in the paper.

'Our generation wants to preserve the past because they don't think we have a present, let alone a future. We're so sick we'd like to preserve Auschwitz, complete with a neat little Garden of Remembrance!' He said this loudly, it was something he was quite prepared for the whole ward to hear. 'Do you know about Auschwitz, Nancy? Or wasn't that something they taught you about in your little mission school out West?'

'What has the priory got to do with Auschwitz?' she asked, smoothing his pillow.

'The priory was a concentration camp, too.' He grabbed at her wrist to stop her fussing. 'A concentration of darkness and superstition and unreason. We're not free of it yet.'

'I've felt a sort of darkness, sometimes,' she admitted. 'I thought maybe it was just because I've been a bit lost and. . . .'

He let go of her hand; it was the only gesture of contempt he was able to make in his present immobile state. 'You've no idea what I'm talking about.'

'Well, what are you talking about, Tudor?'

'Do you know how many homeless families there are on this small island? Yet when a property developer proposes to take over the priory site, the only protests which are raised are from people who want to excavate or keep it as green open space! I'll see about this when I get out of hospital.'

'Until then, ease up, Tudor,' she said with a pretty play of authority. 'You'll only hold up your recovery otherwise.'

He flopped back against the pillows, sweating profusely and more disturbed than he would have thought possible by this further instance of society's irresponsibility. Nancy soothed him, her face radiant as the morning dew. He felt one of his bad spells coming on. Life was slowly draining out of the world, the people in the ward were like puppets seen at the wrong end of a telescope, the view beyond the windows was a little green and blue miniature, brilliant but infinitely fragile. It was a long time since he had felt as bad as this, not since that moment in the churchyard. The terror of that moment gripped him now. He had left Zoe behind in the church hall, standing staring at Vereker as though she had come into the land of milk and honey they had sung about in those far-away Sunday school classes. He had known then that he had lost Zoe. Everything was infinitely fragile, the whole of existence might disintegrate into blackness at any moment. He held on to Nancy's hand like a drowning man, but when she bent over him he could not be sure whether she was not holding him down. He tried to call out, but she hushed him and placed her hand on his chest, pressing him down, down, down, into the blackness.

13

Towards the end of August the weather began to change. There were one or two thunder storms which brought little rain and did not at first bring the temperature down; but gradually, so imperceptibly one scarcely realized what was happening, summer waned. Then, one night the temperature dropped over twenty degrees and when Nancy woke in the morning there wasn't a vestige of summer left. Something else had arrived, unpacked its goods and taken possession, something with its own individual colour, taste and smell. Autumn had come. Nancy liked the word autumn and had looked forward to the season. But it would be a short autumn this year, winter was already waiting in the wings.

Zoe telephoned. 'You'll be wanting to light your fire soon, I expect.'

'Will we?' Nancy thought this business of the fire was childish, but she agreed to help her father collect the logs. It was increasingly important to make him happy in small ways since sooner or later she would have to tell him that she would not be coming back to Coopers Town with him.

Zoe arranged for them to collect logs from the woods owned by Mrs. Mace Cholmondley, an elderly recluse, who lived in one of the large country houses which Vereker thought of as being in the deep heart of the island. Mrs. Mace Cholmondley instructed her game-keeper to see about the logs. The game-keeper was an old man of ninety, nearly blind and stone deaf; the most lengthy part of the whole enterprise was explaining to him what was wanted. Nancy felt sorry for her father who had bought an axe and borrowed a Land-Rover only to find that the afternoon's chief exercise was to consist of shouting and miming for the benefit of this gnarled old man who seemed to be gradually turning into a tree.

When eventually they arrived at what had been referred to as a clearing – although there was in fact more clearing than wood – the logs had already been cut and were waiting collection just as they would have been if they had bought them from Thomas Haines and Son in Marine Parade. Nancy made much of helping to hump the logs and shouted things like 'mind away there – Timber!' to give her father some of the atmosphere he was missing. When they had finished, and the loading took them all of fifteen minutes, he dusted his hands and looked out between the sparse trees at the fields and not very distant houses. 'Of course, it's such a little island,' he said. He sounded as if it had shrunk since he came to it.

Zoe had asked them to tea because they would need refreshment after their arduous labours. As they drove up the path to Carrick Farm it was already dusk and the air had winter's breath on it. The sitting-room curtains had not been drawn and as they glanced towards it they could see warm light leaping on the long wall. 'She's lit a fire for us!' Nancy was amused at her father's delight, but when they were hunched comfortably in the sitting-room warming their hands while Zoe prepared tea, she did admit that there was something especially hospitable about lighting a fire for guests as opposed to flipping a switch; and when her father insisted on building an intricate pyramid of coal on top of the blazing logs she was quite concerned lest he should destroy the magic and disgrace them both.

Later, she watched the darkness deepening outside the window and reached for the last piece of toast with a feeling of well-being. The room itself darkened and shadows flickered and hunched on the walls as one or other of them moved. Zoe and her father talked, the firelight warming their faces so that one could almost imagine that they were looking into a splendid future just as she herself was. She felt extraordinarily happy. A fire was indeed a wonderful thing! She remembered the comforts of childhood; coming home on cold afternoons, her father taking off her boots and warming her toes with his fingers, her mother bringing her hot lemon and honey when she had a chill. Perhaps she would soon be performing these little acts of love for a child of her own.

She had not told her father yet that she was going to marry Tudor. There was no need to rush things : she would hug her joy to herself for a little longer. She stretched her legs out in front of her and half-closed her eyes. The flames had eaten into the pieces of coal and strange faces were appearing. She watched, entranced. She would be twenty soon and youth was slipping away. She must make the best of what was left to her. She would join in this game, collect the logs, light the fire, build up a pyramid of coal; she would make tea for people who had been out in the cold and have hot soup ready for her father when he came back tired after an evening meeting. She felt drowsy and eased back against the crumpled cushions. She decided she wasn't going to make a career for herself after she married Tudor, she didn't want to be a thinker, an instructor, an adviser, she was going to be one of the small-time givers of homely warmth and comfort, the toast-makers of the world.

She wondered where she and Tudor would live when they were married. She was happier than she had ever been in her life; so happy in fact, that there was something a little unreal about it and she could not quite envisage their future together, buying houses and planning a family. The coal shifted in the grate and the faces in the fire changed. It was all a matter of time; she and Tudor would grow into loving, a step at a time.

The next day it began to rain. Tudor was fretful when Nancy visited him. He had written a letter about the use of the priory site to the local paper but it seemed to have had little effect. The archaeologists and the conservationists had made the pattern a little tidier by closing their ranks. Wenfield had agreed to the continued use of the site for hymn singing and had himself attended one or two gatherings, looking genial. The property development company had produced a model designed to show that the proposed luxury hotel would not encroach on the ruins; and a considerably less modest scheme showing every square foot of the site taken up by one structure or another had been leaked to the press.

Day after day rain poured from a grey, wrinkled sky and water lay in the furrows of the fields. The local church leaders breathed sighs of relief, thinking that this would see the end of an outdoor activity which was beginning to affect church attendance. Yet still people came once a week to the priory site; they came in raincoats, anoraks, sou'westers and thigh boots, dragging small children and accompanied by older children who did not need to be dragged because they enjoyed the novelty of being out with their parents. Many came from the mainland. People seemed to enjoy the meetings more now that they no longer represented a holiday pastime. Jarman went down to the priory site one evening to see what it was all about. He reported his findings to the parochial church council when it met to consider a call from the rector of St. Luke's for united action to meet what he termed a "growing threat to true religion".

Jarman said, 'There, poised on one of those broken pillars was young Milo, looking uncommonly like a pagan god in modern dress; but the crowd attended to what he had to say as reverently as if he was the prophet Elijah. He said that the Holy Spirit led the nuns to this island to found a priory; the nuns were explorers of the unknown. The Holy Spirit was working in us today, telling us that we, too, must move out into the unknown. Then he raised his arms above his head and shouted, "The time is NOW" and people groaned.'

One or two members of the parochial church council groaned and a leather-faced farmer pronounced, 'It will run amuck if it isn't put a stop to.'

'Like the charismatics.' Mrs. Hooper spoke the word "charismatic" in her most doomful voice.

Reproachful glances were cast at Vereker. He had preached a sermon the previous Sunday in which he had said, 'I can't pretend that I am in sympathy with the charismatics, but neither can I bring myself to dismiss them. We have pared down our faith until there is nothing in it which could be objectionable to anyone or of much interest, either. Can we be surprised that people cry out for something more?'

The members of the parochial church council now looked at Vereker as though by refusing to condemn the charismatics he had landed them in this trouble with the Holy Spirit. Jarman, in particular, was displeased. Jarman liked religion with the dangerous quality taken out of it, a religion which upheld man's law and order as distinct from God's. Vereker said, looking at Jarman, 'Something new may be stirring here, the Church could make a great mistake opposing it.'

Jarman said, 'I have the feeling that something rather old is stirring, that what we are seeing is just another attack on institutionalized religion. Personally, I believe in institution-alized religion.'

Mrs. Hooper said, presumably referring to the charismatic movement, 'It's the work of the Devil!'

Miss Draisey said in the voice of one introducing a little reason into the debate, 'What *is* worrying is that some of the people who are running these prayer meetings and discussion groups are totally unqualified. It could do a lot of harm. Heresy is very difficult to put down.'

'Yet I think the enthusiasm may be the important thing,' Vereker said gently. 'God will take care of the heresies.'

This caused a little buzz of conversation. The farmer did not think much of that kind of enthusiasm; his cows pastured in the priory fields and one had already been injured by a jagged beer tin left lying about after one of the meetings. Miss Draisey explained about heresies and said that she personally was not happy about Teilhard de Chardin. Donald Jarman eased back in his chair and studied the wall, estimating how much money it was going to cost to repair the cracks which were appearing at the sides of the window. Mrs. Hooper was deeply troubled. Life was precariously balanced on the edge of nastiness and the nuns were proof of it. She could not have argued this but she felt it in her stomach and the feeling was more convincing than any argument.

Vereker said quietly, 'I'd like to think that some of the people who attend these meetings will come to All Hallows, and we shall be able to hold out a hand and lead them on to the next stage in their journey. We all need help in passing from the emotional honeymoon period into marriage; into a state where we have to come to grips with the business of living with other people, of putting into practice day by day and minute by minute the command that we should love one another.'

He had overdone it now, he realized unhappily. Mrs. Hooper's eyes had glazed over; he doubted that she had heard anything after the word "marriage". Old Colonel Maitland had his head on one side and was studying Vereker like a bright, intelligent bird. In Jarman's eyes something flickered; although the face was expressionless, Vereker knew that inwardly Jarman was laughing fit to burst. And, indeed, when the meeting was over, Jarman clapped him on the shoulder and said, 'We'll have to make a book of your sayings, Vicar; you're almost as good at the game as that old heathen, Chairman Mao.' Miss Draisey sat with clasped hands, studying her swollen, arthritic knuckles and thinking perhaps of Delphina whom she had failed to love.

'Christian love *is* difficult,' Vereker said. 'We shall help them and in doing so we shall ourselves be helped.'

He could not reach Miss Draisey any more than he could reach Mrs. Hooper. It was too much to ask; a lifetime of trying to love and failing to love and at the end of it all, the unknown, unknowable God. He felt inadequate and defeated.

'Now, what is happening on the priory site? Think we've got to ask ourselves that, haven't we?' Colonel Maitland was talking. 'Lot of people go along there on a Tuesday evening to sing hymns. Soon won't be able to do that when the clocks go back. As well as the hymn singing, one or two people stand up and say a few things which may seem a bit silly to some of us. No harm in that. Politicians do it all the time. What are we objecting to? Got to be clear about this, y'know, otherwise we're going to make fools of ourselves. Things may get out of hand, but there's been nothing amiss so far. Just what do we think we can do about it? Go along and tell 'em all to go home? It won't wash, y'know. Better to hold our fire for the present.'

The meeting ended shortly afterwards. Vereker and Colonel Maitland were the last to leave. As they closed the vestry door behind them, the old man said to Vereker, 'Think you're wrong, y'know; I think there may be trouble.'

'Then why did you come to my rescue when I was making such a mess of things?' Vereker asked him.

'I don't know.' He hesitated, his eyes screwed up as he looked at the street lamp, blurred in the grey evening drizzle. 'You're a good man, best we've had here since young Penn, and that's a long time. A very long time. So I couldn't let you down, could I?'

14

There was a white frost on the roofs of Carrick Farm when Tudor returned. The sky was a brittle egg-shell and smoke rose straight from one of the chimneys. There was not a breath of wind. In the front garden, the leaves on the shrubs were curled up and there was frost on top of the gate posts and along the rim of the stone wall. It was half-past three in the afternoon, so the temperature would probably fall sharply soon and it would be a cold night.

Tudor paid the taxi-man and pushed open the garden gate. The doctor had not wanted to discharge him, but suddenly he could not stand it any longer. So he was home before Zoe had expected him. She would apologize because there were things she had meant to prepare for him which she hadn't got round to doing yet. He looked forward to being unforgiving. Even now, he had not in his heart fully accepted that she was finished with him.

The first thing he saw when he stood at the front door, key in hand, was a note attached to the letter box. It read, "Fred, could you leave the groceries in the garden shed, please. Key under the flat white stone." Tudor wondered what was the point in leaving the key under a stone if she was going to announce its whereabouts in a note attached to the front door. He let himself into the house.

He knew that this was going to be a bad moment for him, so he did not stand about in the hall thinking how silent the house was or anything silly like that. Instead, he put down his zip-bag and went straight into the breakfast-room. It had been the breakfast-room chimney which was smoking. This was a room they seldom used and he thought she had been foolish to light a fire there. To his surprise, however, he found that the fire was drawing well. This was not the only surprise. She had turned articles out of the rooms which had been her retreat, her bedroom, her studio, and scattered them about the corridors and living-rooms. The sewing machine was open in the breakfast-room with a pattern for a kaftan beside it. A length of cotton hung over one of the chairs; the design was a fretwork of amber and olive green. He remembered her buying the material years ago; he had said he did not like it when really what he did not like was the fact that she had an eye for design and he had not. He had nagged about the material week after week until in the end she had put it away unused. Now, seeing it flung across the chair, he told himself that she had turned it out in a flagrant attempt to hurt him.

He went back to the hall. She must have been out sketching more than he had realized during the summer; there was a series of sketches on the staircase wall, pictures of village life which were full of a vitality the village itself now lacked. The door of the sitting-room was ajar and he could see several sketches in there, too; he went into the room and examined them. They were mostly sketches of children and animals which had the same vitality as the village sketches; some of the sketches of the children, had, also, an unmistakable tenderness.

He went back to the hall for his zip-bag. Her Wellington boots were standing in the corner, thickly coated with mud, and there was a basket beside them full of teasels. Honesty and cape gooseberry branches had been propped up in the bucket which served as an umbrella stand. Her gardening gloves and a pair of secateurs were on the window ledge together with a half-finished flower arrangement. He went into the kitchen to make himself tea. The same evidence of activity greeted him there. The ironing board had been set up and a stack of curtains was in the wicker basket ready to be ironed. A cake was standing on a rack on the table and there was a bowl beside it, covered with a cloth; he lifted the cloth and dipped a finger absently into the icing mixture.

He made tea and walked from room to room, cup in hand, looking at the cheerful chaos created by a woman he did not know. The thing which most impressed itself on him was the craze to make things which seemed to have seized her, clothes, flower arrangements, the cake. . . . He went back to the kitchen and looked in the freezer; it was packed with pies, brawn, pâté, pastry, fruit flans. He felt weak and went up to his room, meaning to rest. She had put one of the damned flower arrangements on his bedside table. At the sight of it, he sat on the edge of the bed and began to cry. Soon, hatred

187

replaced the agony of grief. It was cruel to have put this beastly thing in his room, an overflow of her "making" in which he was included incidentally. If she had excluded him that would have shown that she had considered him. He lay on the bed until the tears petered out, leaving him hollow and listless which was worst of all. He could not stay in the house. It was nearly four o'clock. As far as he knew, nothing happened anywhere on the island at four o'clock on a Saturday. Nevertheless, he must get out.

He took the cup down to the kitchen. He could not bear the smell of cold tea or the stain it left on the cup, so he washed the cup and put it on the draining board. While he was doing this, the telephone rang. He was on his way to answer it when it occurred to him that the caller might be Nancy. If she had telephoned the hospital she would know that he had discharged himself. He stood by the telephone, looking at it until it stopped ringing. He did not analyse his reaction; he simply knew that it would be a mistake to lift up the receiver.

As soon as he was outside in the lane he heard the singing. He had not realized that they came to the priory grounds on Saturday afternoons now that it was too dark to meet there in the evenings. He turned towards the singing. His mind began to nag angrily at the people who were there and the nagging brought a respite from the deeper pain of the loss of Zoe. Before he joined the fringes of the crowd, the singing had stopped. Over the heads of the people in front of him he saw Milo standing on one of the broad, broken pillars. He was shouting : 'Once I was on acid,' which Tudor knew was not true, although he had undoubtedly smoked pot like most self-respecting youngsters of his age. 'But now,' Milo went on, 'I have found something that burns deeper than acid, I have found Jesus Christ.'

Tudor said to the man standing next to him, 'Do you think that Jesus Christ knows that this site is needed for homeless families?' The man looked startled and then embarrassed; he said, 'Is it really? I didn't know . . .' and moved a few paces away. Tudor made good the ground between them. 'Do you think Jesus Christ would be interested?'

'Interested in what?'

'In the plight of the homeless.'

188

The man said, 'Yes, yes,' tetchily and craned his neck to see
if he was missing anything out front.

A well-dressed matron was talking about the permissive
society which was undermining the fabric of civilization.
According to her, the nuns had come to warn people to turn
from the excesses of permissiveness before it was too late.
After talk of discipline and re-dedication and a hail of
alleluiahs, there was a song about coming to Jesus breathed
over a microphone by an intense young woman who looked as
if she wanted to eat every member of the audience. Tudor
saw that one or two people were leaving. He stationed himself
by the gate which opened onto the footpath leading to the
seafront. The crowd was singing :

'When I needed a neighbour, were you there, were you there?
When I needed a neighbour, were you there?'

'I wonder if I could interest you in a scheme to provide for
homeless families on this site?' Tudor said to the first group
to arrive at the gate.

'Sorry. We want to get to the car park before this lot turns
out.'

Tudor put his question more directly to the next arrivals, a
woman and three teenagers. 'What are you doing for the
homeless?'

'I haven't got a spare room, if that's what you're after.' She
urged the youngsters towards the gate. 'How many homeless
people have *you* got in *your* house?' she shouted over her
shoulder.

'When I needed a shelter, were you there, were you there?
When I needed a shelter, were you there?'

Tudor said to a middle-aged man and woman who had
come up to the gate looking guilty as though they were creeping out of a cinema before the national anthem was played,
'What do you think Jesus would have done about the plight of
homeless families on this island?'

'He'd have thought it was a bloody disgrace !' the man said
vehemently.

'Thinking wouldn't have cost him anything. What would he
have *done*?'

189

The woman tugged at the man's arm and whispered, 'Come on, Daddy; don't get in an argument now.'

The man looked over his shoulder to see how many people were behind him. 'Sorry,' he said to Tudor. 'We'll never get on the bus once the crowd breaks up. Anyway, it's your councillors you want to get after. *They're* the fellows who ought to be doing something. You give them a good rousting, and the best of luck to you !'

> '*Wherever you travel, I'll be there, I'll be there,*
> *Wherever you travel, I'll be there,*
> *And the creed and the colour and the name won't matter,*
> i'll be there !'

Tudor produced an envelope and a pencil from his pocket. 'I am collecting names for a petition for this site to be used to house homeless families,' he said to the people who were now coming past him in greater numbers.

'Never sign petitions,' one man said brusquely. Two women said that they would sign and did so. He asked them if they would be prepared to collect other signatures for him. They said no, they didn't think they could do that and looked anxiously over their shoulders to see whether the crowd was breaking up yet.

The crowd sang *"At even e'er the sun was set"* before it finally disbanded. By this time, Tudor had ten signatures. The reason that people refused to sign was not simply that they were in a hurry; most of them resented him. He represented the very thing they had come here to escape from, the nasty, grubby human mess. 'Wherever you go,' one woman said bitterly, 'there's always someone standing around trying to make you feel wretched.' Another woman accused him of using the homeless for propaganda.

'What are *you* doing about it?' asked a young man with a voice to match his immaculately tailored suit. 'Writing a few tear-jerking paragraphs for the local rag?'

'I'm a social worker.'

'*Are* you? Then in that case, you're the chap who should be solving the problem, not standing here asking other people what to do about it. Stop wasting public money putting Pakis up in five-star hotels, for a start.'

Tudor was warmed by these rebuffs which he needed as

some people need kindness. They don't want their new-found togetherness splintered, he thought as more and more people went by; they have those bright unhinged expressions on their faces which are worn by people from the Herrenvolk to the Orangemen who think they have a date with destiny. The thought sent the blood surging through his veins.

It took nearly half an hour for the site to clear. Milo had long since come down from his pillar. Tudor decided it was time to have a word with Milo.

Miss Draisey, for different reasons, had also decided it was time she had a word with Milo. Tudor set out before her, so he had his word first.

There was one light in an upstairs room at the vicarage. Perhaps Nancy was reading in between making telephone calls. Tudor walked quietly round to the back of the house and looked down into the basement. Mrs. Anguilo was at the sink and the two girls were sitting on the table, swinging their legs and shoving each other with their shoulders. Tudor went down the basement steps. Mrs. Anguilo must have seen his shadow on the wall because she came running out, her arms soapy up to the elbows.

'Mr. Vereker is in the church,' she said.

'It's Milo I'm looking for.'

'He's doing his homework.' She pointed to a door to the right. 'He's working very hard. He stays up half the night.'

Tudor waited for her to go back to her washing before he opened the door.

The room was small, ventilated by a grid, and Milo was stretched out on a camp bed reading by the light of a naked light bulb. He looked up, startled, as Tudor came into the room. His face was tired and strained; a poor little waif, he seemed, very different from the orator of the priory site.

'Don't get up.' Tudor found a packing case and dragged it to the side of the bed. 'It's time we had a talk.'

Milo flicked his tongue across his lips. He looked uneasy, if not actually frightened.

'I thought you were still in hospital,' he said.

'I came out this afternoon. It's a wonder I didn't have to go straight back. I nearly burst a blood vessel watching your performance on the priory site.'

'You nearly did that once before.'

191

It wasn't the reply Tudor had expected. He had almost forgotten that there had been a witness to the confrontation in the church. But now, in Milo's eyes, he saw his action reduced to an inept, lunatic gesture devoid of significance. 'You know why I did that, don't you?' he shouted. 'To save *you.*'

Milo gave a short laugh and Tudor struck him across the face. 'To *save* you! I *had* to do it to save you. You stupid little fool.'

Milo said, 'All right; so I'm saved.'

Tudor hit him again.

Milo picked up his book. 'I'd like to get on with my homework. Do you mind?'

'It's your extra-curricular activities I mind about. You will have to stop this business, Milo.' Milo raised his eyebrows. Tudor, provoked beyond bearing, caught him by the shirt front and held him against the wall; he hit him three times, hard. 'All right?'

Milo put the book to one side with the air of someone whose ability to suffer the insufferable is being eroded. 'When I stole from the youth club, you didn't beat me up, did you? You lent me money out of your own pocket. When I was on drugs, you found me an accommodating doctor. And when I had Jenny Britten, your advice was to try for someone a bit more mature; so I got myself Ella Packer with your blessing. Something really horrendous has to have happened for *you* to shout "stop!".' He hunched up on the bed with his feet tucked up in front of him, his back against the wall.

Tudor said angrily, 'The sort of things you did before were. . . .'

'A healthy acting-out of my aggressive impulses?'

Tudor dived at him and Milo shot his feet out catching Tudor in the stomach. Tudor reeled across the room just as Mrs. Anguilo held the door open to admit Miss Draisey.

'The health service is a disgrace!' Miss Draisey boomed as Tudor hunched against the wall, too winded to speak. 'You should never have been discharged from hospital in that condition.' She looked at Milo's bruised face. 'Now, you come along with me, young man, and we'll make some nice strong tea.'

'I can do that,' Mrs. Anguilo protested.

'Yes, my dear, I know you can; but I want Milo to do it. You stay here with our poor friend.' She pushed Mrs. Anguilo into the room and jerked her head imperiously at Milo who followed her with alacrity.

'It looked to me as if there was an argument going on,' she said as he handed her the tea carton.

'Not with him.' Milo was despondent. 'With him I can only argue with my feet.'

Miss Draisey said to Milo's sisters, who were standing goggling stupidly, 'Now I think it would be nice if you two gels went and helped your mother to entertain Mr. Lindsay.'

'In that hole!' one of the girls protested.

'If you don't want to do that, then you must go for a nice walk.' She pushed them towards the door .

'It's cold!' the other exclaimed, even more shrill.

'Then you'll have to walk briskly.It'll be very good for you.' She watched them as they slouched out. They were both dark and sallow; no doubt they took after the Anguilo side of the family.

Milo, who was depressed by the speed with which he reverted to his former unregenerate self in Tudor's presence, had seated himself at the table. Miss Draisey studied him while she waited for the kettle to come to the boil. 'I hope you never do that sort of thing with your boots on.'

He said, 'No, ma'am.'

'Even without your boots, it's no way for a preacher to behave. Even a pop preacher.'

He smiled at that; he had that mischievous smile which is very attractive and not a little corrupting. 'Oh, Delphina, Delphina!' Miss Draisey turned her head away and peered unwisely into the spout of the kettle almost blinding herself.

When the tea was made, she said, 'Now, I'll just take this tray into your mother and then we can have tea, too, because I've come to have a chat with you.'

She returned a few moments later. 'Mr. Lindsay has gone. But your mother has your sisters for company and they will all be quite comfortable in there for a little while.' Milo sipped his tea and Miss Draisey, who for so long had not looked at him because she was afraid of what he might do to her, watched him and was still afraid.

'What do you know about yourself?' she asked. 'How much has your mother told you?'

Milo gazed at her over the rim of the cup, thinking that this dotty old thing had come to tell him the facts of life.

'She *must* have told you *something*,' Miss Draisey persisted.

What did she think his mother could have told him? Facts had always eluded his mother; she had never accepted her pregnancies and was still bewildered by her children.

'Did you, for example, know your father?'

Milo said 'No' because it was impossible to separate the intermittently glimpsed man from his mother's fantasies.

'And your grandparents?'

'I didn't have any.'

'We *all* have grandparents.'

Milo shrugged. 'I'm a one-off job.'

'That's silly,' Miss Draisey said severely.

But he did not think it was nearly as silly as having a father and grandparents; the idea of generation was to him as unlikely as immaculate conception.

'You must have known at least one of your grandparents.'

His mother had been brought up by a maiden aunt, only to be remembered as far as Milo was concerned for one overheard conversation.

'My grandmother,' he said, 'died giving birth to my mother in Shepherds Bush market.'

He had always thought this hilarious and was surprised that it should shock Miss Draisey so much.

She said, in a strangled voice, 'Shepherds Bush market!'

'The police caught her trading clothing coupons and it brought the baby on. It was in wartime, you see.'

He thought the story got funnier as it went along, but Miss Draisey just kept repeating, 'Shepherds Bush market!' Milo supposed that to a snob like Miss Draisey it was inconceivable that anyone could be so undiscerning as to give birth, let alone die, in such a squalid place as Shepherds Bush market.

'Had her parents turned her out?' Miss Draisey asked. 'Was she destitute?'

He did not know anything except that she had died giving birth in Shepherds Bush market. That was enough, surely?

Miss Draisey had come with the confused idea of giving Milo his birthright and thereby expiating her own sin. It was an idea gleaned from the romantic fiction which had filled her head as a young girl and which subsequent intellectual infilling had failed to dislodge. Shepherds Bush market had not featured in the story she had planned to tell Milo. 'I have, in a manner of speaking, been holding something in trust for you,' she had meant to say, rather grandly. Now, she thought, looking at him, 'He would think that funny; he can barely keep from laughing at me as it is.' She got to her feet. It was important that she should go away at once and set about the task of building up the great ramparts of busyness which had to some extent protected her since the day when she sent Delphina packing without even bothering to find out how the girl would be received at home.

'I don't think there is anything I can tell you,' she said to Milo.

He was not surprised, being quite sure that he knew more about the facts of life than did Miss Draisey.

By the time Miss Draisey got home she had realized that Shepherds Bush market, while it could not be incorporated in the story she had planned to tell Milo, must now be incorporated in her own life. 'I must change,' she thought and wondered if she should stop colouring her hair. It would look like chewed string and turn her into a superannuated Meg Jacobs; she didn't think she could bear that. She seriously considered doing without whisky; but that was too drastic. Since Meg Jacobs had come into her mind, however, it might be an idea to see what went on in that place for unmarried mothers.

She lit a cigarette and wandered round the room, pausing to look at one or two of the photographs. She saw Delphina in the back row of the school photograph, but the picture which held her attention the longest was of a young girl dressed severely in a high-necked blouse which had been out-dated at the time when the photograph was taken early in the 'twenties. The girl had the unlined face to which nothing has yet happened, but the eager eyes looked as if they wanted to break out of the restricting frame. Miss Draisey knew even less about the young Genevieve than about Delphina and there was nothing she could do for her now.

Henry was whining in the kitchen. She went out and gave him his supper. Then it occurred to her that she ought to find out whether Tudor had got home safely. There was no answer when she telephoned and her stock of caring was exhausted by now, so she told herself that he was probably resting.

Tudor, in fact, was in the kitchen when the telephone rang. He had returned to Carrick Farm over an hour ago only to find that Zoe was still out. He was tired, but too angry to rest. He went to his study, intending to compose an article for the local paper that would be so savage the editor might refuse to print it, in which case, he would get it printed privately as a pamphlet. Probably he would be sued for libel. He saw himself on trial, pilloried by the press, committed to prison. . . . The images came to mind easily, but the words of the savage attack did not. It was a poor, lamed thing now, this anger of his. In the end, he gave up the attempt to write an article and began to jot down a series of questions. He worked at this for an hour, refining and simplifying, and when he was satisfied he typed a number of copies which he would distribute to those of his clients who could be relied on to make good use of them without resorting to violence. He had just finished doing this when the telephone rang.

He nerved himself not to answer. Things had gone much too far between himself and Nancy while he was in hospital, but the hospital had at least afforded him a refuge. It would be dangerous to take up with Nancy again now that they were both free-ranging. He did not reach this decision without a certain regret. There had been one or two occasions while he was in hospital when he had had the sense of being on the edge of happiness.

When the telephone had stopped, he felt very bad and he thought that perhaps he had made a mistake. He went into the hall and picked up the receiver. After a moment during which he stood staring at the teasels in the basket, he dialled a number. The bell rang four times, then the receiver was lifted. 'Audrey?' he said.

'Tudor! I heard you were in hospital, but I couldn't come to see you, it's been such a hectic term.' School was her community, she did not have time for anything serious outside it. He was safe with her.

15

The congregation filed out and Vereker stood in the porch in spite of the icy wind blowing from the darkness. Nancy stood beside him. They shook hands and made enquiries about sick relatives. Several of the women had woolly hats pulled down over their ears and the youngsters were muffled in scarves. Outside, car windows which had unfrozen briefly during the afternoon were glazed over again. 'At this rate we shall have snow at Christmas,' Donald Jarman said.

'Christmas in two weeks!' Vereker said as he and Nancy walked down the path towards the vicarage. 'And after that, we shall be back in Coopers Town in under ten weeks.'

She did not answer and he was too jolted by the thought to take note of her silence. When they came to Helmsley Island, she had seemed to be the thread on which his life hung, but now it was Zoe who occupied his thoughts. He put his hand in his pocket and fumbled with frozen fingers for the front door key. Nancy jigged up and down beside him. When he failed to get the key in the lock at the second attempt, she took it from him. 'Here, let me do it. This wind is going right through me.' She got the door open at once and switched on the hall light.

'It was good of you to come on a night like this,' he said.

'*You* have to go, don't you?' She slipped off her coat and hung it over the banisters. He noticed how thin she had become. 'I'll put the soup on,' she said and went into the kitchen.

During the summer she had stayed away from church to show that she no longer needed the prop of religion. Lately, however, the duty to support her father had seemed more important and she had made a point of attending one of the Sunday services. She lit the gas ring and put the saucepan over the asbestos mat so that the soup would heat through slowly. She did not know what she would have done during the last weeks without her father to look after.

When she first realized that Tudor was avoiding her, she put

197

it down to the fact that he was having difficulty in reorientating himself to the demands of everyday life. After the second week had elapsed, she told herself that he was having quite understandable doubts about their relationship. Everyone has these ups and downs, she said, and this carried her through the next two weeks. Then she forced him to see her.

'I love you,' he told her, 'but I'm not the marrying kind. I did warn you.' He looked regretful, yet, even while she pleaded with him, she saw that thin face as she had once seen it before, sensitive, fine-drawn, yes, but the face of a man who will never give of himself, and ultimately cruel.

'I don't mind about marriage,' she insisted. 'I don't mind if you come and go. . . .'

'But I have someone else who doesn't mind if I come and go and she doesn't make scenes.'

Everyone has to love and lose, she told herself after that; I am travelling in a great company down a well-worn path. But it wasn't true. No one ever suffers as you have suffered or loves as you have loved; and there is only one person who can deal with your experience and that is you. She had gone into the experience as if it was an initiation rite which would make her one of her generation; and then, quite suddenly, she was swept far out of her depth and she was drowning.

Now here was her father come to talk to her while she prepared the supper. 'You've lost weight, haven't you, honey?' he asked, mildly concerned.

'It's the cold,' she said.

He talked. She saw his lips move and his hands making gestures and it had no relation to her; it was all as incomprehensible as the shadow plays he had performed behind a sheet to amuse her when she was a child.

'There's nothing worrying you?' he asked as they sat down at the table.

'What would I worry about?' At first, when it began to be bad, she had thought she would like to die; then, as it became really bad and she was aware that something *was* dying, she was terrified and wanted nothing more than life. She clung to the longing for life like the survivor of a wreck clutching at a raft. She passed bread to her father. He helped himself to cheese and then said :

'I know you want to be independent, Nan, but that doesn't

198

mean you can't ever confide in me again, does it?' He said it quite lightly so that she didn't have to take him up on it there and then. 'Why, I might even want to confide in you one of these days.'

'What would *you* ever have to confide?' she asked inattentively.

'You make it sound as if I'm as old as Methuselah.'

She said, 'Well, aren't you?' reaching across and absently pressing his hand. Her fingers were ice-cold.

'Now, look,' he said, 'I am going to wash the dishes and make us coffee while you sit by the fire in the sitting-room.'

When they finished eating she went away obediently.

Vereker did the washing-up and thought about the three months which were left to him. He thought about Zoe and how much he wanted her, and of all the little signs she had given which must surely mean that she wanted him. He wondered whether she would also want a child, whether he wanted a child, whether he had the right to put his own happiness before Nan's. He wondered how he would break the news to Nan and ended, as he had every time he had thought about it during the past few weeks, by ridiculing himself for even imagining that Zoe would accept either him or Coopers Town.

Undoubtedly, she would find life in Coopers Town dull. Yet, if he was honest, he knew that this was not the reason why he hesitated, nor was he really concerned with Nan's happiness : it was his own reluctance to put his affections once more at risk which held him back.

'Now, look at it from another angle,' he said aloud as he poured coffee into the jug. 'Imagine yourself going back to Coopers Town without Zoe, imagine yourself there now, alone in the kitchen, washing the dishes, going up to that empty bedroom. . . .'

While his mind was occupied with this bleak prospect, the telephone rang. The bell rang once or twice and then Nan picked up the receiver; she was commendably quick to answer telephone calls, he had noticed.

She came in carrying his windcheater and said, 'Mrs. Jarman says old Miss Harmer is going, they don't think she'll last the night.'

He would not let her drive him to the Jarman house where

old Miss Harmer had been taken to do her dying. When he had gone she walked about the house aimlessly, fighting down the temptation to telephone Carrick Farm so that she could hear Tudor's voice again. She had resisted the temptation for several weeks, but tonight it was too strong. She went into the hall. There was a crumpled questionnaire on the telephone table and she picked it up eagerly. Earlier in the week the police had called on her father to warn him that there was likely to be trouble at the priory meetings. They had said that there was evidence that the crowd was being infiltrated by what they described as undesirable elements. It seemed there was a group of people of mixed nationalities whose mission it was to disrupt the life of the country; they toured from one trouble spot to another. Up to now the island had escaped their attentions. 'At the moment,' one of the policemen had said, 'they are just heckling and handing round these questionnaires, but they won't let it rest at that.' He had handed a copy of the questionnaire to her father, saying, 'Drawn up by Mr. Lindsay, who should have known better.'

Surely she should warn Tudor of what the police had said? He would want to know about these undesirable elements. She picked up the receiver and dialled his number. Zoe answered.

'Nancy, how nice to hear you! I was afraid the call might be for Tudor – he's away tonight.'

Zoe knew. Nancy had suspected it for sometime but tonight there was no doubting it. 'I feel so miserable.' Nancy wept and made grotesque contortions of her features which she could see in the hall mirror; it looked as if someone had stepped on the back of her head and squashed her face breadthways.

'I know what it's like, Nancy,' Zoe was saying. 'I know how bad it is, but one does get over it.'

Nancy snatched enough breath to say, 'If you've got over it, you *don't* know.' Words died away in a long whinny of anguish.

Zoe said, 'You cry, Nancy, We all need to cry sometimes. You go on crying.'

After about ten minutes of this Nancy whispered that she felt better now and refused Zoe's offer to come to see her. 'Pa would wonder why.'

'Don't you want him to know, Nancy? Should you shut him out of this?'

Nancy thanked Zoe for being so understanding and put down the receiver. She could not tell her father about it because that would mean going back to the beginning which was something she could not bear to do. She went to have a bath in case he returned sooner than she had expected and saw her face all blubbery; and also because she was afraid that if it got any colder the water in the pipes would freeze so this might be the last bath until the thaw.

Vereker spent the night at Miss Harmer's bedside and various members of the Jarman family took turns in watching with him.

'She did housework for us for years,' Gwynneth said. 'She used to say we were her family and we always promised her she wouldn't die alone with no one to care for her.'

Barbara made tea and brought a cup to Vereker in the early hours of the morning. She looked at the old woman with an expression of horror on her face. Later, when it was all over, Vereker took the opportunity to speak to Barbara when they were left alone in the sitting-room.

'It was wonderfully good of your mother and father to bring her here instead of letting her go to hospital.'

'She always had to rely on other people's goodness. She never had any love she could take for granted.'

'Yet she always seemed happy.'

'Happy!' Barbara's voice spiralled; she was not nearly so composed a young person as he had at first imagined. 'Nothing happened to her. She might as well not have lived for all that happened to her!'

As he looked at her white, strained face, Vereker was aware that her immediate problem was a sexual one; at the same time, to his surprise, he found that she reminded him of Nan. He faltered and lost his grip on the situation. He was glad when Gwynneth returned. She glanced at her daughter and said with the brusque tactlessness which seemed to characterize their relationship, 'I knew this would be too much for you.'

'You know what she said to me yesterday? She said, "I never expected to go like this", as though she was the Queen! She had so damn little, everything exceeded her expectations.'

Gwynneth made a rueful face at Vereker. 'Don't make a

great drama of it, poppety. She *was* eighty-three. Your father is honouring us by making coffee. So perk up.'

Barbara said, 'Perk up!' and went across to the window. The front door slammed as Jeremy went off on his paper round. Donald Jarman came in carrying a tray and Vereker and Gwynneth talked to him while they drank their coffee. Barbara sat by the window. Her mother was talking about Miss Harmer. The body that Miss Harmer had preserved un-tampered with even to the very end was lying up there on the spare room bed, and her mother was saying how good Miss Harmer had been because she had never found the oppor-tunity to be anything else.

This will happen to me, Barbara thought, but I shan't be grateful for small mercies! For a time, Milo had been unable to decide whether refraining from having sex with Barbara would be a puritan denial of God's gifts, or a first lesson in self-mastery. Self-mastery was currently more attractive. This was not how he had put it to Barbara, but it was how she understood it. While he was toughening his spiritual muscle, she must bear the strain for both of them. 'It has to be Milo,' she thought. 'There will never be anyone else for me. If I don't have him, I'll become sour and withered, like a fruit the frost has got at.'

Her mother said, 'Drink your coffee, Ba. I think that was Doctor Clements' car.'

Barbara flung cup and saucer down on the floor and gave way to hysteria. Fortunately, the doctor arrived at this point and dealt with her briskly and efficiently.

'This has nothing to do with Miss Harmer,' Donald Jarman said to Vereker as Barbara was led away by her mother. 'But I suppose you think that God will take of the hysterics as well as the heresies.'

Vereker was more disturbed by Barbara's display than he had been by the warnings of the police. 'I'll have a word with Milo,' he promised Jarman. He knew that he was being panicked because of that moment when Barbara, in her agitation, had reminded him of Nan. Absurd, of course : Nan had never been impressed by Milo. Nevertheless, even though two agitated youngsters did not represent mass hysteria, perhaps it was time to cool things down a bit. He would see Milo as soon as the boy returned from school.

Milo was late. Vereker sat at the desk in the library looking into the garden; it grew dark and he saw no sign of Milo. He was on edge and opened the window to listen for the sound of footsteps. It was still very cold but the wind had changed direction and he thought, 'I can smell rain.' It was quiet. The island *was* quiet in winter. The feeling of being in alien country came to him again as he stood by the window; it was not so much a sense of something hostile as of smells and sounds that were foreign to him. He had settled into the life of the island easily enough in the summer but now in winter he was more conscious of elements with which he was un-familiar. In particular, he was aware that on this narrow island one was never more than five miles from the sea. Was it his imagination that he could hear the sea whispering up the pebble beach? This was the sound he had heard as a child when he held a shell to his ear, the sound that evoked images not part of a landlocked childhood; shipwrecks on the reef of Norman's Woe and the Kentish Knock, and the more mysterious calm of Homer's wine-dark sea. Tonight, the sea whispered, 'your life will never be the same again, never the same, never again.' He shivered and rubbed the back of his hand, it felt soft and smooth; he licked it and tasted salt.

Another sound jerked him out of this preoccupation with the sea. Something stirred in the bushes. The hair on the back of his neck tingled. It would not be Nan, she was helping Meg Jacobs with whom she spent a lot of time. Milo? One of the sisters? There seemed no reason why they should be in the bushes. He switched off the light and peered into the garden. It was too dark to see anything. He decided to investigate. He went down to the kitchen and out of the back door.

There was a light on in the basement and someone was standing looking down into the lighted room. The picture that was presented of the person always on the outside of life struck at his heart. Then he realised in dismay that it was Mrs. Peters. The particular was at once less heart-rending and more demanding. He was mortified by his failure with Mrs. Peters. She was one of the few people he had met with whom he could establish no contact whatsoever and the awareness of this failure inhibited him so much that each encounter was worse than the last. He said. 'Mrs. Peters? Won't you come into the house?'

Mrs. Peters said, 'Do you hear that, God? Are you listening?'

'I've been wanting to talk to you.' This was near enough to the truth. Tommy had been taken into care and she had sent her husband packing, and Vereker had felt that he should try to do something for her. 'Please come in.'

She came close and thrust her thin face up at him; if there were witches still in England, surely this was one of them! She hissed, 'If you say one word more, God will strike you where you stand because you are a liar and a hypocrite!' She spoke with awesome certainty, and this, added to Vereker's own sense of guilt, made him step back a pace so that he stumbled onto the flower bed. The scene was precariously balanced between the comic and the sinister. He had the feeling, as he pushed a branch of lilac away from his face, that this woman was in a highly volatile state and the slightest miscalculation on his part might precipitate an explosion.

'I'm sorry you feel like this.' He bent down and made a performance of kicking mud off his shoes on the gravel path. When he looked up she had gone, vanished as cleanly as the Cheshire Cat leaving behind a sense of unease if not an actual grin.

He went down to the basement and asked Mrs. Anguilo if she would ask Milo to see him on his return. It sounded like a summons, but a summons might do no harm.

Milo answered the summons readily enough. They talked of this and that for a few minutes and then Vereker said, 'Mrs. Peters was standing outside the basement tonight. She strikes me as being in a rather unstable state.'

'Oh, she is. She comes almost every night.'

'Every night! Are you aware of what you may be doing to this unbalanced woman?'

'I hope I'm doing something *for* her. She comes to me to confess.'

'To confess?'

'She shouts outside the window, repeating all the things people say about her; then she tells me how much it shocks me and what a wicked woman I must think her. Then she goes into details of her wickedness.'

'What do you do?'

'When she begins to repeat herself, I go out and tell her that God loves her.'

'And what does she say to that?'

'Well, at present, it's usually "piss off",' Milo admitted. 'But that's because she finds it so hard to accept the idea of forgiveness, let alone love. I can understand that, can't you? There isn't a lot of forgiveness around. One thing did startle me. She told me, in a roundabout way, that she is the person who digs up her daughter's grave. I couldn't understand that, but I knew I had to do something because it was obviously so important, so I told her she didn't need to do it any more because her sins had been forgiven. The grave hasn't been disturbed again.'

Vereker thought that the grave had not been touched again because, for better or for worse, he had driven Mrs. Peters out of the graveyard. Perhaps it would have been better if he had told her her sins were forgiven. Milo, who had been watching his face, said, 'You're not surprised. Did you know?'

'I guessed.'

'*You* guessed.' Milo was taken aback. 'I would *never* have guessed.'

'You must allow me a little more experience, in some matters, at least,' Vereker said huffily. 'And that,' he went on before Milo could interrupt, 'leads me to another matter.' He told Milo about the visit of the police and his own misgivings about the meetings on the priory site.

'What good reason is there for stopping?' Milo demanded. 'All right, so the site could be used for the homeless. When they are ready to build, *that's* the time to stop; not now, just because people come and chant, "What about the homeless?" There are people who spend their time chanting, "What about South Africa, what about Chile, what about discharged prisoners, old-age pensioners, Rudolf Hess, Northern Ireland. . . ." It's a way of *stopping* people caring.'

'Are *you* making them care?' Vereker asked.

'It's not me, it's God.'

Vereker decided he must form his own opinion on this. Accordingly, on the next Saturday he took the short cut across the field at the back of the church. He had been right about the change in the weather. There had been rain during the week but today it was bright and mild. Ahead of him in the next field he could see one or two people and by the time he reached the priory ruins there was quite a sizeable crowd. He had gone out day after day, making an effort to understand the problems of present-day life on the island, and trying to make some contribution, however small, to the betterment of conditions; as a result he had drawn a handfull of people into All Hallows. All that Milo and his companions had done was to address public meetings on Saturday afternoons and get people to sing a few hymns. Uncharitable though it might be, Vereker could not help but feel that their reward had been out of all proportion to their effort.

Mrs. Peters was standing on a pair of steps near the public footpath to the seafront. She was shouting and waving pieces of paper. From the tone of her voice, it did not sound as though Milo could count her among his converts as yet.

Vereker saw that he was not the only one who had come to hold a watching brief on behalf of his church; at the back of the crowd the Roman Catholic priest was standing shoulder to shoulder with the rural dean. As Vereker joined them, the crowd was singing *Onward Christian Soldiers*.

'My intellectual, liberal-minded parishioners would think I was living back in the bad old days of muscular Christianity if I tried to get them to sing this one,' the rural dean greeted Vereker gloomily.

'Ah, but it has a lovely rhythm,' the Roman Catholic priest said. 'It's the rhythm they're liking, and why not?' He looked around him and waved encouragingly at a woman with three small children. 'Mustn't let them think this worries you, that would never do,' he said to the rural dean whose face fell into lines of worry as naturally as a bloodhound's.

A girl with a fur coat trailing to her ankles was walking towards them. Her hair was long, too, and it was difficult to tell where the hair ended and the mangy fur began. She wove in and out of the crowd as if in a dream and floated down beside Vereker and his companions.

'Say, can you explain this to me?' She had a Southern drawl and Vereker hazarded a guess that she had originally hailed from Alabama but had travelled some way since. She gave them a bright, unfriendly smile and twisted a strand of hair between her fingers. She was not interested in answers; if by any mischance she found herself presented with a satisfactory answer she would shift the ground of her questioning. Disruption was her business and she had been at it so long she smelt of it. 'About God,' she said, pushing hair out of her eyes in a caressing movement as though the greasy strands were spun gold, 'Can you tell me about God? Because I'd like to know just what this is all about.' She let the sentences drop carelessly, she had no wish that anyone should think she was a serious seeker after knowledge; not being serious was much more provoking.

The three men looked at her warily. The Roman Catholic priest said, 'And what sort of idea do you have of Him?'

'Me?' She gave a high, gurgling laugh. '*I* don't have any idea at all."

'But you must have thought about it. Do you think of Him as a person, an old man with a long white beard up there in the sky? Or as a spirit. . . . ?'

She muttered, 'This is bloody silly!' She looked around to see if she was attracting attention and noticed a man staring at her. She called out to him, 'Do *you* know about God? Well, come *on*, join in. That's what the gospels are all about, aren't they? Joining, people getting together, two, or three, or four or more.' There was an edge to her laughter now, the man had turned away and other people were ignoring her; the Roman Catholic priest had given her back question for question. She said to the priest, 'Never talk to a pro.' She turned away, repeating, 'Never talk to a pro. I should have known better than talk to a pro about God.' She began to make her way through the crowd, not weaving in and out now, but pushing and elbowing, laughing when people turned to protest.

Mrs. Peters, leaning from her perch on the steps, watched the girl's progress with as much pleasure as if a troll had suddenly emerged from the marshes and snatched her trade from her.

'What's this got to do with love?' the girl was saying. 'Doesn't anyone here want to tell me? I'm just asking, that's all. . . . I want to know what God's doing about all the people that's sleeping on the beaches, and under the arches. . . .' Her voice was flat and monotonous, her statements calculated to provoke. By now she had clawed her way to the foot of the

207

broad, broken pillar that was used as a platform. A man (identified by the rural dean as a lapsed Plymouth Brother now a member of the National Front) was standing there at the moment. She shouted at him, 'Why don't they listen to me? They listen to other people here, why don't they listen to me? I want to tell them about the people who sleep on the beaches and under the arches. Why can't I come up there beside you and tell them. . . .'

The speaker took no notice of her. It was obvious from his reaction, and from the way the crowd behaved as though she was invisible, that this was not her first appearance. Vereker, looking around, saw that there were several other of her kind moving about in the crowd.

'Anarchists,' the rural dean said. 'Probably from Brighton.'

'Wouldn't it be an idea to give her the platform?' Vereker asked.

'They tried that.' The rural dean winced at the memory. 'She just went on about the people who sleep on the beaches, the people who take the hippie trail across Europe to the East; about people like us who think the hippies are degenerate when really it is we who are finished, but we don't know it. She put it differently, of course.'

The speaker who was a member of the National Front was saying, 'People have come among us whom we find frightening. We ask "Where have they come from? What have we done to deserve this?" I will tell you. They were here a long time ago before the priory was built, in the dark days of barbarism, and we find their relics beneath the earth; but now they are above the earth moving among us. And why? Because for the first time in centuries it is SAFE for them to be out in the open. Yes, I'm talking about you!' He pointed a drama-tic finger at one of the trolls who had been shouting at him. 'The nuns came and drove out the dark spirits, but a new barbarism destroyed the priory. Now, today, when barbarism threatens us again, the nuns have come back to warn us; to ask us to carry on the fight against the dark spirits. My friends, we cannot afford to ignore that call!'

His words were greeted with loud cries of 'Praise be to God' and 'Allelujah!' The crowd then sang "Oh Happy Day" and, perhaps in the face of all this talk of barbarism, the three priests joined in with vigour.

When the singing was finished, the member of the National Front said a short prayer, after which Milo took his place on the pillar. Milo spoke very quietly so that no one could hear what he was saying. Then, at the moment when Vereker thought the crowd would tire of this after the rousing stuff the member of the National Front had given them, Milo put his head back and the most inhuman but beautiful sounds came bubbling from his throat. He raised his arms and spread them wide in a gesture which combined abandon with the most delicate of control, every finger seeming to express a particular joy. The arms curved towards the crowd, holding and embracing them; then, the arms were raised as though making an offering of each and every one of the people gathered here. For a moment, the crowd seemed to hold its breath. Then the woman in front of Vereker flopped down on her knees; the man beside her began to sway from side to side; gradually, sounds rippled through the crowd until the air was filled with a wild, inarticulate babble of rapture and release. Milo turned from side to side, a slim, seemingly frail figure orchestrating this extraordinary doxology. There was nothing coarse, or even distasteful, in Milo's performance; it was sensitive and delicate to the point of the exquisite. This was the quality for which Vereker could not account and which troubled him. Milo's was not a "performance" which would normally appeal to a heterogeneous crowd such as this. So what was it that held them? He looked at the boy. The red hair flamed in the winter sun and it was possible to believe him to be one on whom the fire of the Spirit has descended. Yet Vereker himself felt absolutely nothing, he was stonily rooted to the ground while all around people flopped on their knees or held ecstatic arms to the skies.

'It's sweeping the north, you know,' the rural dean said gloomily, hunching into his raincoat. He might have been speaking of the plague.

'And can you wonder?' the Roman Catholic priest asked. 'Latin and Greek are banished from our services and in our daily speech we have dispensed with Thee and Thou. It's a terrible mistake, so it is. I've told my bishop so many a time. If the people no longer have a special language for God, then they'll invent one, and this is just what these people are doing.'

The rural dean bit his knuckles, unimpressed.

'A movement of the laity, that's what it is. Next thing, they'll be getting rid of the likes of you and me.' The Roman Catholic priest dug his elbow in the rural dean's ribs. He seemed much less concerned than the rural dean. Vereker supposed that the Roman Catholics had been having such a turbulent time lately that gatherings such as this were but a drop in the ocean of their grief.

A discordant noise ripped through the air, parting the ecstatic exaltations. Someone was screaming in terror. Vereker, looking up, saw Milo standing on the pillar, his face a dripping mess of scarlet. People at the front were probably aware of what had happened, but to those further back it seemed that Milo's face had been ripped open. Then another tomato was thrown and the spell was broken. The emotional pitch was high, however, and exaltation changed abruptly to a deep rumble of anger. The woman who had screamed was hysterical. Children were crying. A trumpet sounded the first notes of *"Amazing Grace"* and gradually people began to sing. It had looked nasty for a moment, but now the danger was past.

The Roman Catholic priest strolled over to one of his parishioners. Vereker, not wanting to keep the rural dean company, made a pretence of doing the same thing. In fact, the only person he could see whom he knew was Zoe and she was some distance away. He decided to wait for her near the path to Carrick Farm. But it was Tudor and not Zoe whom he encountered.

'The stage has lost a great actor,' Tudor said.

The light was fading now and street lights were coming on in the distance. Vereker and Tudor stood together, looking back at the crowd. 'That was an ugly little scene,' Vereker said.

'It's an ugly little world.'

'But something dreadful may happen.'

'Something dreadful *has* to happen. How little you understand.' People were peeling away now, but the tight knot at the centre held. Tudor took out a packet of cigarettes and made a gesture of offering one to Vereker. He was thinner than ever. 'It doesn't matter what happens on the priory site, or anywhere here on this island. We can't go on. Our time has run out. Your God's time has run out. Everything has to be scraped clean to the bone. Then there can be a fresh start. Not for us, of course. We're finished here in the Western world. *That's* the message those hippies on the Eastern trail are carrying.'

The crowd was falling apart now. 'Like a lot of maggots,' Tudor said. A few villagers walked past them, but most of the people were heading in the other direction. Now that the centre of the site was deserted they could see the jagged walls of the cloisters. Vereker thought he could see Zoe walking between the walls. Tudor said 'I wonder how she feels now that her nuns have been taken over.'

Two boys went by, one carrying a guitar. The one with the guitar called out to Tudor, 'Are you better?' Tudor joined the boys and they walked together down the lane. Vereker waited until their voices had died away and then he walked towards the solitary figure in the cloisters. The crowd had dissolved and the priory grounds were as he had first seen them, a pastoral scene cluttered with the leavings of the past; and because the past here had been broken into unrelated pieces there was the sense of something more than ancient, of archaic structures to whose identity modern man did not have the key. Vereker walked cautiously between the broken stones, while Zoe waited for him looking composed as though for her past, present and future were held in this moment. When he came to her, she said, 'I saw you,' explaining her presence here.

Vereker looked around him, seeming unprepared for being alone with her in spite of having sought it.

'I've been talking to Tudor,' he said.

'Oh, Tudor. . . .' She turned her head away indifferently.

'He has stirred up a lot of trouble with all his inflammatory propaganda; but while I was talking to him just now I got to wondering whether something else isn't at the bottom of it all.'

She put her head down on the stone and watched an insect crawl between her fingers.

'There is something here,' Vereker dug his heel in the ground 'that is destroying him, although he thinks that he is the destroyer.'

She said, 'Possibily,' still watching the insect. Then, without looking up, 'Did you realize that it was he who damaged the altar and the church window?'

They were silent. Vereker looked at her face, familiar and yet mysterious. The questions posed by Tudor seemed no longer important and he did not pursue her statement. At last he asked, 'Do you still see the nuns?'

She shook her head. 'I don't look for them any more.'

He took her hand and said, 'Well, now, let's just stroll over to the field's edge, shall we? I've never been that far since I came here and I think the light will hold.'

They began to walk across the grass. The mist was patchy and late sunlight fell on the broken stone pillars in which specks glinted like black diamonds. A seagull glided beneath one of the arches.

On the other side of the hedge lay the marshland : behind them, the layers of history; ahead a place that seemed as yet untouched. It was like looking into the future, full of possibility and promise, but giving nothing away, offering no assurance of good or ill.

Vereker said, 'I'll be going home soon, but I won't belong there the way I did before. Things will never be the same again.'

The sun was low now and in the level light the marshes merged into the sea, a grey-green expanse with no clutter of houses, fields or hedgerows to distract mind or eye.

'Why won't things ever be the same again?' Zoe asked.

'For one thing, I won't be the same. For another, I suppose you never really see a place clearly until you've been some place else.'

They looked across the marshes for a time in silence, standing close, Zoe leaning against Matthew's shoulder. Soon, the flowers of the marshes would bloom, there would be the rich gold of marsh marigold, the pale lilac of Lady's Smock, the scarlet Ragged Robin and the wild rosemary; the grass would be greener than it was now, and thicker, so that, although there were paths through the marshes, they would not be discernible and there would be nothing to indicate where the ground was firm, where it was treacherous : a beautiful and dangerous place in which every step would involve a risk.

Matthew sighed. 'It's just that I'm afraid you'll find Coopers Town very dull."

'That's for me to worry about. All *you* have to decide is what you want.'

'I know what I want,' he said cautiously.

She pressed her fingers in the palm of his hand. 'That will be enough to begin with.'

She sounded quietly confident, as indeed she was. Life was just beginning, she could feel it moving in her body; it was slow and gentle, but it had a rhythm and the rhythm was insistent. Later, as they walked back across the dark field, she marvelled at the great force that was within her. I am alive, she thought; I, Zoe Lindsay, am alive and dangerous. Is that what you want, Matthew? Oh, I do hope it is what you want.

16

The news that Zoe Lindsay was to marry Matthew Vereker added spice to the Christmas fare. It was received charitably enough on Christmas Day, but after Boxing Day, when turkey and goodwill were pared to the bone, and the wine had turned sour in their stomachs, most of the islanders agreed that it was at best a ludicrous, at worst, a disastrous match.

'I suppose she had to find a priest to keep all those nuns in their place,' Donald Jarman observed. A smile creased the flesh around the triangular eyes, but whereas usually one had the impression of laughter bubbling up from deep inside him, this time the merriment was all on the surface.

'Poor Donald!' Gwynneth commiserated. 'Did you think you were the only love of her life?'

'I think she could have done better for herself than marry Matthew Vereker.'

Colonel Maitland, on the other hand, thought that she was not good enough for Matthew Vereker, a sentiment which aroused resentment in his wife.

'Are you aware, Herbert, that your habitual reaction to holy matrimony is that the man is throwing himself away?' The Colonel busied himself folding his copy of *The Times*.

Mrs. Hooper said, 'And his wife not two years in her grave.' She spoke as though the late Mrs. Vereker had been a personal friend whose betrayal she had long anticipated.

The one person about whom Matthew and Zoe were concerned was Nancy; and it was, therefore, a great joy to them that she expressed unreserved approval.

Nancy was indeed pleased. At a time when she intended to relinquish her charge of her father, a replacement had been found, and she was genuinely delighted that the replacement was Zoe. But in spite of the fact that he was now in good hands, she still put off the moment when she would tell him that she would not be returning to Coopers Town. 'It's the words,' she told herself, 'I haven't found the right words yet.' But really, it was the heart that was not ready.

The heart was still in a good deal of trouble although Tudor was less at the centre of the trouble than he had been. Gradually, some instinct of self-preservation fastened on those weaknesses in him of which she had always been aware and began relentlessly to destroy his image. She saw that he was neither child nor adult, so he could neither accept a woman's loving protection, nor sustain the man's role. This was her salvation and his damnation.

Yet although Tudor's importance gradually diminished, the hunger for something in life which seemed to be denied her increased. What *was* life about? She wanted there to be a purpose, and to find her particular purpose; not a worthy purpose, not something she had to grub away at to make the world a better place, but the thing which would fire her into life. She had wanted to arrive in the adult world like a rocket; but she had no propelling power and sometimes, in the drab anti-climax of January, it was hard to fight the fear that Nancy Vereker was a very ordinary person with an ordinary person's potentialities, and it was true, what all the clever people said, that you had to accept this and adjust your vision accordingly.

She made a few minor adjustments. She had discovered that provided she was doing something constructive, she got along very well with people; it was when she was just being social that the difficulties arose. She increased the amount of time that she spent helping Meg Jacobs.

Meg had acquired another helper in Miss Draisey. In the realm of the underprivileged and the unfortunate, Miss Draisey would never make a good field worker. She was, however, an excellent organiser and, where fund-raising was concerned, she had formidable qualities of initiative and what Meg described as 'sheer bloody cheek!' Meg said to Nancy, 'When you are giving out like I have to every day, there isn't anything left for the bookwork. But dear old Genevieve responds to the profit and loss on an account sheet as if she is reconciling a broken marriage.' The fact that she had a sympathetic and uncritical listener in Nancy made it easier for Meg to accept Miss Draisey's efficiency.

The weather in January was mild and the meetings on the priory site continued. It was a wet month, however, and because of this people parked their cars as near to the site as possible instead of using the official car parks. Residents complained that their driveways were frequently blocked, that their normally quiet neighbourhood reverberated with the banging of car doors, that people threw litter into their gardens and lowered the tone of the area by standing around gossiping after the meetings. 'What will it be like in the summer if this goes on?' they asked.

Worse was to come. The trolls camped out on the island and their numbers increased. They lit fires on the beach and roamed up and down the seafront shouting obscenities, so that residents were afraid to allow their children to go anywhere near the sea. When the police turned the trolls off the beach, they took over some of the derelict property in the fairground area and even the squatters were afraid of them. During the day, they trailed around the shopping centre or draped themselves on the pavement. Mrs. Peters, and those who were homeless because they hadn't got a place to live as distinct from not wanting one, resented the trolls bitterly. There were several angry exchanges in the shopping arcade and on one occasion windows were broken and the police had to be called in. When the miscreants came up before the magistrates, one of the trolls stood up in the gallery and said that England was a Fascist state and the chairman of the magistrates was acting under instructions from the Special Branch. When the police (who had rather enjoyed the remark about the chairman of the magistrates) came to restrain him, he climbed onto the balcony rail. No one believed he would jump, but in fact he did; he stepped out into space quite nonchalantly as if it was of no concern to him whether he broke his own or another person's neck. It was not a high balcony and he did not hurt himself, but he created panic among the people sitting below and heightened the feeling of insecurity which had gripped the islanders.

The crusade which Tudor had started was taking an ugly turn, but he refused to condemn the growing violence. When Vereker spoke to him about it, he said with quiet bitterness, 'My days of speaking out are finished. It gets you nowhere; I've learnt my lesson.'

'What kind of a lesson is that?' Vereker was angry. 'You are letting other people do your fighting for you.'

But Tudor could no longer summon the passion for a fight;

direct confrontation must be left to others now. He shrugged his shoulders and said bitterly, 'I should lose my job if I got in a fight; jobs aren't easy to come by these days.'

Surprisingly, one person who persisted with peaceful protest was Mrs. Peters. Day after day she paraded through the market and the shopping arcade, causing considerable embarrassment to shoppers but keeping always on the move and restraining her language so that it was difficult to decide what law she was breaking. A person can't be arrested for talking out loud, even if people don't like what she is saying. Certainly, the shoppers did not like it when Mrs. Peters shouted, 'That's a nice little girl you have there, Madam – you, Madam with the purple hair. Have you got a nice house, Madam, a nice house to live in with your little girl?' She would walk on past several stalls, so that she could not be accused of harassing the Madam with the purple hair, before she continued. 'Keep an eye on your little girl, Missus with the smarty pants. Don't let her out of your sight. If anything happens to her, they'll take your little boy away from you as well.' Then on briskly to the secondhand clothing stall where she inspected the items, shouting as she did so, 'Once you're on a losing number, it's all up with you. "From those that hath not, even that which they have shall be taken away from them." That's what the Bible says, and it's true. God doesn't forgive the losers. Don't look so shocked, Admiral,' shaking a finger at an elderly man in a navy blazer, 'I'm only witnessing to the truth of the Bible.'

'Drat the woman!' Colonel Maitland's wife said to Zoe when they met in the market. 'If we all handed our houses over to her kind tomorrow, in five years' time they would be homeless and we should have found somewhere to live.' She beckoned to the owner of the fish stall and pointed to a piece of haddock. 'Where was that fish caught?'

'Beautiful fish,' he said. 'Fresh and....'

'I daresay; but I don't want any fish that's been caught off the West Point where the sewage pipe comes up.'

'It troubles me when I think how fortunate I have been, living all my life at Carrick Farm,' Zoe said.

'I don't know about fortunate; I expect you've paid for it ten times over in taxes.'

They parted soon after this and Zoe went to the estate agent and told him that she had decided to take Carrick Farm off the market.

'I think I should leave the house to Tudor,' she told Matthew. 'He can use it to try out his ideas about a commune for problem families.'

Vereker only half-listened to what she was saying. He was concerned about an article in the local paper. The writer of the article said that during the last year life on the island had changed in such a way that unless drastic action was taken "we may find that we have seen the last of life as we have known it here – quiet, peaceful, some might say dull, but a life free from the violent excesses which are part of the life of many of the large towns on the mainland."

Vereker went to a group discussion in the house of his parishioners, Mr. and Mrs. Hanley. There were several young people there, including Milo. To Vereker's surprise, the man who was a member of the National Front was there, too; Mrs. Hanley whispered to Vereker that her son had invited him. 'We don't really approve.'

Someone mentioned the article in the local paper and Mrs. Hanley, avoiding her son's eye, said that perhaps the meetings on the priory site had contributed to the increased violence.

'How can that be?' The National Front man had a high-pitched, staccato voice which although not pleasant had a hypnotic quality. 'People come with their kids. Our movement starts with the family, right where Jesus started. True, it has attracted trash; but we shall get rid of the trash.'

'We shouldn't try to convert them?' an earnest girl suggested.

'We have to begin in a small way. Helmsley Island is our immediate family. The English people are our extended family. You have to get things right in your own family before you can take on anything else. Jesus came for the Jews, *they* were His family. When the Canaan woman wanted a portion of what He had to give the Jews, He said, "It is not fair to take the children's bread and throw it to the dogs." '

'The Canaan woman did not go away unanswered,' Vereker said.

'He said, "It is not fair to take the children's bread and throw it to the dogs." ' The man held up a stiff cautionary finger. '*That* is the important thing. We shouldn't wince from the things He said which seem harsh to us. There are times when it is right to take a line which seems harsh. We shouldn't flinch from it.'

'What in particular shouldn't we flinch from?' Vereker persisted.

'There are words we've allowed ourselves to be brainwashed into being ashamed of using – morality, standards of conduct, values.' The lips moved faster but the expression did not change, it was like watching a puppet speak. 'The Church has been very weak, meddling with things it doesn't understand, whoring after Marx, canvassing the immigrant vote, and failing to assert its authority over things which really matter.'

'Such as morality, standards of conduct, and values?'

'You see, you can't bring yourself to speak the words without a sneer. No, no, don't try to justify yourself, my friend, you sneered! And so do they all, the arrogant intellectuals, the trendy bishops, they all sneer. But that's not how the people feel, the real people of this country who have been stifled for so long *want* morality, standards of conduct, and values; they want to be masters in their own house.' He gazed at Mr. Hanley who looked uncomfortable. 'So, we start with the family and work outwards. When you have a united family, you have a disciplined society, a society that wants law and order so that people can walk in the street without fear, day or night.'

There seemed to be signs of disunity in this particular family and Vereker felt that he was increasing the tension by his presence. He left the meeting early. To his surprise, Milo, who had been very quiet, decided to leave with him. There was no reason why they should have taken the long way home across the priory fields, but Milo turned in this direction and Vereker fell into step beside him. They walked in silence for a few minutes, then Milo said, 'All right, then; I admit things aren't turning out the way I hoped.'

'What did you hope for, Milo?'

'You said in one of your sermons that our world is a dim reflection of God's Kingdom, that we ourselves are dim reflections of the complete person He will have us be. I wanted people to get *that* message, to see that we had a whole new continent to explore within ourselves.'

Vereker kicked a stone out of the way, not best pleased to have his sermon quoted back at him out of context.

Milo said, 'When I came down here that night I had such an extraordinary feeling as though a misted glass had cleared and the world was radiant. It was something outside time and I knew that I was outside time, too. There was such joy, such unimaginable joy!'

Vereker said drily, 'And now?'

'Now!' Milo stopped close to the great hooked pillar. 'It's all gone dark again. So what do I do? I started this; am I supposed to call it off at the first sign that it's going sour? Is that what you do when people misunderstand what you are saying to them?'

There was a deep regret in Milo's voice; but whether it was for a lost pagan delight or for a spiritual experience he had had in this place, Vereker did not know. But whatever had happened to Milo, and whatever he might do from now on, Vereker was convinced that some change had taken place in the boy and that Milo was frightened by it.

Vereker said, 'How long before the next meeting?'

Milo's fingers moved along the base of the pillar, exploring the cracks where the valerian grew. 'Five days.'

'Then you have five days to pray about it.'

Should I have suggested we should pray together? Vereker wondered. No, we are too unlike. I have learnt at last that there isn't going to be one blinding moment when I meet God face to face : mine is the Emmaus road. For Milo, it may be different, but that is not my business.

The next day, Zoe told Matthew that she had decided to let Carrick Farm to Meg Jacobs. 'It will make a much better home than the house she has at present; they can keep that for people who need a room for a short stay.'

Tudor had reacted angrily to the suggestion that he should establish a commune at the farm. Carrick Farm was a place which he could not incorporate in his professional life; ghosts would indeed have walked there had he tried to do this. He was even more angry when Zoe said she would let the house to Meg Jacobs.

'You realize it may be difficult for you to get it back if you want it?'

220

'But I shall never come back here.'

'That's how it seems to you now. But you won't be able to live in this little hick town he's taking you to. I can see you have to find that out for yourself; and, of course, I *hope* it's going to work out for you. But I think that with your history you need to take precautions. You're not the kind for whom a bad marriage is better than no marriage.'

While he talked Zoe looked at his taut, anxious face and she thought, how could I have blamed him for all that happened between us? I was content with our relationship because it suited me to be the one who gave the most : as the giver, I could set limits and make sure I was not drawn out of my depth. It was a dark world that we shared but I felt safe in it. I clung to the darkness as a protection from joy. Joy is dangerous, one has to open oneself to joy.

'You're not the kind for whom a bad marriage is better than no marriage,' Tudor repeated. 'You're not sufficiently robust to survive that kind of failure and if it happens you will need somewhere to run to.'

'You are right, Tudor! You are right!' she cried. 'I have been talking about *letting* the house so that it will be there as a security for me. I shall *give* it to Meg!'

Meg was shattered by the gift of Carrick Farm. 'I couldn't cope,' she told Nancy and Miss Draisey. 'It's too much. The present set-up suits me.' There had been times when she had lain awake at night worrying about the present set-up, but she forgot that now. 'It's grown up around me, it's my size.'

Nancy and Miss Draisey tried to prove to her that Carrick Farm would solve some of her problems rather than create new ones.

'I *like* to be cramped and crowded,' she insisted. 'And I hate change. Change really bugs me.'

Miss Draisey said, 'I shall work out how this can be done with the minimum of change. The whole operation must be planned very carefully, and I promise you that a year from now you will be complaining that not enough has changed!'

Meg shrivelled beneath the glare of Miss Draisey's confidence. 'You always hope for something really tremendous to happen, and when it does, it's never quite what you wanted,' she said later to Nancy. 'It's the wrong time, or the wrong place, or you're the wrong person for it to happen to.'

Nancy saw that the thing which troubled Meg the most was that there were now too many possibilities open to her. She remembered how frightened she herself was whenever she thought of all the freedom stretching ahead of her, vast and empty, with no small tracks in it for small people. 'I guess if we didn't have limitations, we're the kind who'd have to construct them,' she said to Meg.

Meg was cheered. 'Bless you, my dear. It's so uplifting to know that other folk make a balls-up of life, too.'

Vereker took little interest in the future of Carrick Farm. On the following Saturday he went to the priory to see what Milo would do. He realized that even if Milo wanted to turn back it would be a very difficult undertaking now.

He was earlier than on previous occasions and found himself carried well to the front of the crowd. In spite of himself he was infected by the excitement of those around him. There were times during the week of the fair when he had felt that the island was coming alive at last. Now, on the priory grounds, the experience of the fair was being extended. Here, there was no longer the separation of performer and spectator, here all participated, donating their small amount of enthusiasm and energy to something that was bigger than themselves. They were no longer fragmented, unco-ordinated, uncentred particles, they were one people and this cohesion gave them strength and power that was far beyond anything they could have achieved individually.

Inevitably, there were some who were less than enthusiastic. On Vereker's right, an old woman grumbled to her middle-aged companion, 'I don't *want* to live for ever. You wouldn't if you were my age.' She sounded aggrieved, as though a privilege had been withdrawn.

Then, there were the police; a new element, moving in the crowd in quite large numbers. There were new faces among the trolls, while on the perimeter of the site a group of people with shaved heads hopped about ringing handbells. Vereker was reminded of the strange creatures which framed the prisoners in Zoe's drawings.

Mrs. Peters was prowling round, shouting, 'You're a lot of

slops!' and she had brought a reeking slop bucket to give pungency to her account of the insanitary nature of the accommodation provided for the homeless.

Jeremy Jarman and his group had arrived and Barbara was with them. The group began to play *"I like that old-time religion"*. The crowd sang, full-hearted, faces alive with wonder. The old woman looked around her unimpressed. During the prayer that followed the singing she said to her companion, "Arry Plumb! Fancy 'Arry Plumb being 'ere, then. 'As 'e given up the drink?'

The prayer was followed by the testimony of a severe teenage girl who had brought her worldly parents to God. The prodigal parents stood looking awkward and out-of-place in well-tailored suits while the girl said that now they brought everything to God each morning at breakfast. This family was followed by a husband and wife who vied with each other for the major share in what had been a bad marriage, she had been a shrew, he had been unfaithful, she was mean, he was spendthrift; but now they had found the Lord Jesus Christ and love and order had come into their home.

The old woman said sceptically, 'If 'Arry Plumb's given up the drink, I'll live for ever!' and Mrs. Peters screamed 'Shit!' and waved her bucket to prove it.

When the husband and wife had departed, Milo came forward to hold out a helping hand to a young girl whose appearance caused a thrill of excitement to run through the crowd. Vereker heard the name "Betty Arnold" repeated in tones of amazement.

The girl, who looked very frail, remained at the foot of the pillar supported by friends, while Milo climbed to the top of the pillar to recount how, early one morning, this girl who was paralysed had awoken greatly moved by the beauty of the world. She had looked out of the window. There was a lake in the garden of the house where she lived and a heron was standing motionless by the lake. She watched the heron until it flew away and after that she remained by the window for a long time thinking about the heron. It was only when her mother came into the room and cried out that the girl realized she had walked to the window. Milo spoke of the power of the Holy Spirit as a divine madness, making nonsense of man's limited ideas of reason and order.

Vereker, feeling a movement beside him, turned his head and saw the girl from Alabama. She said, 'Say, can you tell me if this is true. This old planet Earth revolves on its axis because there are two currents way out in space....' She had a can on a string in each hand and she swung them as she talked as though they were the currents and she was the earth. People told her to be quiet, but she went on, 'If God decided He didn't like what He'd done here on this old planet Earth, if He thought it was all a Goddam cock-up, do you think He might blast those currents apart, just like Samson pulled down the pillars? Do you think He might do that?' A man nearby shouted, 'Praise the Lord!' and the cry was taken up all around the field. The girl raised *her* voice several notches. 'Don't you think God sometimes feels the whole thing's got so bad it doesn't even make Him laugh any more? Don't you think He wants to cancel it, blast those currents apart....' As she spoke, she swung her arm and let go of the can she carried in her right hand. It sailed over the heads of the people in front and landed in the small area of open space at the feet of Betty Arnold. Immediately she had done this, the girl turned and disappeared into the crowd. Someone screamed, 'It's a bomb!'

As Barbara Jarman had once noted, Milo's reactions were very quick. He had leapt from the pillar and picked up the can before most of the people realized what was happening; the crowd to the rear of the pillar was thin and he turned and ran that way. He was out into open space, and people had let their breath out to cheer, when the bomb went off. It had been an effortless, elegant performance and it seemed at first that he had got away with it. Undoubtedly the bomb had left his hand before it exploded; his limbs were intact when they got to him, although there was blood on his face. He was not concious, but breathing quite easily. He came to in the ambulance and said, 'I can't see.'

'That's shock,' they soothed him. 'You'll be all right. You've been very lucky.'

He was not lucky. When Vereker took Mrs. Anguilo to the hospital to see him, the registrar would say very little. Ten days later, when Vereker saw the consultant, he learnt that the most Milo could ever hope for would be that he would 'see a blur which he will know is a person.'

224

'Does he know this?'

'Yes.'

Milo was in one of the amenity rooms off the main ward. There were several vases of chrysanthemums and other winter flowers which did not give off a strong smell. Milo was sitting up in bed, humped against pillows. He turned his head when Vereker came in and said, 'Hullo. I recognized your footsteps.' He went on, without giving Vereker time for a greeting, 'Will you look through the cards and letters on my table? I need to thank people who have written and sent flowers.'

'Would a tape recorder help?' Vereker asked. 'You can have mine and I could arrange for people to hear the messages.'

'A tape recorder would be marvellous. But as for the thank-you letters, my sisters will write them for me. It passes the time for them untearfully when they come to see me.'

Vereker began to sort through the pile of cards and letters. Milo folded his hands on his knees and Vereker was painfully conscious that the boy was restraining himself from talking with some difficulty; the temptation to build a wall of words around himself must have been very strong. In the corridor a trolley squeaked and rattled on its way to the ward and a cheerful voice shouted, 'Oh, *very* natty, Mr. J. I *like* that. But don't overdo it, dear.'

'I wonder what Mr. J. has been up to,' Vereker murmured, and then wished he had not said it because this was how things would be from now on for Milo, listening to the passing show off-stage.

Milo said, as though to demonstrate how acute were his other senses, 'You mustn't feel sorry for me. That won't help me.'

'Of course I feel sorry for you. Don't be silly.'

'I shall manage, though. You believe that, don't you?'

'Yes. You will have to manage. Others do.'

'You cut me down to size so nicely. You always have.' He settled into a more relaxed silence.

When he had finished sorting the correspondence, Vereker said, 'Do you want me to read the more recent ones to you?'

'No. Someone else can do that. It's very necessary to keep visitors occupied otherwise it's a great strain on them . . . and on me, too. How do you overcome this business of people talking to you in a special way, as though you had lost your wits as well as your sight?'

'I suppose you have to impose your will on theirs. That was something you were always rather good at.'

'Too good, do you mean?' Milo was composed now. 'I think you are right about that. I can see myself more clearly now than ever before. It will be good for me to have to depend on other people, to use their gifts instead of always being at the centre of everything myself.' If he was afraid his followers might drift away, he did not show it.

Vereker said quietly, 'Do you *really* believe this is good for you, Milo?'

Milo laughed. 'Oh, I shall miss you so much when you leave Helmsley!' He turned his head in Vereker's direction. It was no longer possible, now that the brilliant eyes were dulled, to catch a glimpse of the mischievous sprite which had once dwelt in Milo. Vereker switched off the table lamp and concentrated on listening. 'Did they tell you how I spent the first three days here after I knew that I had lost my sight? You must listen to this; it's a very inspiring story. I refused to see anyone, or to eat anything, and when they came in the room they found me in an attitude of meditation. They were terribly impressed, I heard them talking in the corridor (they think I am deaf now, too); they thought that I was committing myself into the hands of God, praying for courage and strength. It pleased me that they thought this, it pleased me that what they thought sacred was in fact profane. I spent my time hurling every abuse and obscenity I could think of at God, spewing out everything beastly that I had stored up inside me waiting for just such a day, and not only girls and drugs and the sailor who got at me in the subway in Portsmouth, the sort of thing that happens to everyone; but the things I could throw in the face of Christ about what *His* life was really like, with women washing His feet with their hair, and the disciple whom He loved resting on His breast.

'It didn't work. I used to think of God as someone "out there" who intervened when necessary. But when I had spewed out all that anger and resentment, I knew that He wasn't outside at all. He is in me. I have all that I shall ever need in me. *That* is my light. Some people will laugh when they hear it, some will be embarrassed, some will be sceptical, but some will believe.'

Vereker was aware of the pressure being put on him to say 'I believe.' He wanted to give way to it; he was a priest and surely this was the least he could do for Milo who needed comfort so much at this moment. But while he wanted to respond to Milo's need, he could not say, 'I believe' to a personal god who knows nothing of the God of the thunderbolt, of earthquake, fire and flood; the God who created the lion as well as its prey, who cares as much about the bomb thrower as the victim. He said, 'That's fine, just so long as you don't ever lose your sense of something beyond your reach. Hang on to your unease.'

Milo said sadly, 'You have very little faith.'

It was after eight o'clock when Vereker left Milo and he was surprised to see a dark figure standing in the window alcove at the end of the corridor.

The next time that he visited Milo he told him about his grandparents. He thought that Milo had a right to this information. Milo thought it was a very funny story. Although he had shown such surprising ability to sway a crowd, his understanding of individual relationships was limited.

'You find me unfeeling?' Milo asked. 'But you must know that the time when I needed a family was when I was a child. It's nothing to me now.'

There was a brightness about Milo, in spite of his blindness. Vereker, looking at him, wondered how long this inner light would burn. Would it last until he came out of hospital and tried to come to terms with his blindness, until interest in him died down, as it well might? Or would it burn, as Vereker believed it could, for all eternity? He was not sure, as he had never been sure of anything about Milo.

When he left Milo, Vereker saw that once more there was someone waiting in the corridor. There was a row of chairs against the wall where visitors could sit while they waited to be admitted to the main ward and a woman was seated on the furthest chair. It was late in the evening, well after visiting hours, but if a patient was on the danger list relatives were sometimes allowed to spend the night at the hospital. Vereker was surprised that a more comfortable place had not been found for this woman. He hesitated, wondering whether to speak to her. She was a sombre figure, draped in a dun-coloured cloak which looked as if it had been inexpertly made of a blanket. Her face was turned away from him, but something about the way she sat, quite still, legs apart, hands resting on the knees, gave him such an impression of rock-like durability that he could not imagine she had any need of conventional consolation. In fact, there was something intimidating about the way she kept her lonely vigil. 'I'd be rather frightened to inspire such devotion,' he thought, looking at the unyielding mass of the body and the hands, thin and strong, the splayed fingers like the roots of a tree. He had seen those hands before. He walked down the corridor and looked at the woman's face and saw that it was Mrs. Peters.

'There's a woman waiting in the corridor,' he said when he managed to find the night nurse. 'I didn't speak to her because she seemed ... well, rather absorbed. ...'

'Now how did she get in this time!' the nurse exclaimed crossly. 'She gets on my wick, sitting outside his room all the time like that. If I had my way, I'd hand her over to the police!'

Vereker left her to deal with Mrs. Peters as best she could and sneaked down the back stairs.

Nancy was really in on the caring business now, ferrying Mrs. Anguilo to and from the hospital, helping to look after the Anguilo girls, bolstering up Meg Jacobs, rejoicing with her father and Zoe. She even had to act as confidante to Barbara Jarman.

Barbara had been to see Milo once. 'All I got out of that was to be told I should be studying for my A-levels!' she said to Nancy. 'So, that's that. It'll have to be medicine after all.' She said it just as some people say. 'There's always teaching.' 'I'll become a doctor, and marry a doctor, and we shall have four children and make dismally bad parents, the way professional people do.' She sounded very hard, but there was despair behind the façade. The bomb episode had shaken her into realization that there were things in herself to which she did not want to give expression. Her mother and father had reached an accommodation, but their two natures still warred in Barbara and she could not marry them: one must go to ground. Her mother's was the more unacceptable by today's standards; it had had its romp and nearly frightened her to death, and that must be the end of it. Soon people would be saying 'Barbara's herself again' by which they would mean she was crisp and hard as a piece of celery.

Nancy was surprised that Barbara, who had seemed so competent and had the course of her life planned out so carefully, should allow herself to be unsaddled before she'd even got under starter's orders.

She told her father about Barbara. It was the nearest she could get to telling him of her own exploits. 'You'd think she'd just put it down to experience, wouldn't you?' she said. 'Try to be a bit more discriminating next time.'

'Yes, I would have thought that,' he agreed, thinking about Barbara Jarman and not about his daughter.

Nancy wondered whether to pursue this line. She had had her first love affair and she had come through it without laying any burdens on her father; it was the only pain she had ever kept to herself. If ever she was up against something bad in the future, it might be a help to know she'd managed this alone. She said, 'Anyway, Barbara will be going to university next fall. It will do her good to get away from her parents for a year or so.'

She knew by the way he took off his reading glasses and laid them carefully on the desk that she had her father's full attention now. She did not know quite how to start, and he said gently, 'What is it you want to say, my dear?'

'I don't want to hurt you.'

He smiled. 'I promise not to be hurt.'

'I'm thinking of staying behind when you and Zoe go; I'll stay with Meg at Carrick Farm. She and Miss Draisey don't get along awfully well, but I can cope all right with each of them and I think that would be a help.'

'It would be a help to them.' She sensed that the idea did not appeal to him. He said quietly. 'I'd like to think there was something in it for you as well. Miss Draisey is doing this at the end of her life, and Meg is half-way through hers, but you are at your beginning. Don't you think this might be the time to train for something?'

'And have my life mapped out for me by other people before I've had time to find my way around?'

He looked down at the desk, rubbing a forefinger across his

forehead in a way he had when he was collecting his thoughts. 'What are you going to use for money?' he asked.

She bit her finger nail and thought how sordid life was. It wouldn't have been so sordid if she herself hadn't cared about money, but the thought of not having enough money to keep a roof over her head filled her with dread. 'I reckon I can manage for about a year on what Mother left me,' she said. 'After that, I might get to be a nurse. I've an idea I need something fairly structured, I don't think social work is for me.'

'You could train for a nurse at home,' he pointed out.

'Yes, I know.' How could she say that if she came home she would never be free? Her mother had been ill for so long that she had invested too much in her father; now, when she had started withdrawing it, little by little, she dared not stop. 'It's just that I have to do things on my own. There was a time when I thought I wasn't ever going to make out as a person.' It was touch and go now, but she didn't add that.

He flipped the hook of the glasses, jigging them about on the desk. 'This is what we're really talking about, isn't it? Not Meg and Miss Draisey needing help, but you needing to make out on your own? Don't look so upset, my dear. It makes more sense.'

'We'll be able to enjoy each other more when I've got myself straightened out,' she said unhopefully. Love and the fear of losing seemed to her to be so inextricably entangled she found it hard to believe that if she loosed the knot that bound her to him love would survive.

He picked up his glasses and put them on. 'That's settled then?' he said. 'You'll stay at Carrick Farm and I'll quite envy you that. I had the feeling I'd have liked to stay there myself once.' He was drawing his book towards him as he talked.

'You want to get on with your old sermon,' she teased. She kissed the top of his head and went out.

Vereker sat with his finger on the page, not reading, after she had gone. You saw all these youngsters bumming around, thumbing lifts through life, and you never thought it was going to happen to your child. Your child was going to grow up nice and steady, be processed through the educational machine and emerge a teacher, a chemist, a librarian, it didn't

230

matter what so long as it was something which satisfied you she had a good future. He thought : at least Nan wants to do something for people. But it did not console him. "Doing something for people" is sometimes the refuge of the inadequate : he prayed that in her case it meant accepting the discipline and responsibility of nursing.

Zoe was sympathetic when Matthew talked to her about his fears for Nancy, but she was nevertheless conscious of a slight irritation that Nancy's problems should intrude so soon on her own happiness. She had overlooked the fact that there was an area of Matthew's life into which she could not enter fully. She had never intended to come between him and his daughter, but she had tended to see them as living in a harmonious relationship, united yet particular, rather like the Blessed Trinity. Fortunately she had time to bring herself down to earth and make a more realistic assessment of their relationship.

'One of the things I lack,' she said to Matthew, 'is a sense of proportion. You will have to remind me of that from time to time.'

17

February was cold and grey; February was always a dead time of the year on the island. A few people went to the priory grounds on the first two Saturdays after the bomb incident and hung around hopefully but eventually they were discouraged. It seemed that the movement was unlikely to survive the combined challenge of the bomb and February.

Vereker and Zoe had decided to be married in Southampton on their way to the boat. They wanted a quiet wedding away from both the island and Coopers Town. Nancy was glad about this. Although she continued to be cheerful about the marriage, she did not want to share her father with a stepmother during his last weeks on the island. It was agreed that she would drive Zoe and Vereker to Southampton, attend the wedding and see them off on the boat.

Tudor left the island in the second week of February. He had a talk with Nancy before he went. He suggested that from time to time he might spend a night at Carrick Farm and they could continue to be lovers on a casual basis if that appealed to her. Now that he would be living with the school teacher, he felt he would need a woman on the island as well. Nancy declined.

'I just don't have the urge.' She was surprised that she had the nerve to say this to him. If she had said that she was in love with another woman, or with her father, Tudor would have accepted it, but he would find this answer beyond belief. She hoped he would not take it personally; she did not want to damage his self-esteem. But he began to tell her that she would never develop properly as a person, that she would be unable to enjoy anything fully, music, art, poetry, all would be closed to her; in time she might not even enjoy her food or be able to sleep. So she knew he had not taken it personally. Poor Tudor, she thought, looking at his taut face. He had scoured himself clean of every weakness, of which he believed love to be one, and now only anger moved in him : it had worn him to the bone. She cried for him that night, but after that she did not think much about him.

There was a farewell party in the church hall for the Verekers. Then Nancy and Matthew had the churchwardens and their families to dinner; and the following Saturday they went to lunch with the Maitlands.

After lunch, the Colonel's lady permitted the men to go for a walk. They turned automatically in the direction of the sea front. It was high tide and there was a stiff breeze coming off the sea, blowing spray in their faces. The Colonel told Vereker about the mistakes which the English generals had made during the War of Independence. Somewhere a radio was switched on and a brass band provided martial music for his discourse.

There were only a few people about; the island attracted no visitors in February. A woman passed them accompanied by an elderly dog with faded eyes; a man and a woman with three children to tire before tea headed purposefully towards the harbour; an old man stooped at the sea's edge, collecting shells for his grandchildren.

The Colonel was talking about Bull Run; he must have switched to the Civil War while Vereker was watching the people coming and going, like sparrows making the best of things after the crowds have gone. The band was nearer. The Colonel stopped talking and the two men stood listening as the sound swelled. 'I thought it was on the radio,' the Colonel said. At first, it was difficult to tell from which direction the music was coming; then, far down the seafront, wintry sunlight glinted on brass. The doors of houses were opened, people came out into the gardens, looking from right to left. Children scampered onto the seafront; parents followed carrying the children's coats. The band was playing *"In the name of Jesus every knee shall bow. . . ."*

'Well, I'll be damned!' the Colonel said, 'Someone must have called the Army in.'

'I should have thought they'd have other things to do,' Vereker said, not understanding. Then, as they came nearer, he saw the band of the Salvation Army. A woman and a child were walking in front of the band, and behind it marched a long, orderly column with only a few Salvation Army uniforms

here and there. There was no hand clapping, no shouts of
Alleluiah; although their feet marked the rhythm of the
music, there was no swagger in their bearing, and they did not
shout to onlookers to join them. Their countenances proclaimed that to be of their number was a privilege and one
must comport oneself accordingly. People ran forward, tug-
ging on raincoats, putting scarves round their heads, looking
not so much eager to join as afraid of being left behind. As
soon as they were in the ranks, any exuberance was quietly
but firmly restrained; they seemed at first overawed and unsure, skipping from one foot to the other, constantly changing
step; then gradually, they became calm as they realized what
was expected of them.

The band was nearly abreast of Vereker and Colonel Maitland. The woman in front loped along, her head poked
forward slightly. In spite of the blare of the trumpets, the clash
of cymbals, she walked with no suggestion that she was taking
part in a military parade but rather with the resourceful air
of a housewife with a hard day's shopping ahead of her.
Neither Vereker nor Colonel Maitland recognized her until
she was quite close to them. If she had walked barefoot in
rags, or worn the hair shirt of the penitent; if she had dressed
in scarlet and laughed like a mad woman, or been sombre in
friar's habit, the impact would have been no more arresting
than the sight of Mrs. Peters in a navy raincoat, too broad in
the shoulders for her, but giving nevertheless the overall impression of neat respectability. It was as though, having no
riches to give away, she had renounced the obvious signs of
her poverty.

To Vereker and the Colonel's embarrassment, the procession
halted at this point to give the long column an opportunity
to close ranks. While they waited, the marchers stared ahead
of them. One look at their faces told the onlookers they would
not be thanked for a laugh and a cheery greeting. These were
people who had discovered a sense of responsibility and they
were feeling its weight on their shoulders. As one looked from
one face to another, it seemed that they were saying, 'Enough
is enough. No more permissiveness, no more improvizing, ex-
temporizing, no more impromptu living. Life is too important
to play it by ear. All the nonsense is over; now let's get down
to business.'

Tommy, holding his mother's hand, looked about him pleased and proud. Vereker dreaded that his mother would do the same. Suppose she turned to him and challenged him to march beside her? But "joining" was not as easy as that : a forfeit must be paid. When she did turn to look at Vereker, she called out, 'Join us, brother. But first throw that collar away, there's no place for it in the People's Movement.' She looked at Colonel Maitland consideringly and then said, 'Leave your wife, Colonel.'

The band struck up *"Mine eyes have seen the glory of the . coming of the Lord"* and the procession moved off. Colonel Maitland cleared his throat and said to Vereker, 'Remarkable woman, that!' The trumpets blared, the cymbals clashed; the voices of the marchers were loud and strong. But it was all very disciplined. These were people who felt they had a long way to go, who knew that strength must be conserved and that spiritual ecstasy is rare as water in the desert not one drop of which must be wasted. It was not the singing which was the most impressive thing : it was the sound of the marching feet. Vereker, listening, was afraid.

> *"He hath sounded forth the trumpet that shall never*
> *call retreat. . . ."*

Colonel Maitland said to Vereker, 'You're not going to throw your dog collar away?' He sounded wistful, perhaps he was thinking that he wasn't going to leave his wife. They watched the people marching by. There were a lot of them. Afterwards, they learnt that the procession had started on the mainland, marched in good order across the causeway and right round the island before it reached this spot. In the middle of the column and towards the rear, there were men with fifes and drums who kept the rhythm going when the sound of the band faded in the distance.

> *"Oh, be swift my soul to answer Him; be jubilant*
> *my feet! . . ."*

Colonel Maitland said to Vereker, 'My feet want to follow them.'

They turned and walked slowly away, their coats flapping in the salt breeze. They could still hear the drum-beat but the people had gone and the seafront was deserted, except for a seagull perched on the top of a shelter, indifferent as a pirate in the riggings of a doomed ship.

In his last sermon, Vereker said, 'Keep the faith, be of good cheer, don't be frightened by what you see happening around you, by changes which seem to threaten the Church. Change *is* life and life is dangerous because everywhere we are exposed to God, there are no hiding places and we are always at risk. We are travellers. On our journey, we may pass through a land of milk and honey into a barren country; we may pass from a democracy to a totalitarian regime; we may travel fast, in good company and fine health; at other times, we may move slowly because we are sick and alone. But of one thing we can be sure, life will be change all the way; we could not expect it to be otherwise, for here we have no continuing city.'

As the congregation filed out, Mrs. Hooper was heard to remark, 'I've had a bellyful of change. Thank goodness Mr. Roberts comes back next week.'

Others were more charitable in their comments and genuine in their good wishes; but most of them would by now be relieved when Vereker had gone. Americans had never understood the English. 'Talking about totalitarian regimes as though this was Germany!'

Before they left, Nancy and Zoe spring-cleaned the vicarage and took from dark stores bowls of hyacinths and crocuses ready to greet the Roberts family who would be arriving early the next week. In spite of their efforts, the house did not seem as peaceful to Vereker as when he had come to it.

He looked for the last time from the library window. The trees were not in leaf yet, but there was a froth of snowdrops on the lawn and the daffodils were in bud. What would happen here after he had left? Would his fears as to what might grow out of the meetings in the priory grounds be justified? Would Milo regain control of his movement and what part would the formidable Mrs. Peters play? It seemed wrong that he should go away now. As a child, he had been told, 'Once you start a job, you must finish it,' and he had spent the rest of his life learning that we seldom have a chance to see anything through. It didn't make sense. But it was no use worrying about making sense of life : we come in after the beginning and we have to leave before the end.

They made their farewells, promised to write, invited the

Maitlands to visit them in Coopers Town. Then, before Zoe had time to realize she was looking her last on childhood scenes, or Vereker to wonder who would be living in the luxury town houses which now rose like a grey envelope pasted against the sky, Nancy was driving them across the causeway. When they reached the mainland, they craned their necks, searching the island eagerly for a visual image to stimulate their feeling for it, to pin it for ever in their minds. It was small and flat and looked like a large grey whale. Then the road took a sudden twist and the next time they looked back, the island had disappeared.

They drove along a three-lane road with unfamiliar heathland on either side. Vereker sat back and stared out at the tangle of gorse and heather, and then at parkland intersected by a long drive at the end of which stood an imposing, porticoed mansion. He looked serious and absorbed. They drove on through a small, ugly town and into gently wooded country, past a village with wide streets and pleasant grass verges; and on and on until they were travelling through narrow, grimy streets and over the roofs of the squat houses they could see cranes and the masts of ships.

Zoe took Matthew's hand. 'What are you thinking about?'

'I was wondering what Roberts has been up to in Coopers Town.'